THE AVENGERS

DEATH IN DOWNING STREET

THE AVENGERS

DEATH IN DOWNING STREET

A NOVEL BY

DAVID CRICHTON

TITAN BOOKS

The Avengers: Death in Downing Street
Print edition ISBN: 9781835416198
E-book edition ISBN: 9781835416204

Published by Titan Books
A division of Titan Publishing Group Ltd
144 Southwark Street, London SE1 0UP
www.titanbooks.com

First edition: July 2026
10 9 8 7 6 5 4 3 2 1

A CIP catalogue record for this title is available from the British Library.

EU RP (for authorities only)
eucomply OÜ, Pärnu mnt. 139b-14, 11317 Tallinn, Estonia
hello@eucompliancepartner.com, +3375690241

Designed and typeset in Bembo MT Std by Richard Mason.

Printed and bound by CPI Group (UK) Ltd, Croydon, CR0 4YY.

For Becci, Sophie, Millie, Margot, Ian and Marie.

In loving memory of Bill and Irene, Eric and Dorothy.

1

HAROLD WILSON HAD made the short journey hundreds of times before. Maybe even thousands. Bundled into his royal blue Rover P5 outside the Palace of Westminster and manhandled back out again a few minutes later at his Downing Street home, fresh from the weekly interrogation at Prime Minister's Questions, or else exhausted from rabble rousing his colleagues and desperately trying to keep his government united. Two years – and two general elections – after he'd first come to power, the novelty of office had long since worn thin.

He could still remember his first visit to Downing Street. Not as prime minister, or even as a parliamentarian, but as an eight-year-old boy on a day trip with his father, James Herbert Wilson – a chemist who had himself dabbled in politics and worked with one Winston Churchill back in his days in the Liberal Party. Harold Wilson had never forgotten posing for the camera on the world's most famous doorstep, with no inkling of what the future might have in store.

As mundane as today seemed, Wilson knew destiny beckoned. This time next week, Britain would submit its historic application to representatives from Belgium, France, West Germany, Italy, Luxemburg and the Netherlands to ask – nay, *plead* – for a second chance to join the European

Economic Community, otherwise known as the Common Market.

The decision hadn't been an easy one. Wilson had never been what you might call an "emotional European" and he knew only too well how divisive the topic was. Barely a day went by when the ghouls of Westminster weren't plotting to overthrow him for even daring to think that Britain could unite with its neighbours and heal the divisions of the past. But the House wasn't the problem – Wilson had spent his whole life persuading people on the back benches. And only an hour ago, his whips had run the numbers, and confirmed he could comfortably get Wednesday's all-important vote through Parliament, even allowing for a modest rebellion. No, it was the people outside of the establishment that were harder to bring along. The armies of lobbyists from big business, the militant trade unions. Not to mention Joe Public. The topic was at best controversial, and at worst incendiary.

Today was no different. Leaving Westminster, Wilson could see the usual scores of protestors lining the streets, chanting in an inharmonious dirge, inaudible to the ear but piercing to the soul – waving placards around like angry mobsters. But Wilson's resolve was stronger than ever. He never doubted he was making the right decision – he'd vowed early on to follow his instincts, wherever they took him, and at whatever the cost. But like every leader before him, he often found himself wondering whether it was all worth it.

Reading the placards through his window, it was clear he couldn't win either way. No politician could. How could you reconcile people waving placards that read, "Keep Britain Out!" and "Non, Nein, No!" with ones saying, "Get in to get on," and "Great Britain equals Great Europe." There were only three viable options for any leader: back either side and be a hero to half the country or sit on the fence and please nobody.

As per usual, the roads around Whitehall were closed because of the protests, so Wilson's chauffeur took the "scenic route" around St James' Park. The Prime Minister sometimes wondered if his aides deliberately told his driver to take him round "the back roads" to avoid the protestors' venom. Why he couldn't just walk the six-hundred-or-so yards between his House and his home defeated him, but that was the security services for you.

As expected, the crowds started to thin around The Mall, but the Prime Minister knew it would be short respite, as the horde would inevitably be back when they reached Downing Street. He took a deep breath, steeling himself for what was to come. Any minute now, he'd be bundled out of the car and into Number 10, like McCartney or Jagger entering a concert hall – only the crowd enveloping him would be baying for blood.

As the heavens opened, the gentle pitter-patter of rain on the car roof helped Wilson to finally relax. He settled back into his seat and lit his pipe. The foreboding weather meant he could see his reflection in the car window. It was a man he barely recognised. The stresses of the job had aged him prematurely and made it almost impossible to control his weight. The last remnants of his striking dark hair were fading to silver by the day, but he sought comfort that, unlike many of his contemporaries in Parliament, at least he still had his hair.

Had the journey been longer, Wilson might have nodded off, but his talkative driver had other ideas. Thomas Kilpatrick was a stoic and weedy sort of man in his early forties who wore an ill-fitting suit and sported black-rimmed spectacles with lenses thicker than a glass ashtray, prompting many to question whether he should even be on the road. Kilpatrick had been the Prime Minister's principal driver for the past six months, but today Wilson was in no mood for small talk, and the words went in one ear and out the other. He desperately wanted to pull up the privacy screen and drown him out, but politeness – as his mother had so often told him – cost nothing. So, he offered just enough stock responses to feign interest. Yes, he'd had a good day. No, he wouldn't take the placards to heart. Okay, he'd rest when he got home. After that, the words became white noise. What Wilson was really thinking about was about his steak supper and the bottle of '58 Merlot waiting for him at home.

They stopped at a red light for what seemed like an eternity, and by now the Prime Minister was deep in thought. Remembering that small boy in 1924 and dearly hoping his father was proud. Surely that's what every son wanted? He couldn't help but think that the journey from a terrace in Huddersfield to leading Her Majesty's Government must surely fit the bill.

As the Prime Minister's car started to speed up, Wilson snapped out of his thoughts and realised that they were driving dangerously fast. The car took a bend at breakneck speed, which jolted Wilson – wresting the pipe from his hand and spilling tobacco embers on the car seat.

'What the devil?' snapped Wilson, in his usual high-pitched – almost squeaky – tone. His words were spoken in standard RP, but his Yorkshire lilt bled through.

'Sorry, sir,' said the chauffeur, as the Prime Minister picked up the pipe and emptied the remaining contents into his custom-made ash tray.

'Care to explain what that was all about?'

'Something and nothing, sir,' the chauffeur said in a thick continental accent that Wilson could never quite place. 'I just had the feeling we might have been…'

The sound of crashing metal resonated throughout the

car. Wilson spun round to see what was happening. Behind their car, he could see two of his motorcade riders lying helplessly on the ground – shunted off the road by a white van. Presuming an accident, Wilson enquired whether they should stop to help.

'Sorry, sir,' Kilpatrick shouted, 'that was no accident.'

The car accelerated at speed. Wilson checked his escorts out front were still in place. They were, and both cyclists turned a one-eighty to spring into action, removing their Colt revolvers and turning back to confront the pursuing van. As they passed Wilson's window, one of the leather-clad security men gestured for the Prime Minister to get down, while the other signalled for the chauffeur to accelerate further.

Wilson's heart was racing. Part fear, part adrenaline. He'd planned for this kind of scenario of course. Goodness knows, he'd sat through enough briefings and training exercises. But this wasn't America. In Britain, politicians were verbally excoriated day after day, but thankfully physical threats were rare. Wilson tried to calm down, reminding himself that his car was bulletproof – or "bullet resistant" whatever that might mean – and that he had one of the best security details in the world. But as his driver manoeuvred round another corner, he saw the last of his motorcade spiral into the curb, accompanied by the sound of a shotgun ricocheting down the street. Now only one thing stood between Wilson and his would-be assailants: his chauffeur. A man who was effortlessly dashing through the streets of Westminster, seemingly undaunted by the task in hand.

'What's the plan?' the Prime Minister asked, unsure if he should be distracting his driver at such a critical time.

'The police'll be all over it, sir,' he said calmly. 'We've just got to hang on until they get here.'

As every second passed, Wilson started to feel a little safer.

The distant sound of sirens gave him some small comfort. Surely, they'd evaded their pursuers by now? Slowly, he started to sit back up and summoned the courage to take another look. The coast was clear. He could only see a handful of drivers and pedestrians looking thoroughly disgusted by the speed the car was reaching, unaware of the occupants.

'Okay,' said Kilpatrick. 'Let's get you back to Downing Street.'

As the driver took a warren of backroads back to Westminster, Wilson knew they were only minutes away from safety. But as the car squeezed down a tight lane between two buildings, Wilson saw Kilpatrick's unflappable demeanour slip. He glanced ahead and saw a second white van blocking the road. Two armed men, wearing blue boiler suits and balaclavas, were each pointing a shotgun squarely at the Prime Minister's car.

Wilson felt powerless. Despite what the movies said, MI5 *didn't* equip government cars with secret rocket launchers, ejector seats, or wheels that kept turning with blown-out tyres.

'Hang on, sir,' said Kilpatrick, finding his calm. He threw the car into reverse and sped backwards, narrowly avoiding the blaze of gunfire and making good their escape.

When the sound of police sirens rang nearby, Wilson saw the van turn in the opposite direction as his pursuers conceded defeat and at last, the car reached Downing Street and sanctuary. The Prime Minister didn't say a word. Confusion and shock rendered his face immobile, as if he couldn't yet process what had happened.

The second the wheels stopped spinning, a dozen aides huddled around the car like mechanics at a pit stop, bundling the shell-shocked prime minster into Number 10 and clearing people away from the area. With Wilson indoors, and police roadblocks surrounding Downing Street, the danger was over for now.

Inside Number 10, the prime minister's chief aide, Roger Tully – a dour, unremarkable man, suited and booted and drenched in Old Spice – sat Wilson down and poured a large brandy. 'Drink this, sir,' he said. 'Doctor Summers is on his way.'

Wilson barely registered the drink, and Tully practically had to clasp the man's hands around it. He paced up and down the room urgently. Something wasn't right. He'd seen Wilson fuming, sarcastic, irritable, elated – and all too often frustrated. But never mute, and never morose.

Another aide, Lyle Jesson, came over to Tully. A similarly inconspicuous man, albeit with a more commanding presence. 'Must be shock,' he said.

Tully hoped that was true.

'Are you hurt, sir?' Jesson asked. There was no reply. Wilson's gaze was elsewhere – somewhere and nowhere – lost in his own thoughts. 'Prime Minister. Are you hurt?'

This time his question registered. But it wasn't the firm commanding tone that stirred a response. Rather the words.

'Prime Minister?' Wilson said, barely mustering a whisper.

'You've been in an accident, sir. You're in shock.'

Wilson couldn't comprehend Jesson's words. But eventually found his reply. 'I think there's been a mistake…'

Tully and Jesson exchanged glances. 'Sir?' they echoed in unison.

'I'm not the prime minister,' said Wilson. 'Where's my family? I want my family!'

'Mrs Wilson's out at bridge, sir,' Tully replied. 'She's on her way back.'

'I need her,' he pleaded. 'I need my mum.'

'I meant your wife, sir. *Mary*.'

'Mum's Ethel,' said Wilson, 'I don't know a Mary.'

Jesson turned to Tully. 'Go and find that doctor. And make it quick. The Prime Minister's clearly hurt.'

'Please – why do you keep calling me that?' asked Wilson. '*The prime minister*?'

Tully couldn't believe what he was saying. 'Because it's true, sir. You lead Her Majesty's Government.'

For the first time Wilson looked Tully straight in the eyes. Trying to understand whether the man standing before him was a liar or an idiot. 'But how can an eight-year-old be prime minister?'

DEATH IN DOWNING STREET

STEED BECOMES PRIME MINISTER
EMMA LEADS THE OPPOSITION

2

EMMA PEEL SAT alone in her apartment. A striking auburn-haired woman in her late twenties, she was dressed in a bright scarlet trouser suit that perfectly complemented the gloss red piano she was playing in her stylish loft-style apartment in London. It was a tastefully decorated flat with powder-blue walls and vibrant accented orange decorations. Modern bench seating contrasted the handful of antique collectibles she'd acquired from her many travels. Contemporary and traditional working in harmony.

Nothing helped Mrs Peel unwind more than a quick tinkle on the ivories, but recently she'd found less and less time to indulge her old passions. It was her own fault of course – when she'd started working with Steed on an informal basis a couple of years ago, it was precisely to get away from the monotony of her everyday life and the crushing pressure of maintaining her status as a "captain of industry" – flying the flag for women and earning plaudits and criticism in equal measure. Back then, the press had called her "ambitious", sometimes "emancipated". One headline in a broadsheet even declared she was the "New face of the British woman". The world saw her as driven, but she'd rapidly recognised the signs of becoming a workaholic. The truth was she was an obsessive thrill seeker. She thrived on challenge and adventure, and although she missed her husband Peter, and clung to the hope he might one day be found alive, marriage had been a struggle for her. Not because she and Peter didn't get along – but the role of "dutiful wife" was never going to be one she excelled at. It was no secret that the past two years spent working with Steed had been the best of her life.

As she played the third movement of Beethoven's *Moonlight Sonata*, a handful of dropped notes told her it had been far too long since she'd last practiced. And if she wasn't very much mistaken, her middle E string was slightly flat. There was a time when she'd have repeated the piece over and over again, honing and perfecting it until it was just right, but that kind of motivation escaped her today. She was killing time. Waiting for her next fix. Her next big adventure.

As if on cue, her doorbell rang. She opened the door, but no one was there. Beneath the elaborate chrome doorbell that bore her name, she found a red briefcase. The chamfered edging and gold monogramed crest told her instantly what it was. What she didn't know was *why* somebody had delivered a ministerial box to her apartment. Opening the briefcase, she found a white envelope.

Inside, on Government-headed paper were four words that got her heart racing: MRS PEEL – WE'RE NEEDED.

3

MRS PEEL FELT a pang of nervousness as she drove towards Downing Street. Her association with John Steed never failed to take new and unexpected turns. It was her first visit to Number 10, and she knew Steed would have had to pull some strings to bring her onto the case. The Ministry turned a blind eye to Steed's penchant for partnering with "amateurs", but this was in a different league.

She didn't know the details of the case yet – only that something was wrong with the Prime Minister and that she needed to come at once to Downing Street to assist. That necessitated the highest level of security clearance, which as an outsider, she simply didn't have. The fact she was being brought in to help reminded her just how much sway Steed still had with the establishment.

In the time Mrs Peel had spent with Steed, they'd worked on all manner of cases with the Ministry – they'd foiled foreign agents, stopped automatons from wreaking havoc on polite society, and prevented any number of diabolical masterminds from taking over the nation. But they seldom got mixed up in working for the top brass.

Mrs Peel guessed they'd either been invited due to desperation, or by request, because they'd inadvertently thwarted a plot to blow up the Prime Minister's train not so long ago, which had put the pair on the government's radar – and no doubt cemented their reputation as problem solvers.

The rain, which had been tiptoeing around all day, took a turn for the worse as Mrs Peel's powder-blue Lotus Elan turned off Whitehall onto Downing Street. It was an unassuming kind of road that looked much like any other row of Georgian houses that you might find in London, but for the distinctive exteriors that had started life as traditional London Yellow brickwork and had darkened over the years due to pollution, later being painted in a coal black to make the dramatic effect permanent.

As Mrs Peel parked up outside the doorstep of Number 10 and exited the car, she could see herself perfectly reflected in the mirror-polished black door. As a child she'd always wanted to play Knock, Knock, Ginger at Number 10 – and had often imagined the look on the Prime Minister's face as he opened the door to find nobody there. The thought of finally knocking the polished black lion that hung dramatically on the door brought a brief childish thrill, but when the door swung open from the inside before she had a chance, she was deprived of the opportunity. The bright light shining from within was in sharp contrast to the overcast weather outside and the silhouetted figure that stood in the doorway to greet her was unmistakable. Sporting an immaculately tailored Pierre Cardin suit, dark blue bowler hat and Whangee Cane Crook umbrella – John Steed was always a welcome sight.

Sixteen years her elder, Steed embodied almost everything she thought a man should be: strong but gentlemanly, cunning yet principled, respectable but flawed. And a mind that could – almost – rival her own. Though she'd never have told him that.

'Mrs Peel!' He beamed, as though he hadn't seen her for years.

'Steed,' she replied in a tone which, to the outsider, might have seemed cold.

But Steed could read the underlying affection. 'How would you like to meet the Prime Minister?'

Mrs Peel's look said it all – her opinion of politicians was well known to him.

Inside Number 10, she found a modest reception room. The reverse of the famous black door was the perfect inverse of the outside, painted in high gloss white. And the pale cream walls and chessboard floor were littered with antiques and collectables from the building's long history.

'What seems to be the problem?' Mrs Peel asked, picking up a taxidermized stoat and looking at it incredulously, as if trying to wake the poor creature from its century-long sleep.

Steed's expression turned serious – gesturing for her to walk with him and away from prying ears. He led her through a warren of rooms, each statelier than the last. Mrs Peel thought the building was certainly impressive, but not on the scale of Buckingham Palace or some of the other magnificent buildings she'd visited around the world. It seemed deliberately more austere – more utilitarian.

Out of earshot, Steed brought her up to speed. 'Someone took a shot at poor old Mr Wilson. Quite literally it seems.'

'Isn't that a job for Security?' asked Mrs Peel.

'Well, it would be. If…'

'If?'

'If the Prime Minister didn't think he was an eight-year-old boy.'

'Ah.'

'Ah exactly, Mrs Peel.'

'I thought you were all eight-year-old boys!'

'Fun loving and young at heart?'

'Immature, reckless and impulsive.'

'You've been spending time with the wrong sort of men.'

Mrs Peel looked Steed up and down. 'You can say that again.'

Arriving at the foot of the famous Downing Street staircase Mrs Peel took a moment to take in her surroundings: a cantilevered wrought-iron staircase wrapped itself around the heart of the imposing building, which ran across three floors. And a black and gold lamp-post scaled the entire height of the building, dominating the area as its centrepiece. The painted honey-yellow walls were decorated with contrasting monochrome portraits of every prime minister all the way back to Walpole.

As Steed and Mrs Peel climbed the stairs, Steed gave a running commentary on each of the famous faces – summing up their tenure in a single word: 'Philanthropist… womaniser… hero… villain… hero *and* villain,' and on the list went, 'and him,' he said resting on a single portrait. 'I can't even remember him! The great and the good, Mrs Peel. What do you think?'

Mrs Peel could sum them all up in a single word. 'Men,' she said.

'Well, play your cards right, Mrs Peel, and there could be a space up there for you.'

'No thank you.'

'Oh, come now, Mrs Peel. You wouldn't fancy being Britain's first female prime minister?'

'In my experience,' she replied, 'politicians are deceitful, arrogant and self-interested. Give me foreign agents any day. At least they let you know where you stand.'

'You're getting more cynical by the day,' Steed said.

'Hmm. I have a good teacher,' she replied.

Outside the Prime Minister's chambers, Doctor Summers and Wilson's aide, Jesson, briefed Steed and Mrs Peel while the Prime Minister was sleeping, courtesy of a gentle sedative to make sure he got some rest.

'He can't remember anything after 1924,' said Jesson. 'Back when he'd have been eight years old. Keeps asking for his damn parents. Doesn't even remember his wife. He thinks we're playing some kind of elaborate practical joke on him.'

'So, what are we looking at, doctor?' asked Steed. 'Some kind of head injury?'

'That's just the thing, Steed,' Summers replied. 'There's not a mark on him. And the chauffeur's *sure* he wasn't hurt. Not physically anyway.'

'The driver pulled off quite an escape by all accounts,' said Mrs Peel.

'Absolutely,' said Jesson, 'He'll be fast tracking his way to the top of the honours list as we speak, I shouldn't wonder. His quick wits undoubtedly saved the Prime Minister's life.'

'Some kind of shock perhaps,' Mrs Peel asked, 'leading to amnesia?'

'At this moment, your guess is as good as mine, Mrs Peel,' said Doctor Summers. 'If it is, I've never seen anything quite like it, and nor have my colleagues.'

'Either way,' said Jesson, 'upshot is... the Prime Minister's incapacitated.'

'And how many people know that?' asked Steed.

'Oh, strictly hush-hush, you understand.'

Steed placed his finger to his lips, his eyebrows furrowing agreeably.

'So that's our *first* problem,' Jesson continued.

'First problem?' asked Mrs Peel.

'Quite,' he replied. 'In a few days' time, the Prime Minister needs to give the performance of his life. The Government's knee-deep in preparations to join the Common Market. He's leading the negotiations personally, and he's due to sign off on our application next week. I don't need to tell you how well things went last time we tried to join, do I, Steed?!'

Steed vaguely remembered the fuss it generated at the time. Back in 1961 when the Conservative Government of the day, under Prime Minister Harold Macmillan, had tried to join the EEC it had the door slammed in its face by the French President, General de Gaulle, citing incompatibilities between Britain and the fledgling union. Macmillan had ended up with considerable egg on his face, and the current Labour Government would inevitably be keen to avoid a repeat performance.

'The Prime Minister is confident he can talk de Gaulle around this time,' said Jesson, 'but to say things are precarious is an understatement. Too much work has gone into this to fall at the final hurdle, Steed.'

'So,' said Mrs Peel, 'you need us to find whoever's responsible for the assassination attempt, bring them to justice, find a way for the Prime Minister to regain his memory, and make sure Britain joins the Common Market... all in under a week?'

'Oh no, Mrs Peel,' said Jesson, 'much sooner than that. The documents need to be signed, sealed and delivered by then, but the Prime Minister still has an awful lot of cajoling to do. Our European neighbours are prepared to consider our seat at the table, but they're a long way off pulling the chair out for us.'

'Well then,' said Steed, 'we'd better get started. We need the Prime Minister out of Downing Street for the time being.'

'Yes, I agree,' said Doctor Summers. 'We can send him to Chequers to recuperate.'

Steed nodded. 'Mrs Peel, I need you to go to the hospital to speak with the injured security guards please. See if they saw anything that could be helpful.'

'Right,' she replied.

Steed turned to Jesson and Summers. 'Let me know when the Prime Minister's up and about – I'll need to talk to him. See if he remembers *anything*.'

'Good luck with that!' said Doctor Summers. 'We've not been able to get any sense out of him.'

'Don't worry about that, gentlemen,' Steed said – full of impish charm, 'I'm good with children.'

4

TO THE NORTH of the river Thames, the London skyline resembled a Lowry painting. Warehouses and factories intersected like badly fitting jigsaw pieces. It was a landscape born of manufacturing necessity, and devoid of architectural charm.

The headquarters of TG Travis & Son was easily missed. An old brick-built building that looked like it was probably Victorian but bastardised almost beyond recognition: 1930s outbuildings were bolted on unsympathetically, 1950s chimneys had been added for ventilation, and half a dozen roof patches just about kept the place dry. The green shoots of any number of indomitable creepers burst through spalled brickwork and crumbling mortar, reclaiming the land that industrialists had stolen a hundred years before.

It was the perfect base for Bill Jacobs. A middle-aged man who looked much older than his years. Dressed head to foot in camel-coloured overalls that had seen better days, he stood on the overhead footbridge that connected two outbuildings, like a lion surveying the savannah beneath. Waiting for his men to return and explain themselves.

Nobody really knew what Jacobs' business actually did. Not even his staff. There were deliveries, there was mysterious inventory, and there were wage packets each week, but the specifics seemed purposefully vague. The company had originally manufactured munitions and made its fortunes – unsurprisingly – during both world wars. Jacobs had dropped out of school early, like most in his class, and had worked his way up to foreman and ended up inheriting the place when the founder's son became a conchie during the War. Something his father could neither understand nor forgive given war put food on their table. The eponymous Travis had issued an ultimatum to his son: come back into the fold, or the business would go to his number two. The son refused to back down and the men never spoke again.

By the time Jacobs got the deeds to the business in '52, after poor old Travis had succumbed to emphysema, the proverbial arse had well and truly fallen out of the business, as the new world order began to shun the conflicts of the past, and alliances like NATO were born. He pivoted as best as he could – putting his machinery to use making pen casings, hinges and fitments instead of bullets and bombs – and turned his hand to anything and everything else that could earn him a living. But then the international markets started to open up and more and more buyers were shipping things in from overseas. But the 'glory days' had given Jacobs just enough money to get by and pursue his other interests. It had also given him a warehouse full of surplus vintage weapons and ammunition.

After three hours and forty-five minutes, Jacobs finally spotted a swarm of beaten-up vans heading back towards the factory. Seven of his so called "best men" returning from their failed mission, tails firmly between their legs. He knew, and they knew, that they were in for a pasting, and justifiably so. They knew how important the mission was. There were no second chances. For Jacobs, *or* his boys. But as much as he'd have liked to take these halfwits outside and shoot every last one of them, he needed them, so today words were the only weapon in his arsenal. That and an assault on their pay packets.

Jacobs strode up to the group's foreman, Manson, and pushed him to the ground.

'It wasn't our fault, guv,' the man pleaded.

'It's true,' said another called Timpson. 'It's the driver, see, he'd have given Jim Clarke the run-around.'

'Excuses,' Jacobs snapped, 'always the same excuses.'

'We did everything like we were s'posed to,' said Manson, 'just like you told us.'

'Just like I told you?' Jacobs laughed. 'Did I tell you to let Wilson give you the slip? Did I tell you to leave eyewitnesses and breadcrumbs strewn across the whole of sodding Westminster? Did I? *Did I?*'

The men kept their heads down.

'You told me you were professionals.'

One of the men looked like he was about to reply.

'That wasn't a question.'

The chap, a Scottish man-mountain called Geiger, persisted, 'It's fixable.'

'Here we go,' said Jacobs. 'The brains of the operation has spoken up.'

'I'm just saying,' said Geiger, 'is ripping us a new one helping?'

'It's certainly making me feel better,' Jacobs replied. Then, through a dirtied window, he spotted a lone motorcycle heading towards the entrance. He slapped Geiger's arm and pointed to the heavy concertinaed factory doors behind him. 'Open it up,' he growled, and the men scrambled to comply. A Triumph Bonneville T120 motorbike slid through and came to rest less than a foot away from Jacobs. The biker, dressed head to foot in rider's leathers, removed her helmet and freed her flame red hair. The woman, Cynthia Turner, kissed Jacobs on the cheek and squeezed him on the arm to try to calm him down. She knew all too well what he was like when he was in a rage, and instantly recognised she needed to pull him back from the brink.

'I've got good news,' said Cynthia. 'Seems your dear friend, the Prime Minister, didn't escape unscathed after all.'

Jacobs' eyes widened, like a child finding a shilling on the street. 'He's injured?' he asked.

She nodded.

'Bad?'

'My contact doesn't know,' said Cynthia, 'but they've sent for a Dr Thomas Summers. A neurologist.'

Jacobs could almost feel his blood pressure coming down in real time. 'A brain injury?'

'Maybe,' she replied. 'Looks like we did more damage than we thought.'

Jacobs smiled and turned to Manson. 'Find out,' he said, 'and quickly. I need to know if I'm planning a mop-up or a rerun. Either way, I want the job done, *tonight*.'

5

THE COUNTRY ESTATE at Chequers in Buckinghamshire had been a home from home for prime ministers since 1921 and Harold Wilson was no exception.

The sixteenth century red brick building embodied the splendour of Elizabethan Britain – a glorious symphony of stone windows and chimney pots gave rise to a building that looked like it was straight out of an oil painting. Rumour had it that the ghost of Lady Mary Grey – the sister of the Nine Days Queen – roamed the corridors of Chequers, after she'd been imprisoned there for two years from 1597. A stone inscription above the garden gate, which read: "All Care Abandon Ye Who Enter Here", further romanticised the grand old house.

Chequers had hosted politicians, presidents, kings and queens, but today's visitor arrived in a six-litre racing green Bentley from the 1930s. The sound of Dunlops pummelling the gravel beneath reverberated around the beautifully tended grounds and dispersed the birds which had happily perched on the building's rooftops. Steed had been to Chequers once before, during a skirmish some years previously involving an Armenian diplomat, a Russian spy and a case load of highly classified stolen transistors that promised to revolutionise Western defence systems. It was one of the more prosaic cases he'd worked on over his long career and lacked the sheer ingenuity to earn Steed's respect. His philosophy was simple: if you were going to break the rules – whether they be morals, conventions or legalities – then it was incumbent upon you to at least do it with a degree of panache. Anything less was barely worth his time.

Steed dropped the car outside the front entrance and hopped out like a show horse jumping a hurdle. Though his knees had been playing him up recently, and he wondered how long it would be before he'd need to find a motor more forgiving for his forty-five-year-old joints.

Climbing the steps, Steed took shelter in the stone-built vestibule before giving the wooden door a firm but friendly rat-a-tat-tat. After thirty long seconds, a gentleman in his sixties or seventies appeared. He was impeccably dressed, wearing a dark suit and black bow tie. He instantly spotted Steed's car, which had been abandoned not five yards from the front door at a displeasing angle.

His words said 'Welcome to Chequers' while his body language said something altogether different. The man, a housekeeper called Renley Leamington-Stork, led Steed through a labyrinth of wood-panelled rooms and corridors, beautifully adorned with portraits, landscapes and precious antiques. When they arrived at the library, the man reached down, as though to retrieve a book from the shelf; instead he pulled a discreet brass handle which – like something out of an Agatha Christie novel – unlocked a hidden door that swung open. Inside, Steed spotted Harold Wilson, perching on a stool by the window.

'Prime Minister,' said Steed cheerfully, practically shutting the door in Leamington-Stork's face before removing his bowler hat, setting his umbrella to one side and extending his hand. Just the two of them alone in a big sitting room, complete with ornate fireplace and hand-carved furniture.

Harold accepted the shake tentatively, like a child who'd been told to play at being a grown-up. 'That's what they keep telling me,' he answered, lighting his pipe and inhaling the sweet tobacco.

'You've had us all quite worried, sir,' said Steed. 'Are you feeling any better?'

Harold exhaled the mouthful of nicotine and tar. 'Other than forgetting who I am, you mean?'

'Oh, I don't know,' quipped Steed, 'I happen to know a few men who'd quite like to forget their sins.'

But Harold wasn't paying much attention; he was busy fidgeting with his pipe.

Steed walked over to a decanter by the bay window. 'May I?' he asked.

'If they've said it's okay.'

'They?' asked Steed.

'Whoever's in charge here.'

'I think that's you, Sir.' Steed replied.

'I'm really not you know,' said Harold, his voice squeaky and unsure.

Steed poured two brandies and passed one to the Prime Minister.

He shook his head. 'Mum said I oughtn't.'

'I won't tell if you won't,' said Steed in a whispered tone. 'I dare say she'd have something to say about her eight-year-old smoking too.'

This stopped Harold in his tracks. He looked at the pipe and instantly dropped it. Like he'd lit up purely on autopilot and had been snapped back into "reality".

'Relax,' said Steed, bending down to retrieve the pipe. 'Look, why don't we both sit down and talk.' Steed gently but firmly placed Harold in a chair. Then he dropped the pipe back in one hand and a glass of brandy in the other. 'Much better,' he said.

Harold now didn't seem to know what to do with either.

Steed took the seat opposite. 'So, tell me what *can* you remember?' he asked.

'I've been through all this with the quacks,' he replied, the frustration clear in his voice.

'Humour me,' said Steed.

Harold spoke in a monotone. Fed up with recanting the events. 'There was a car chase. They said I must have bumped my head or something. They took me to Downing Street of all places. And suddenly everyone's saying I'm the Prime Minister!'

'That must have been quite a shock,' said Steed, trying to empathise.

'You could say that,' he confirmed.

Steed retrieved a battered photograph from his pocket. 'What can you tell me about this?'

Harold looked at the image. It showed a young boy dressed in a grey suit jacket and shorts with knee-high socks and a flat cap. 'That's me,' Harold answered.

'That's right,' said Steed. 'You had this very photograph on you this morning. They said it's something of a good luck charm.'

Harold shrugged.

'How old do you think you were when this photograph was taken, Mr Wilson?'

'It can't have been more than six months ago,' he replied. 'So, seven or eight. My birthday's in March.'

'Okay. And can you tell me how old you are now?' asked Steed.

'Eight. I just said that. It was back in the summer if I'm remembering right. I wanted to see the Prime Minister, Mr MacDonald.' He summoned an ironic laugh.

Steed stood him up and turned him towards the mirror atop the fireplace. 'Look, I don't want to be impertinent, Mr Wilson, but...' He held the photo up to the mirror, so the Prime Minister could see both faces side by side. The contrast was significant. 'You must be able to notice the difference,' said Steed, 'otherwise that's one heck of a six months!'

Harold seemed bemused. 'I don't follow?' he said.

'You're telling me that you can't see *any* difference between these two images?' Steed pointed at both figures in the mirror.

Harold took another look. The face he saw reflected was youthful and carefree. But the more Steed spoke, the more the illusion snapped – just for a second – and he began to see another face bleeding through. A much older man with a round face, greying hair and dark eyebrows. This scared him and he jolted back away from the mirror.

'Mr Wilson?' enquired Steed.

'What kind of witchcraft is this?' the Prime Minister asked.

'Witchcraft? Did you see something in the mirror?' asked Steed.

Harold shook his head furiously like a toddler trying to shake off a nightmare.

'What did you see, Harold?' The words stuck in Steed's palate because he was a stickler for formality and courtesy, but calling an eight-year-old "Mr" and "Prime Minister" was patently absurd. At least from the perspective of the man-child before him.

'An old man,' Harold replied.

'And did you recognise him?' asked Steed.

'I don't know... Maybe.'

'That's good. We're making progress. Can we try again?' Steed enquired.

Harold shook his head, visibly scared.

'It's okay. I won't let anyone hurt you,' said Steed, fidgeting in his pockets and retrieving a coin. 'There's two bob in it for you if you do?'

Harold's eye widened and Steed helped him back up to the mirror, hoping the illusion would be broken. 'Can you see him? The old man?' Steed asked.

But Harold couldn't. The reflection was younger and more energetic than ever. A lad proud as punch at receiving half a crown. 'He's gone,' said Harold.

'The boy or the old man?'

'The old blighter,' said Harold. 'I'm glad – he was terrifying. Looked like my Old Man. Just rounder in the face.'

Steed found it hard to conceal his frustration.

'Who was he?' asked Harold.

Steed collected his bowler and umbrella and headed for the door. 'He was the Prime Minister, Harold. And I'm going to help you find him.'

6

MRS PEEL HAD been interrogated more times than most. She'd been tortured by tyrants, manhandled by maniacs and shouted down by sociopaths. Therefore, the motley crew of middle-aged windbags that sat across from her didn't feel particularly intimidating. Each man was fairly indistinguishable from another – a veritable sea of receding hairlines, bulging waistlines and pasty white complexions which looked like they hadn't seen a spot of sunshine in decades. The room smelt strongly of smoke, whisky and mediocrity.

Considering the importance of some of the decisions that had been made within its four walls over the past century or two, the Cabinet Room was surprisingly plain. The walls were white, the floor sported a simple patterned rug, and the room was dominated by an oval table, with twenty-three upholstered chairs surrounding it, covered in vivid green billiard cloth. Some had described it as boat shaped, while others affectionately called it "the coffin".

Today, there was only one seat empty, but it wasn't for Mrs Peel, it was the chair nearest the fireplace at the centre of the table – the Prime Minister's seat.

Mrs Peel stood by the door impatiently as the men exchanged pleasantries, seemingly impervious to her presence, until they were finally called to order by the Chancellor of the Exchequer, James Callaghan. He was a rather cheerful looking chap with puffy cheeks and slicked-back greying hair.

'Gentlemen, may I introduce you to Mrs...' Callaghan turned to their visitor.

'Peel,' she replied, 'Emma Peel.'

'That's right, Mrs Peel, she's from the Ministry.'

'That hardly narrows it down,' said George Brown, the Prime Minister's Foreign Secretary who shared his name with one of Wilson's footballing idols, and bore a passing resemblance to Harold himself if you allowed for the black spectacles. '*Which* ministry?'

'*The* Ministry,' said Callaghan.

'Ahh.' Brown replied.

'Perhaps you'd be so good as to enlighten us about the reason for your visit, my dear.' said Callaghan.

'Gladly,' said Mrs Peel, the disdain in her voice clear for all to hear, 'I'll be brief... We're trying to establish what exactly happened to the Prime Minister this morning – and why.'

'I thought you were going to tell us,' said Roy Jenkins, the Home Secretary, another well-spoken man with bushy eyebrows, receding hair and lines on his forehead that betrayed his age like the rings of a tree.

'Are we sure he hasn't just been on the bottle?' added a voice Mrs Peel couldn't quite place, from the far end of the table.

'I've been saying for years he needed to slow down,' said another.

'We're working on the assumption the timing *isn't* coincidental,' Mrs Peel asserted.

'The Common Market, you mean?' asked Callaghan.

'Yes,' she replied.

'You think someone's out to sabotage it?' he replied.

'We don't know. That's why I'm here. Are you aware of anyone that would go to these lengths to prevent Britain signing up to the treaty?'

There were chortles around the table, which Mrs Peel found in poor taste.

'Only half the country, Mrs Pier,' said the only other woman in the room, the red-haired Transport Secretary, Barbara Castle whose very presence seemed to command attention from her colleagues.

Mrs Peel let the mistaken nomenclature slide. 'Anyone who'd *kill* for it?'

'The EUNOCs I suppose,' Castle replied.

'I beg your pardon?' Mrs Peel asked.

'The European Nation Opposition Campaign. A funny sort the lot of them. Factory workers, trade unionists, you know the type.'

'Careful, Barbara,' said a voice from the back of the room. 'That's half of your constituents.'

'And one hundred per cent of yours,' she replied acerbically. 'A barmy idea in the first place if you ask me – and I've said so, repeatedly, to the Prime Minister.'

'*Repeatedly*,' said Jenkins, rolling his eyes.

'I take it you're not all dyed in the wool Europhiles then?' asked Mrs Peel.

'Not at all,' Callaghan replied. 'But that's par for the course around here.'

'Collective responsibility I think is the phrase, Mrs Peel,' said Jenkins. 'Unified in public, feral in private.'

'So, what happens now?' asked Mrs Peel. 'Will the application be delayed?'

'Absolutely not,' said Jenkins. 'It can't be. We've worked too hard for too long to have a second throw of the dice as it is. A delay is unthinkable; it would be another decade – at best – until we'd have another chance. Not to mention how it would look to the public.'

'And what are you telling your dear electorate?' Mrs Peel asked.

'Nothing,' said Callaghan. 'Or as close to it as we can get. Word's out that *something*'s amiss, but nobody's terribly concerned… at least not yet.'

'We'll arrange for Wilson to be seen walking in and out of buildings, a few paparazzi getting a shot off in the car, that sort of thing,' said Trevor Lloyd-Hughes, a quirky looking chap with a prodigious nose and thin moustache who could have passed for a spiv during the War. He served as the Prime Minister's Press Secretary and had been invited to cabinet to help handle the situation. 'Proves he's alive and well, while swerving well… you know what.'

'And who does know the truth?' asked Mrs Peel. 'Outside this room, I mean.'

'A handful of trusted staffers and medics,' said Callaghan. 'Her Majesty of course. And *you*.' The final word was enunciated indignantly.

'I'm honoured,' Mrs Peel replied.

'You should be, missy.' Callaghan snapped back. 'I'm not best fond of bringing outsiders into Government business I can tell you. But this Steed fellow's got quite some sway in *very* high places indeed, so I'm prepared to go against my better judgement.'

'Seems to me she's just as clueless as the rest of them,' came a voice near the window.

'I feel like we're wasting time,' said another member of the Cabinet.

'Send her on her way and we can get back to the business of the day,' added Castle.

Mrs Peel strode across the room in her bright red

one-piece. She refused to be spoken to like that by anyone, even elected officials. She walked over to the Prime Minister's chair, pulled it out from under the table and plopped herself down on it defiantly. The sounds and sights of open gasps reverberated around the room. 'Gentlemen… and lady,' she said, 'Let me be *very* clear. You asked for my help, which I'll gladly provide. But make no mistake, unlike your prime minister, I am not a child, and nor shall I be spoken to like one. So kindly afford me the respect I've shown you.'

Barbara Castle smiled. She'd underestimated the young woman. She liked a lady with a bit of piss and vinegar. 'I apologise, Mrs *Peel*. Perhaps we let our emotions run a little high.'

Callaghan made a sound – a sort of grunt – which Mrs Peel interpreted to mean he was also conciliatory. 'But you really can't sit *there*,' he added.

'Rather than postulating on posteriors that can or cannot grace a chair, perhaps – if I may – we should focus on the matter in hand.'

'What more can we tell you?' asked Jenkins.

'Who's taking over the Common Market negotiations for a start?' she asked.

'I am,' came a voice from the back of the room, a man who'd been standing the whole time, because there weren't enough seats left around the table. He raised his hand to catch her eye. 'The name's Hagley. Lord Hagley.'

'Well then, my lord,' Mrs Peel replied, somewhat sardonically, 'I'd recommend you keep a security detail with you at all times.'

'I hardly think—'

Hagley was cut off at the pass. '*If* the attack was motivated by the question of Europe,' Mrs Peel explained, 'then logic dictates they'll try again.'

Callaghan agreed. 'I'll make sure we look after him.'

'Is there anyone else who could be responsible? A foreign power perhaps?'

Callaghan shrugged. 'Possible but I'm not convinced. Some see European integration as a threat you understand, but assassinating a sitting prime minister is an act of war in anyone's book. It's a lot to risk to stop what is – for all the hoo-ha – a glorified trading agreement.'

'Don't be so sure,' said another unseen voice, 'There are plenty from the Eastern Bloc that see the EEC as a threat to communism, you mark my words.'

'Perhaps,' said Callaghan, 'but we'd have heard whispers if something was brewing. I'm sure of it.'

'What about the fanatics?' said Castle.

Mrs Peel's ears pricked up.

'That strange lot up at the lodge?' clarified Callaghan. 'It's their life's work to *join* Europe, I hardly think they'd do anything to scupper it.'

'Tell me more,' said Mrs Peel.

'They're based on Wimbledon Common, from memory,' said Castle. 'Never stop banging on about European integration. They think we should hand *everything* over to the Continent: our armies, gold reserves, coal. *Everything.*'

'Perhaps my private secretary can sort you out with the details…' said Callaghan, keen to move on with the business of the day. 'On the way out.'

Mrs Peel gladly accepted the hint.

'Thank you,' she said vacating the chair and very slowly replacing it to its original position. 'Good day,' she said walking towards the door without looking back. 'It's reassuring to see the country's in such good hands…'

7

GOVERNMENT HANDLERS WERE ill-accustomed to being driven at sixty miles an hour down a single-track country lane in a vintage open-top car that probably should have either been in the scrapper's yard, or else a museum, a good twenty years ago. Especially when the night was drawing in. But accepting Steed's offer of a lift back to London in the Bentley was the fastest way Roger Tully could get home in time to see the children before their nanny put them to bed. And besides, it gave him some time to – as delicately as he could – broach the matter of Mrs Peel.

The phone line at Chequers hadn't stopped ringing since the cabinet meeting had ended. A succession of frustrated ministers all complaining at the manner in which Steed's "aide" had behaved when addressing their hallowed group. Personally, Tully found Mrs Peel perfectly charming when they'd met. In his opinion, she was fiercely bright, refreshingly forthright, and eminently capable, but she'd clearly upset some of the old guard who didn't like to be challenged, especially not by a woman – and an unelected one at that. It was no great surprise that the only minister who spoke in her defence was Barbara "Babs" Castle who said the girl had "bigger balls than most of her colleagues" and looked forward to seeing "more of her type" on the team.

Steed could tell there was something on Tully's mind. They'd spent the first twenty miles parroting small talk by rote. If there was a book of Great British Pleasantries, they'd almost certainly have exhausted it. They'd talked about the weather (unusually cold for the time of year), the decline of the British motorcar (American imports were simply not built for English roads) and mused whether or not jam should be placed above or below the cream on a scone (Steed's penchant was always to spread the preserve first). When the gentle chitchat petered out – culminating in a particularly anodyne comment from Tully about the ideal tyre pressure for front wheels in winter – the silence that followed felt like blessed relief for both parties.

'Steed, do you mind if I speak openly?' said Tully at last.

'I'd expect nothing less,' said Steed.

'Look, I know you don't like to work alone,' Tully said, 'but it seems Mrs Peel's got a few backs up.'

'Oh?' said Steed.

'Oh indeed,' he replied. 'Addressed Cabinet this evening,' Tully expanded. 'By all accounts, by the end she was practically running it.'

'That sounds like Mrs Peel,' said Steed, adopting a smile that betrayed his amusement and pride.

'Well, that's the point, isn't it,' Tully said. 'She's a loose cannon and right now I can't afford liabilities.'

'What would you have me do?' said Steed, momentarily taking his eyes off the roads to look Tully square in the eyes.

'They're saying she's off the case,' said Tully. 'I'm sorry, Steed. Honestly, I am – it's nothing personal, you understand, but you're going to have to go this one alone.'

Steed slammed on the brakes and pulled into a lay-by. The shock on Tully's face was clear to see.

'What on earth are you doing, man?' Tully asked.

'Recusing myself from the case?' said Steed.

'Don't be ridiculous, Steed,' said Tully, 'we need you. We're in the middle of a national emergency.'

'You need *both* of us,' said Steed. 'I'm afraid you don't get to pick and choose.'

'This won't play well with the Ministry, Steed. A secondment is a secondment.'

'I'll worry about the Ministry,' said Steed. 'You worry about the 47B.'

'The what?' Tully asked.

'The bus to High Wycombe,' said Steed. 'We passed one about half a mile ago on its way out of Great Missenden. I'm sure there'll be a stop around here somewhere.' Steed leaned over and opened the small hatch that passed for a door on the Bentley's passenger side.

'Listen. A joke's a joke and all that, but we need to be getting along,' said Tully. 'I'm due back in London before the hour.'

'I'd love to help you and all,' said Steed. 'But unfortunately, I'm no longer heading in that direction. As of a few moments ago, I'll be taking a long overdue holiday. I'm thinking of trying my luck on the slopes. Or... you'll like this... I've been meaning to visit the States and see Mrs Gale's beach-house. You remember Cathy Gale, don't you Roger? Another one of my outspoken partners. I seem to remember you took quite a shine to her.'

'Okay, Steed,' said Tully, 'you've made your point.'

'Have I?' said Steed.

'Adequately.'

'Well, that's wonderful news,' said Steed, reaching across Tully's waist and pulling the hatch closed. 'I'll tell Mrs Peel the good news as soon as we're back.'

'She'd better be worth it, Steed,' said Tully.

'Oh, she is,' said Steed earnestly. 'She most definitely is.'

8

STEED HAD NEVER cared much for jigsaws, and this one was no exception. His second cousin thrice-removed, Cousin Herbert, had sent it to him in this morning's post, along with a cryptic message: "Identify the car and what do you see? Your share of Uncle Robert's inheritance is hidden plain as can be." Now probably wasn't the right time to be sorting his edge pieces from his middles – given the country was in the midst of a diplomatic nightmare – but Mrs Peel was still ten minutes away, traffic permitting, and a man had to while away the time *somehow.* There wasn't a photograph on the shoebox the jigsaw had been sent in, but Steed quickly established it was some kind of countryside scene. There were pieces of sky, shrubs, a body of water – probably a pond or lake – some bricks, and a bright red race car that Steed thought was probably a Bugatti.

Why Uncle Robert wanted him to have it, however, was a mystery. As was how there could be much of an inheritance in the first place, given the last time Steed had seen his old uncle, he'd been practically penniless, owing to a taste for expensive wine, wheels and women. As he tussled with the Bugatti, try as he might, he couldn't work out how the exhaust connected to the car's rear bumper, and he suddenly remembered exactly why he found puzzles so frustrating. Just as he was contemplating giving up on the whole thing and chucking the pieces into the four-foot high tuba which sat in the corner of his apartment – an elegant oak-panelled first-floor flat with a rich purple carpet – the doorbell rang, and Steed welcomed Mrs Peel, who was soaked from the rain which hadn't let up all day.

Steed grabbed a towel and passed it to her. 'You look like you've been through the wringer,' he said, instinctively walking to the decanter to pour her a drink. She gladly took it from him.

'In more ways than one,' she said, taking a seat at the table and surveying the jigsaw puzzle.

'Let me guess,' said Steed. 'You were awestruck by the well-lubricated wheels of democracy?'

'I was positively charmed,' she replied, picking up the "exhaust" and instantly recognising it was a wing mirror, which she slotted into place, much to Steed's chagrin.

'I'm guessing the visit to the hospital didn't get us anywhere either?' asked Steed.

'One motorcyclist deceased,' Mrs Peel replied. 'One on life support, and the other two bodyguards didn't know what hit them.'

'As I feared,' said Steed.

'How was the young prince?' Mrs Peel asked.

'Decidedly immature,' he replied. 'I can't see him snapping out of it any time soon. He's utterly convinced he's eight years old and won't hear a word otherwise.'

With one wing mirror in place, Steed readily identified the other and gave Mrs Peel a "your turn next" gesture, as if they were playing chess.

'Any history of psychosis in the past,' Mrs Peel asked, 'other than his choice of career?'

'Nothing in the files,' Steed replied. 'Yesterday he was fit and well. Today he's practising his times tables.'

Mrs Peel began to assemble the bricks that surrounded the Bugatti. Steed looked impressed.

‘I looked over the files Dr Summers sent over,’ she said, ‘I’m not an expert in neurology, but psychosis is usually a response to brain injury, disease or medication.’

‘All of which we’ve ruled out,’ said Steed.

‘Precisely.’

‘How did you get on?’ Steed asked, ‘any idea who we’re looking for?’

‘EUNOCs,’ she said, without the faintest hint of irony.

‘Mr Peel would be pleased,’ quipped Steed.

‘You should try it,’ she replied. Then she playfully tossed a jigsaw piece at him and added, ‘Maybe you already have.’

‘I always knew they couldn’t be trusted,’ Steed replied.

Mrs Peel looked wearingly at Steed. His humour was as predictable as his tailoring.

‘The European Nation Opposition Campaign,’ she said. ‘*Apparently*. One half of our cornucopia of crack pots.’

‘And the other half?’ Steed asked.

Mrs Peel withdrew a curled-up poster from the inside of her thigh-high boot. ‘This lot.’

The advertisement featured a painted Greek goddess called Europa, riding a bull. Atop the image were the words *YOUR CONTINENT NEEDS YOU!* And at the bottom it read: *EUTOPIA. The European Unification Taskforce Office – Promoting Integration and Accession.* The poster ended with a call to action: *Lobby your local parliamentarian to show your strong support for joining the Common Market.*

‘One group fighting to unify Europe, and the other fighting anyone who tries,’ she summarised.

‘Anyone willing to kill for it?’ asked Steed.

She pressed a final piece into the puzzle to complete the Bugatti, then she turned to Steed and said, ‘I suppose we should find out.’

9

STEED PULLED UP to the headquarters of EUTOPIA and slipped the Bentley into neutral, an awkward process which meant sticking his hand outside the car and cranking a huge metal lever, not unlike operating a steam train. The building was unassuming, an old community hall that had been cobbled together with simple bricks and timber. On the tin roof were six flag poles, representing each of the Common Market's founder members. There was the Bundesflagge of West Germany, the Tricolore flags of France and Italy, the Belgian Government Ensign, along with the Netherlands' Statenvlag and Luxembourg's Rout-Wäiss-Blo which, confusingly, were nearly identical. In the centre, was the Union Flag with its world-famous triple crosses representing England, Scotland and Northern Ireland. The fourth nation of the United Kingdom – Wales – was conspicuously missing from the flag because it was considered part of the Kingdom of England back when the flag was created in the nineteenth century.

The second Steed set foot on the overgrown concrete pathway that led up to the lodge, he heard a cheery voice greeting him.

'Good morning traveller,' said the voice. It belonged to a raggedy man wearing a bobbled suit. 'The name's Reginald Noble.'

'How do you do?' said Steed, tipping his bowler as he was led inside.

'Welcome to our little slice of continental bliss,' said Noble.

Steed smiled politely. The lobby was timber clad, like a hunting lodge, and was sparsely furnished with a single wooden desk, a wastepaper bin, one filing cabinet and seven internal doors. Each had a country's name on it.

'Here for the tour, are you?' asked Noble.

'If it wouldn't put you to any bother?' Steed replied.

'Not at all. Visitors have been few and far between of late, tell you the truth. What with all the scaremongering that's been going on.'

'The *conman* market?' said Steed.

'I beg your pardon?'

'It's written on your gates.'

'The little devils…' said Noble, his grimace suggesting this wasn't the first time.

'I take it not everyone in the community's a fan of your…' Steed struggled to find the word.

'Society,' Noble answered, 'of like-minded folk who believe the *only* way to stop a third – and some would say final – war in Europe, is to heal our divides and take on the Yanks and the Soviets as a *united* empire. A *European* empire no less. Just imagine it: British strength, German engineering, French ingenuity. If the *whole* of Europe came together, we would be unstoppable.'

'Unstoppable,' said Steed, mirroring the man's language enthusiastically.

'I take it you *are* here to join the fight?'

The words piqued Steed's interest. 'The fight?'

'To get Lady Britannia to take her seat amongst the new order of course. You *do* believe in the great unification?'

Steed dodged the question. 'I'm here to educate myself,' he replied, 'getting all the information, so to speak.'

'Sensible, dear boy. Veracity not mendacity.'

'Facts not facsimiles,' said Steed.

'I can see we're going to get along swimmingly, Mr… er…' It dawned on Noble that he hadn't even asked his visitor's name.

'Steed.'

'I can see your wit is as sharp as your suit, Mr Steed.'

'You said something about a tour?'

Noble sprang into action. 'Yes of course. Listen to me wittering on,' he said retrieving a wooden box from under the desk. 'My wife used to say I'd forget my manners if I had any.'

'Used to?'

'Left me,' said Noble, 'for a foreigner would you believe!'

'Not… a *European*?' Steed asked.

'Certainly not…' said Noble, 'perish the thought – he was antipodean.' The man began rummaging through the box for seven labelled keys. 'It's a self-guided tour,' Noble said pressing the keys into Steed's palm, 'start with France and work your way round.'

'Thank you,' said Steed, turning the lock and stepping through the first door, which was engraved with the words *Liberté, égalité, fraternité*.

Inside, the room was decorated like a French chateau, adorned with intricate plaster work, gold leaf trim, and exquisite furniture. A giant chandelier drew the eye as it dangled gracefully above the Savonnerie-style rug at the centre of the room.

It didn't take Steed long to spot the attractive brunette woman draped across the chaise longue, wearing an elaborate eighteenth century get-up that wouldn't have looked out of place on Marie Antoinette. Steed's face betrayed his penchant for French nobility.

'*Bonjour*,' she said, '*je m'appelle Jeannette, bienvenue au Chateau Lombarde*.'

'*Enchanté*,' he said, '*je m'appelle Steed*.'

'*Parlez-vous anglais?*' said Jeannette.

Steed nodded. '*Mais, bien sûr*.'

'Then welcome, Monsieur Steed,' she said, affecting a French accent. 'Our tour today begins in the glorious Première République – the world's most visited country. Home to the iconic Eiffel Tower, the Louvre, Notre Dame, the Arc de Triomphe! Birthplace of Monet and Renoir, Debussy and Saint-Saëns, Eiffel and Braille.'

None of this was news to Steed who had spent a lot of time in France during the War.

'Please tell me you have a French cellar?' he asked.

'I can see you're going to be trouble, Monsieur Steed.'

'That's what my French mistress said,' he replied.

She looked intrigued.

'My *school* mistress,' he clarified. 'I failed languages I'm afraid.'

'Perhaps you'll fare better over the border?' she said. 'The peaks are exceptional.'

Steed could well believe it.

Next, Steed entered door two – Italy – which read *La Dolce Vita*. Inside, he found himself in an ancient Roman villa, like something from Pompeii. There was a stone fireplace replete with statues, and coloured marble columns flanking the doorway. Steed marvelled at the pure theatricality of it all as he heard an ominous drumbeat, getting faster and more intense. When the sound stopped, a woman wearing a revealing toga stepped through some curtains at the far end of the room.

'*Salvē*!' she said.

As the woman lifted her head, Steed instantly recognised her. 'I don't suppose you have a twin, do you?' he said, addressing the woman he'd met a few moments ago in the other room.

'My name is Janetta,' she said, now producing a Latin accent. '*Fac me ridere*.'

Steed's eyes widened.

'It means… you make me laugh.'

'Pity,' he replied.

She blushed. 'Welcome to Italy. The home of da Vinci, the Roman Empire, the Colosseum. Of Raphael and Venice, Michaelangelo and Lake Garda, pizza and Pisa. If Italy is a boot, Signor Steed, then its footsteps have been felt across the world.'

'*Bellissimo*,' said Steed.

'Speaking of which,' Janetta said, 'how about we slip you into something more comfortable?' She gently removed Steed's jacket and wrapped a toga around him.

'I'd love to,' he said, 'but I've an appointment in Belgium.'

Door three's inscription read *Eendracht maakt macht*, meaning "unity makes strength". Inside the room, Steed found himself in a lacemaker's workshop. Unsurprisingly, he found a familiar face at the work bench, wearing a white apron.

'*Welkom in België*,' she said in Flemish, a language Steed didn't know. Instead, he simply removed his bowler.

'My name is Janna,' she said in a pidgin Flemish accent. 'Would you like to see how we make lace?'

'Absolutely,' said Steed.

Janna sat at a stool on her workbench and began spinning bobbins like a pianist playing a master concerto, overlapping them at breakneck speed to twirl the lace into an incredibly delicate pattern. Steed was transfixed.

'Very impressive,' he said.

'Can you guess what I'm making?'

The bright white lace garment was small and dainty. 'I can only imagine,' said Steed.

'Do you know how soft lace feels against the skin, de heer Steed?' she said, placing his hand on the material.

'I do now,' he replied.

She held the lace up to her bosom before handing Steed the pocket square.

Next came Castle Schapp of Luxembourg, emblazoned with the words: *Mir wëlle bleiwe wat mir sinn.*

'It means, "We want to remain what we are,"' said an old friend.

'Let me guess,' said Steed. 'Jeanelle?'

She shook her head.

'Jeanitt?'

'No.'

'Jenittle?'

'My name is Jang, Hr Steed,' she said at last.

'Naturally,' replied Steed. 'Pleased to meet you, Jang.'

Steed's guide wore a headscarf, and a red and white dress with ribbons. This time, Jang barely spoke any Luxembourgish, which suggested even Noble's staff had their limits.

Following Luxemburg was a doorway marked with the phrase: *Einigkeit und Recht und Freiheit*, which meant *Unity and Justice and Freedom* and led to a tavern in West Germany, overseen by a fräulein, who wore a blue, black and white flowing dirndl and offered a wide array of German ales.

'*Altbier, Helles, Kölsch*,' she said, which Steed took to be another national motto of some import.

'Beer,' she said, pointing to the three labelled kegs beneath her.

'Ah,' said Steed, 'I see. Which would you recommend?'

'It depends,' she said. 'Do you prefer it sweet, rich, or with a little bitterness?'

'I've dated all three,' he joked.

'I think we'll go for the Kölsch,' she said, pouring him a taste.

'I'll drink it outside if I may,' said Steed.

'Of course,' she said, 'but don't be a stranger, Herr Steed.'

'Certainly not,' he replied, doffing his hat and crossing the border.

The last of the founder states was the Netherlands where Steed was introduced to a clog-wearing street-seller trading tulips from her wooden *sjees* – a traditional horse and cart hand-painted with the words: *Mevrouw Jeanet's Tulps*.

Steed patted the wooden horse that lay at the end of the reins affectionately.

'*Je maintiendrai*,' said Jeanet, which translated to "I will maintain", the official motto of the royal family of the Netherlands, which adorned the doorway to Holland.

'Isn't that French?' Steed asked.

She offered him a flower. 'Shall we go Dutch?'

'I wouldn't hear of it, Mevrouw Jeanet,' Steed said, removing a green one pound note from his wallet and passing it across the table. 'An English gentleman always pays his way.'

'Gulden, Dhr Steed?' asked the woman, feigning ignorance of the British currency she'd been handed. 'Only the Queen's Shilling for me, I'm afraid,' Steed replied.

From her cart, she poured two glasses of jenever, a Dutch gin. Clinking glasses, the two downed the clear spirit and shuddered as the pleasing burn registered in their throats.

With a tulip in both hands and fire in his belly, Steed headed for the exit.

Back in reception, Reginald Noble opened the final doorway marked *Keep Calm and Carry On*.

'Are you ready for the climax?' he asked.

'Always,' Steed answered.

'Then, Mr Steed, I give you the newest member of our community – God willing – Lady Britannia.'

Inside, Steed found himself in a British pub with a cockney barmaid wearing a chequerboard miniskirt.

'Janet,' she said, introducing herself. 'Did you enjoy meeting my sisters?'

'It was quite an *experience*,' he answered honestly.

'I can imagine. Go on then… who was your favourite? I shan't tell.'

Steed shook his head, 'A gentlemen never tells.'

'A lady likes to know,' she replied.

'Well, I do have a soft spot for a good Englishwoman,' he said.

'Good choice,' she said. 'Drink?'

'Not for me, thank you,' said Steed, fearful of adding Brahms and Liszt to the catalogue of European luminaries.

'Do take a seat,' said Noble, pulling up bar stools for himself and Steed. 'Jean, why don't you join us?'

'Right you are,' she said, removing her blonde wig and unclipping her loud hooped plastic earrings. 'Did you like our little show?' Jean asked, her accent switching to perfect Queen's English.

'Very much,' said Steed, admiring the sheer effort they'd gone to, albeit confused as to the reason why.

'So do you see yourself as a EUTOPIAn?' Noble asked.

'I shall certainly give it some thought,' Steed said diplomatically.

'Please do,' said Jean, 'I'd be devastated if you – of all people – became a EUNOC.'

'Not as sorry as I'd be,' said Steed earnestly. 'You've heard of them then?'

'Heard of them?' she replied. 'How ever could you not? They don't stop telling anyone and everyone who'll listen that the country's finished if it dares to get into bed with Europe. You tell me, Mr Steed, have we given you any cause to worry?'

Steed may well have been happy enough to get into bed with any one of the six nations, but he chose not to say anything. Instead, he threw out a conversation starter to see if it provoked a reaction: 'I've heard whispers that the Government might delay?'

'Not a chance,' said Noble. 'Now they've *finally* seen the light, they daren't risk a U-turn. The press would have a field day.'

'*Finally*? They haven't always been so "enlightened" then?' Steed asked.

'Good heavens no,' said Noble. 'It's been like pulling teeth. But we're on the right side of history, you mark my words.'

'And now?' said Steed.

'On the same page, at last,' Noble replied, 'I'm no fan of the Labour Party, Mr Steed, but when it comes to Europe, we're singing from the same hymn sheet.'

'So, you can't think of any EUTOPIAns who would be out to cause trouble?'

'None whatsoever,' said Noble, 'but it's an odd line of questioning if you don't mind me saying. Usually, applicants want to know how much membership costs and whether they'll have a vote at the AGM…'

'I never like to be predictable,' said Steed.

'That you are not,' Noble agreed.

'Nor you,' said Steed, 'I do have some more conventional

questions if it helps… like, how many members do you have for instance?'

'Nine hundred and fifty-two,' said Noble. 'Fifty-three if you pay your subs today.'

'Anyone I'd know?'

'Can't tell you that, old boy. Not until you're a member.'

Steed admired Noble's perseverance. 'Let me sleep on it,' he said.

'Very well, Mr Steed,' said Noble. If you have any questions, you know exactly where we are.'

'To the nearest continent at least,' said Steed.

Noble and Jean smiled, intrigued but suspicious.

'Thank you again for your hospitality,' Steed continued, locking eyes one last time with Jean, '*all* of you.'

10

MRS PEEL DROPPED her Elan half a mile from the headquarters of the European Nation Opposition Campaign. Unlike Steed's more direct approach, Mrs Peel preferred the element of surprise, especially as the EUNOCs were on the Government's watch list. In fairness, so were Steed's lot – the EUTOPIAns – but from what she could tell, that was a minor skirmish at a march. Apparently, someone from the group had been caught trying to hang a blue flag with circular gold stars – an emblem that was fast becoming synonymous with Europe – from the Downing Street railings. The EUNOCs had a much more violent history and operated out of a former munitions factory, so she wanted to tread lightly.

After parking her car in an old dock on the edge of the Thames, she hopped out of her open top car and jogged the journey she'd just driven, back to the estate of TG Travis & Son.

The six-foot gates were rusted wrought iron with decorative spikes, but thankfully not barbed. She hopped up and over them with relative ease, dropping to the ground stealthily like the manoeuvre came entirely naturally. As she wandered through the machine graveyard that surrounded the factory, she found little of interest, but the overgrown shrubs that had started life as tiny weeds in the cracks of crumbling masonry comfortably hid her from view. The main building seemed to be over to the east, and she could see some lights and hear a hubbub of activity coming from that direction.

However, before she headed over there, and risked being caught, she decided to explore the outbuildings to the west of the complex. Most were full of wooden crates that she couldn't open without a crowbar, but the third or fourth ramshackle barn she tried seemed to be some kind of garage. Inside were a handful of dusty cars, some that looked older than her, mothballed away, unlikely to ever see the road again. But at the front of the unit was a bigger vehicle, covered in a tarpaulin. It grabbed her interest, because – unlike everything else in the space, which looked like it hadn't been disturbed for decades – the bright blue plastic sheet covering the vehicle seemed fairly new. A spot of colour amidst a sea of monochrome. Unhooking the tethers that held the cover in place, Mrs Peel removed just enough to recognise what was underneath. A white Bedford CA that matched the description of the van that had pursued the Prime Minister yesterday.

That was more than enough for Mrs Peel to know she needed to get out of there and summon reinforcements. Even if nobody had been able to take down a number plate at the time to prove it, it didn't take Sherlock Holmes to know it was more than likely the same one.

Her instinct to leave was spot on, but her timing wasn't. As she headed for the exit, three burly men in boiler suits jumped out from behind a rusty piece of equipment that looked like it belonged in a museum. After one of them made an initial lunge, Mrs Peel dropped to the floor, making the attacker think he'd got the upper hand. Instead, she had the advantage and used her low position to swipe the man's ankles and send him crashing into a pulley. Next, the other two attackers coordinated their response. This posed Mrs Peel a greater problem as one grabbed her arms, while the other delivered a blow to her abdomen.

Doubled over in pain, she crumpled to the floor and her assailants let go of her as she fell, underestimating the fight she still had left in her. As she curled up into a ball, nursing the ache, she took the opportunity to scan the room for anything that could be used as an improvised weapon.

'Up,' one of the men commanded.

She feigned ignorance.

'I said get up,' he yowled.

This time she complied but kept her hands interlocked over her stomach, forcing the men to grab her by the elbows, giving her the opportunity to grab a spanner and hammer from a work bench on the way back up to her feet, which she simultaneously tossed over both shoulders in a single uninterrupted motion, thwacking one man's cheek, and breaking the other's nose.

It gained her a few seconds' respite, but by now, the original assailant was back on his knees and Mrs Peel realised she was playing a game of deadbeat whack-a-mole. If the fight had remained three against one, she was confident she'd have *probably* prevailed. But hearing the commotion, a fourth man arrived and darted towards her – tipping the odds. Mrs Peel realised she was outflanked and decided to surrender and conserve her energy. As skilled as she was in self-defence, the combined force of four meatheads was just too much to repel.

Inside the factory, Mrs Peel was dragged in front of Jacobs.

'Is this how you treat a member of Her Majesty's

Government?' she asked. The words stuck in her throat a little, as at most she was a freelancer, not a paid civil servant and – heaven forbid – certainly not a politician. But it felt the most useful line of attack in the moment, and she *had* been granted a temporary security pass from the highest levels to work the case.

Jacobs' expression showed he was sceptical.

'It's true,' said Manson, showing Jacobs the Government ID he'd confiscated from Mrs Peel.

'Then for goodness' sake let our visitor down,' said Jacobs.

The two men holding her relaxed their grip, and Mrs Peel dusted herself down.

'You'll have to excuse the rough treatment,' said Jacobs.

'Will I?' she asked.

'A turn of phrase, Miss?'

'*Mrs*… Peel,' she corrected.

'What I mean to say, Mrs Peel, is that I hope you'll overlook this indiscretion. Clearly if we'd known the Government of the day had such a fascination with our… establishment, we'd have been only too happy to cooperate. Though I must admit, you'll need to enlighten me as to why an agent of the Crown would be prowling around my property. To the best of my knowledge, our taxes are paid, our books are clean, and our rights are inviolable. At least for now. Unless the Government is interested in procuring lawful munitions, in which case I'd very much welcome a conversation.'

'I'm here about your extra-curricular activities,' said Mrs Peel.

'Oh?' Jacobs asked.

'I was told this is where I might find EUNOCs,' Mrs Peel looked the men up and down, 'and you didn't disappoint.'

'Oh, I see,' said Jacobs. 'You'll understand why I was

confused, Mrs Peel. You won't be surprised to hear that most people who share our beliefs come through the front door.'

'Perhaps you need better signage,' said Mrs Peel.

'Perhaps. Well, do take a seat,' Jacobs said, offering her an old wooden stool splattered with dried paint, which she accepted reluctantly.

'What is it exactly you'd like to know about our little group?' he asked.

'Not so little, by all accounts,' she said. 'The Ministry seems to think you've got a membership in the thousands.'

'And growing daily, Mrs Peel.'

'That's a lot of people who want to keep Britain out of Europe.'

'And you'd be very welcome to join us, Mrs Peel,' Jacobs said.

'No thank you,' she said emphatically.

'So, you're a paid-up Europhile, I presume? Much like the rest of your government.'

'I'm nothing of the sort,' she replied. 'And they're *not* my government.'

'So, you are a like-minded soul after all?'

'I can't say it bothers me one way or the other,' said Mrs Peel. 'Frankly I have more pressing things to worry about.'

'Such as?' Jacobs asked.

'Such as why someone tried to kill the Prime Minister earlier today in a van that looked exactly like…' She stood up and walked across to the window. Even through the murky glass, which looked like it had never been cleaned, she could still see the bright blue tarpaulin flapping in the wind. She pointed at it with her thumb and forefinger, miming a pea shooter, '… that one!'

Jacobs smiled. 'And why would we do that, Mrs Peel?' he asked.

'You tell me?'

'There's nothing illegal about activism, I can assure you.'

'And how about your members?' Mrs Peel asked.

'Carefully vetted. We're not in the habit of letting crackpots into our organisation.'

Mrs Peel wasn't so sure, judging by her treatment to date. 'So, who are your members?'

'People of all ages. All walks of life,' he answered, 'some of them businessmen like me, ex-forces, nurses, doctors, teachers – good honest people who're fed up of being sold down the river by successive governments, each inepter than the last. Folk who see the Common Market as the *final* insult.'

'The government seem to think you could be dangerous,' Mrs Peel ventured.

'Well, they would, wouldn't they,' Jacobs snapped, 'because they despise hard-working people like us.'

'That sounds like fighting talk,' said Mrs Peel.

'Oh, it is, Mrs Peel, it is.'

'I thought you said you were benign?'

'Look around you, what do you see?' Jacobs asked.

She reviewed twenty or so blue-collar men, all looking every bit as threatening as their master. 'You won't like my answer.'

'Veterans, Mrs Peel,' he replied. 'Not me, I was an armourer during the War. I'm just a footnote in history, but these men – Evans, Masters, Timpson, Haynes, even Geiger here. War heroes. Manson over there took three bullets for His Majesty.' Jacobs traced the location of each gunshot wound with his finger to emphasise the point – one to the sternum, another to the navel and a third to the left leg. Then he walked over to Evans, an emaciated soul with gaunt cheekbones and thin hair. He placed his hand on Evans' shoulder, 'Tell Mrs Peel here your story, brother.'

'I was a POW,' Evans said, 'nine months in Italy. Starved. Beaten. Humiliated. They had me labouring twenty hours a day.'

'And it's the same story for hundreds of our members,' Jacobs continued. 'They fought Europe and *fought for* Europe, Mrs Peel. So that we could keep that most precious commodity. Our freedom. Our independence. As *Great* Britain. A *United* Kingdom. And our glorious prime minister is prepared to give that all up, not twenty years later, to the Germans and the Italians. Something Hitler himself couldn't even achieve! No Mrs Peel. We say *no*.'

'A compelling argument,' said Mrs Peel. 'But you can see why the government might be a bit suspicious of a group of ex-soldiers with a chip on their shoulder. And I can't say my treatment here will do anything to reassure them.'

'Perhaps not,' he replied. 'But you *were* trespassing, Mrs Peel. And the last time I checked, we're still well within our rights to defend our property.'

'How about you, Mr Evans?' asked Mrs Peel. 'How far would *you* go to fight for the cause?'

'More or less whatever it takes,' Evans replied, peering into her soul, unblinking.

'More or less?'

'I'll fight for my country, Mrs Peel. Like I did in '39. I'll die for it if needs be. And I know these men'd do the same… but if you're asking me if I'd *kill* for my country. Then no. Not anymore.'

Mrs Peel couldn't tell if she believed him, but she'd taken the conversation as far as she could. The only question was whether they were going to let her leave. 'Then I'll be on my way,' she said, using the words to test if she was now guest or captive.

'Of course,' said Jacobs. 'We'll even show you to your car.

You'll find it's much quicker if you leave through the main entrance.'

'I'll remember that for next time,' she said, relieved she was getting out of there.

Jacobs smiled. 'I'll look forward to it.'

11

SWEENEY TODD WAS considered the most barbarous resident of Fleet Street. But the literary transgressions that generations of journalists had committed there over the years would have given him a good run for his money. Newspaper editors did more damage with a sharp pen and printing press than Todd's fictional razor blades ever could.

Fleet Street today was an odd ensemble of buildings. A clash of architectural styles from Georgian to Art Deco to Brutalism. It was the land of tabloids and broadsheets – even Reuters.

Jeffrey Lamb had spent his whole life in journalism. Working his way up from a dogsbody working obituaries, to a photographer and investigative reporter at *The Gazette*. He'd dreamt of prize-winning exposés and bringing down monsters and moguls, but most weeks he had to make do with depressing op-eds about the state of the pound, or outlandish technology pieces, like the half-written article on his typewriter about a man who thought he could transplant a heart.

Lamb was restless by character and didn't like to conform. He wore a light grey suit jacket that was at least two sizes too big and an open collar shirt because ties were for schoolboys and bankers – not artists like himself.

Not for the first time this week, Lamb was sat outside the

office of his editor, Peter Gauge. Gauge had been heading up *the Gazette* for nearly twenty years and many people – including Lamb – thought it was time for new blood. The scene reminded him of his days at school. Waiting for the headmaster to give him a stern telling off. Only instead of being ritually humiliated by fellow schoolboys, here he was being hazed by a roomful of reporters, all clack-clacking their typewriters at a hundred decibels. A dirge that could drive anyone mad. The press room was a grim affair. Not like some of the more upmarket broadsheets that were starting to kit out their offices with glass booths and IBM Selectrics. *The Gazette* had to make do with tobacco-tinged asbestos ceiling tiles, and back-achingly uncomfortable chairs that would have made a taxi rank look positively salubrious.

Finally. The surrogate headmaster's voice boomed through the door.

'Come in,' he said.

Lamb dutifully obeyed and took a seat opposite the boss.

'Right. I'll make it quick,' said Peter, a rotund man who wore tartan braces. 'I need you on Wilson today.'

Lamb deflated like a balloon that Gauge had just extinguished with his cigarette. This was not how he saw his career going all those years ago.

'Pete, I've spent months on his back,' pleaded Lamb, 'and nothing. I'm telling you. He's the electoral equivalent of a cheese sandwich.'

'Trust me on this,' said Gauge.

'You're barking up the wrong tree there, boss.'

'I'm hearing whispers.'

Lamb rolled his eyes, 'What kind of whispers?'

'Something's going on over there. Wilson's been rushed to Chequers. Cancelled all appointments apparently.'

'Probably some visiting dignitary or other,' said Lamb.

'That's what I thought until I saw his guest list.'

Gauge passed Lamb a typed list of names.

'Bloody hell,' said Lamb scanning the list. 'That's half of Harley Street.'

Gauge smiled. 'Yes, it is!'

'Okay then,' said Lamb, slapping his thighs and rising from his seat, 'you command, I shall obey. But if it turns out to be nothing, I want you to let me run that piece on the risk of devaluation.'

'Deal,' said Gauge. 'Find me something that'll sell papers and I'll take a look at whatever the hell you like.'

'Let's find out what our dear prime minister's been up to then.'

12

STEED WAS A familiar face at every embassy in London. Some of the staff loved him, some of them loathed him, but all of them respected him. When anything happened that threatened Britain's security or its standing on the world stage, it almost always paid to consider the usual suspects.

On one level, it was all pure theatre. There wasn't a chance that any of them would either confirm or deny their involvement, but Steed wasn't there to listen to what they had to say, he was there to gauge how they *behaved*. To study their body language and their subtle reactions. Were they surprised, confused, worried, or excited by what he was telling them?

His first stop was Kensington Palace Gardens to visit the Soviets. A beautiful late-Georgian three-storey building with Corinthian windows. It was no secret that the Russians were strongly opposed to the European Economic Community, lest it rival their own union and threaten the spread of communism. And it stood to reason that the more countries that followed the six founders, the bigger that threat became. But this didn't feel like the work of the Eastern Bloc. It was too loud, too brash – and, frankly, too ineffective. Steed couldn't help but think that if the Soviets wanted Wilson dead, he'd have been lying on a slab, not learning how to crayon inside the lines. As diplomacy dictated, his contact inside the embassy – an amiable, if somewhat ill-tempered man named Mikhail whose sartorial finesse rivalled Steed's own – was cordial.

'An attack, you say?' Mikhail was considering what Steed had told him, which was a carefully curated version of events: there had been a wholly unsuccessful attempt on the Prime Minister's life, which understandably warranted a detailed investigation. It was a delicate balancing act. Tell a foreign power nothing and you ended up talking in riddles, tell them too much and you become the informant. Steed rationalised that the worst the Russians would do with the information would be to leak it to the press, which would likely inevitably happen in the coming hours and days anyway, so it was a necessary device to begin a meaningful conversation.

'The Prime Minister was never in any real danger, of course,' blagged Steed, 'but he's not too happy knowing he's in someone's crosshairs. Wanted me to ask around, take the temperature so to speak.'

'Absolutely, Steed,' said Mikhail, 'I'm sure I can speak for Mr Brezhnev in offering the USSR's warmest wishes to Mr Wilson. We're relieved nobody was hurt.'

It was a perfectly perfunctory response, but Steed's gut confirmed that this wasn't the work of Mother Russia. Mikhail's demeanour had betrayed a smug pleasure at this turn of events, but it also suggested this was the first the USSR was hearing of it.

Steed's next appointment was with the Americans in their majestic building in Grosvenor Square, a hop, skip and a jump away from the Russians, over on the other side of Hyde Park. A delightful walk along the Serpentine lake delivered him to the imposing building designed by the prominent American architect, Eero Saarinen, featuring a giant golden eagle statue perched atop the rectangular building made up of interlocking oblong windows that looked like it had been built of Lego. Before Steed's rubber soles had passed across the embassy's threshold, Thomas Jennings, a happy-go-lucky American diplomat with a smile that would rival the Cheshire Cat's, came bounding up to him at speed, shaking his hand like he was trying to pull it clean off. He brought an aide with him called Lilly, who Steed had only met once before.

'You were expecting me?' asked Steed.

'Sure,' said Jennings, offering a window into exactly what Steed was up against. 'We saw you with our "friends" from Moscow across the road and I said to Lilly, I said he'll pop in to us on his way back. Didn't I say that, Lilly? Didn't I?'

Lilly looked nervous, like she was trying her best to learn the ropes but finding it challenging. 'You did, Mr Jennings,' she said, 'he said "Steed'll pop into us on his way back".'

'D'you see, Steed,' said Jennings, 'what did I tell you?'

'That I'll erm…' They all spoke in unison this time, 'pop in to see you on the way back.'

Steed smiled politely, conceding internally that the only thing he could "see" was that the embassy was giving their employees too much caffeine.

'Let me guess,' said Jennings, leading Steed to a side room where he was offered a seat, and a decent Scotch from the nearby decanter. 'You're here about that nasty business with Old Harry?'

It came as no surprise at all to Steed that the Americans were already across this. The Ministry used to have a running joke that if you needed to get access to Britain's deepest and darkest secrets, the best course of action was to ask the Americans.

It went without saying – to most – that the USA was one of Britain's greatest friends, at least ever since the two powers had got over that nasty business at the Boston Tea Party. And even through the eyes of a born sceptic like Steed, there was absolutely no question of the Americans having been involved in an attempt on the Prime Minister's life – or at least if they *had* then frankly the country had bigger issues to worry about than how many candles Wilson popped on his birthday cake. No, the point of Steed's visit was to gauge whether the Americans had picked up any "noise" which indicated another foreign power may have been moving against the United Kingdom. This wasn't only helpful for matters of national security, it was also born of sheer pragmatism, because over eighty countries had an embassy in London, and Steed had neither the time nor the patience to visit every one of them.

Steed decided the direct approach was best with the Americans. 'How long have we known each other, Tom?' he asked.

'Oh, gotta be twelve or more years, Steed,' said Jennings.

'Exactly,' said Steed, 'ever since that business with Mr Johnson's…'

Jennings blocked Lilly's ears and interrupted Steed immediately.

'Hey there, pal,' said Jennings, 'let's remember that discretion is the better part of valour.'

'That's Shakespeare. Henry the Fifth if I remember rightly…' Steed replied.

'I've had to assimilate,' said Jennings.

'Fourth!' said Steed. 'Henry the Fourth, it *has* to be.'

'Where are you going with this?' Jennings asked.

Steed's face became more serious. 'We've always been honest with each other. Yes?'

'Right,' said Jennings.

'There's nothing that happens around here that you don't know about. You know it. We know it. You know we know it. And we know that you know that we know. But we don't talk about it. Because Britain and America are friends, just like me and you.'

'And?' said Jennings.

'And, just this once, I need you to be straight with me,' said Steed. 'If you're hearing whispers, I need to hear them too.'

'There's nothing,' said Jennings. 'Radio silence.'

'The Middle East?' asked Steed.

'On the verge of their own war,' said Jennings.

'Japan?'

Jennings turned to Lilly who specialised in Far East relations. 'Their economy has risen like the phoenix, Sir,' she answered, 'they're going great guns.'

'Great guns,' Jenning's parroted. 'Britain's of no interest to them right now.'

'The Europeans?' asked Steed, clutching at straws.

'They're all falling about themselves trying to get a piece of the Common Market pie themselves,' said Jennings. 'I'm telling you Steed, if someone's got Wilson in their sights, we haven't heard about it, unless he ends up – how do your cockneys say it, brown bread? In which case we absolutely knew and we did our best to warn you. At least that'll be the official line.'

Steed didn't look happy. He desperately needed a lead, however small. Jennings picked up on the silence.

'Look, Steed, I don't know what to tell you. I can give you a list of people that are trying to enter the UK illegally, no problem at all. I can tell you every aircraft and boat that's pushed their luck over your waters. I can probably at a push even dig out a couple of bomb threats, tell you where there's a riot brewing, or maybe, just maybe, help you detect a bit of good old fashioned insurance fraud. But I'm telling you – and believe me when I say I've got no reason to hide this from you – I ain't seen *anything* about a plan to take out the Prime Minister.'

Steed nodded. He had no reason to doubt what Jennings was saying and he'd always found him a *fairly* trustworthy individual to deal with. That wasn't to say the Americans weren't more than happy to lead the Brits up the garden path if it suited Uncle Sam, but with global tensions being what they were right now, Steed couldn't see any reason for them to antagonise the British.

In public, the Americans supported the Common Market as they were keen to keep the Western influence on Europe stronger than the competing pull from the East. Even so, there were some inside the American Administration that were also a little worried that if Europe became too big, too successful, too *powerful*, it could produce another power bloc to rival the USA's position as de facto world leader.

'If anything changes…' said Steed, finishing the last sip of his drink.

'You'll hear from me,' Jennings confirmed, 'you can bet on it.'

'I'll hold you to it,' said Steed.

'You better,' replied Jennings.

'Our special relationship is my number one priority,' said Lilly with a pleasing smile.

'I'm very glad to hear it,' Steed said, finding the prospect particularly appealing. Then he doffed his bowler and disappeared through the revolving doors.

Steed's final destination was the Chinese embassy in Portland Place, less than a mile or two from the American embassy. It was the most modest of the three buildings to look at, but no less elegant for it. Inside, he was greeted by Xian Yong, who Steed had been dealing with since the day he first arrived at the Ministry. Yong had seemed old to Steed even back then; by now he looked positively ancient, though he kept himself in good shape, and his bright white hair was perfectly curated, with barely a strand out of place.

'Good afternoon, Mr Steed,' said Yong, greeting his visitor like an old friend, and grasping Steed's fingers with both hands.

'Good to see you, Xian,' said Steed, 'long time and all that.'

'Too long,' said Yong, 'you don't write, you don't call...'

Steed smiled. 'We've had a spot of bother over at the Ministry Xian. One of our government drivers was ambushed in central London. Managed to get away unscathed, but it's left us nervous.'

Steed studied Xian's reaction. He'd thought it best not to mention the connection to the Prime Minister on this particular occasion. Yong gave little away.

'I'm sorry to hear that, Mr Steed,' he replied. 'Is there any assistance me and my team can offer you in your... investigation?'

Steed thought he'd try a different tack.

'Thing is, Xian,' he said, 'the driver's passenger was on his way to a negotiation regarding the European Economic Community. In case you don't know, Britian's keen to try to join.'

Again, this was all part of the rigmarole of diplomacy. China knew perfectly well that Britain – and frankly half of Europe – was keen to forge a union. And unlike the Americans, they were honest enough to openly admit their misgivings.

'Well, you know our official line on this, Mr Steed,' said Yong, 'but it hopefully goes without saying that the People's Republic of China would never interfere in the sovereignty of your nation.'

'Naturally,' said Steed, continuing to enjoy his old acquaintance's company. Yong was the kind of man that would pretend he couldn't find the English word for something whenever he was being pressed on an issue he didn't want to explore, despite his command of the English language far exceeding Steed's, by his own admission. Yong was always more talkative after a few drinks at the local pub, but Steed didn't have time for that today.

'Then I'd like you to do one thing for me please, Xian,' said Steed.

'Simply name it,' said Yong, 'if it's within my gift to grant, it shall be yours.'

'I want to know who has a score to settle with the British Government. I'm not talking about eggs and placards, I'm talking the nasty kind – threats, physical violence, insurrection. You know the sort of thing. The kind of people you'd happily reach out to if it… suited.'

'Careful, Mr Steed,' said Yong, 'it's no secret I like you, but don't give me reason to parrot the official line.'

'I'm sure, in return, I could… circulate that it wasn't the mighty Americans, or the iron fist of Russia that helped us repel this appalling attack on our sovereignty, but the talons of the Red Dragon,' said Steed, 'That's a nice bit of PR for you amongst the embassies, wouldn't you say?'

In fact, Yong *would* say. Indeed, he liked the idea a lot, 'Okay, Mr Steed,' he said, 'here's what I know…'

13

JACOBS WAS FURIOUS. Manson and Geiger had seen their boss's blood boil over more times than either could remember. But this was positively volcanic. Jacobs had ripped the outfit to shreds. He told Timpson he was a workshy wastrel, like his father, and that he should be grateful he'd not finished the job the Germans started back in '44 when a bullet had grazed the left side of his skull and left him half an inch from death. Paulton didn't come out of it any better – he'd had to dodge a stool, launched across the room and a tirade of spit-filled abuse for good measure. But Galton got the worst of it, for his part in letting Mrs Peel past the perimeter gate. Jacobs had simply stared, speechless, like a disappointed parent, too furious to find the words. Scary when he was speaking, Jacobs was positively terrifying when he wasn't. For the past hour, he had locked himself away in his gantry office and nobody had dared disturb him until they had some good news. Or an end to the endless bad news. And at last it came.

Manson had been given the unenviable job of rousing his boss, as it had long been established by the company faithful that he was "the chosen one" – the employee every business had that could seemingly do nothing wrong and spent their life brown-nosing their employer.

Manson gave three knocks that were firm but not aggressive.

'Come,' came the reply.

Manson stepped through the door. Jacobs looked much less irate, but the large pile of discarded butts on the ashtray he'd cleaned out for his employer that very morning told him it was a nicotine-induced calm.

'And?' Jacobs asked, not bothering to turn to face Manson, instead preferring to stare intimidatingly at the men beneath through the patinaed fog of the glass windows.

'Sorted,' said Manson. 'The problem's gone. I saw her crushed myself.'

'Well, that is a relief,' said Jacobs, sarcastically, 'I trust Mrs Peel didn't suffer.'

'You know what I mean, Mr Jacobs,' said Manson. 'The Bedford. No one will ever find it.'

'But they *did* find it, didn't they Manson,' Jacobs said.

'Let 'em try proving it.'

'They don't need to prove it, do they? Not when they've got the word of a government agent?' Jacobs said. 'You haven't just shut the door after the horse has bolted, my apprentice. You've buried the bloody mare after it's already run rampant.'

'At least we know Wilson's injured though, boss,' chanced Manson. 'That's got to be something?'

Jacobs' chair turned 180 degrees at rapid speed, his face crumpled like he'd been stung by a nettle.

'It means *nothing*,' said Jacobs. 'Less than nothing. Like that lot out there.'

'Surely, it'll buy us some time?' argued Manson. 'If it's bad enough to hide him away, he's hardly going to be on the next plane to Brussels, is he?'

'He doesn't need to be, does he?' said Jacobs. 'Some fool by the name of Hagley is stepping in for him.'

Manson looked quizzically. Sometimes he had no idea how Jacobs found this information out. It'd taken four hours of deep digging to find out the Prime Minister had even been hurt. And he'd had to pull in every favour he possibly could to find that much. Even then, he was none the wiser as to what was actually wrong with Wilson. As ever, Jacobs always seemed one step ahead.

'Why wouldn't they put one of the front benchers on it – Callaghan or Jenkins?' Manson asked.

'Scared we'll pick them off too, I shouldn't wonder,' Jacobs replied.

'So Hagley's a fall guy?' Manson asked.

'Well, it stands to reason, doesn't it?' Jacobs explained. 'You need to keep things moving, while drawing out your opponents.'

'So, we *don't* target Hagley?' Manson asked, confused.

'Oh, we absolutely *do*,' said Jacobs. 'If the Government offer me a sacrificial goat, it would be rude to decline.'

'But you said it was a trap?'

'Only if we get caught. And I have no intention of that happening.'

'Won't they just keep replacing him though. And plough on regardless?'

'Almost certainly,' said Jacobs, 'but we need to play for time. It's not about the Government being wounded, it's about them being *seen* to be wounded. To make things altogether too toxic for de Gaulle and his cronies to go anywhere near this.'

'I see,' said Manson, though his face disagreed.

'That's why all this is for nothing if they suppress the information.'

'Can't *we* go to the papers?'

'Already done. But they'll need to find proof. Hence, we need to up the ante.'

'So we go big with Hagley. Make it a spectacle?' asked Manson, keen to earn back his boss' favour.

'Already taken care of,' said Jacobs.

Manson visibly took umbrage.

'Oh, don't look so wounded Manson. You can hardly blame me for bringing in backup. I need the bloody SAS, and I've got the Sally Army!'

'You can't keep ripping them a new one every time something doesn't go to plan, boss,' said Manson. He knew he was pushing his luck, but if he wasn't prepared to say what everyone else was thinking, then who would?

'Well, if isn't Field Marshal Montgomery,' Jacobs replied, 'I'm honoured to have you in my office.'

'All I'm saying is… the men are loyal,' said Manson, 'to you, and to the country. But every man has his breaking point…'

Jacobs' expression showed his had been reached a long, long time ago, but he chose to drop the rope instead. One of the reasons he grudgingly admired Manson and saw him as his successor was precisely because he had the balls to stand up to him. And Manson was right. His men were loyal to the cause and could comfortably endure the odd beasting because of their time in the forces. But he'd lost men before by pushing them too hard. He thought for a moment and pressed the intercom on his desk.

'Yes, Mr Jacobs?' said a nasal voice.

'Cancel my meeting with Mr Parker,' he said. 'Tell him we're going in another direction.'

'Of course,' came the reply.

Jacobs unlocked a small drawer in his desk using a brass key that he kept in the breast pocket of his overcoat. Inside, he retrieved a small black wooden box and passed it to his colleague. Manson knew exactly what it was, and what he was being asked to do. And he wasn't excited by either. He pondered whether he should have put up and shut up after all.

'Time to prove me wrong then,' said Jacobs, 'but it's last chance saloon. Fool me once, shame on you. Fool me twice, shame on me.'

14

LORD HAGLEY WAS a dutiful if unremarkable sort of chap. A tall, slight gentleman who'd spent his whole life in politics. Local councillor aged twenty-five. MP at thirty. Cabinet by forty-five. Put out to pasture in the House of Lords by sixty. It was Harold Wilson who'd put him there after his colleagues had started talking about Robert Hagley as a leadership contender. And many – himself included – had wondered if the "honour" had been a blatant attempt by the incumbent party leadership to extinguish a future threat. Not least because there were plenty of other fish swimming around the Prime Minister, waiting for their day in the sun.

Truth be told, it didn't matter anyway. Hagley harboured absolutely no intentions of becoming leader, which was precisely what made him appealing to so many backbenchers who derided the idea of the career politician. But he firmly believed he still had a role to play in public service and had been honoured – if a little taken aback – by the request to handle the EEC negotiations in the Prime Minister's absence.

That said, he knew the issue of the Common Market was something of a poisoned chalice. One best handled with extreme care. Yes, it might bring economic prosperity to the country, but at what cost? He had nothing against people on the Continent. Indeed, he'd built a career building relationships with the Germans, French and Italians during his work in the Foreign Office after the War. But they were different to the Brits. Not just the language or the culture, but their mindset. It had only been twenty years since Europe was blowing itself to pieces over who controlled the Continent. Were European nations truly ready to let bygones be bygones? But it didn't matter what he thought. The party line was clear, and if political life had taught him anything, it was the importance of *never* airing one's dirty laundry in public. If he had any reservations at all about taking the country into Europe, one thing was for sure – nobody would be any the wiser. For Hagley, the stiff upper lip wasn't just an English stereotype, it was a way of life.

Lord Hagley's journey to Westminster had begun like every other, despite it being his day off. Ablutions – or a shit, shower and shave as his army chums used to call it back in his days as a cadet – then he'd pick up his copy of *The Times*, visit the station shoe-shine, and catch the six o'clock tube from Sloane Square with plenty of time to spare. Albeit today, the powers that be were summoning him at six o'clock in the *evening*, which, in addition to disrupting billiards, meant fighting his way into central London when everyone else was fighting their way out. Apparently, this new mission they were lumbering him with "absolutely couldn't wait" – oh how the Cabinet loved their drama.

Thankfully, the train was mercifully quiet, which afforded Robert a seat, for which his sciatica was eternally grateful. He opened his copy of the broadsheet and voraciously consumed an article about the Americans' incredible plans for the Apollo space programme. Soon, he'd be knee deep in negotiations with de Gaulle and his merry band of men. So for now, it was his slice of calm before the storm.

Half a second before the train doors slammed shut, a final passenger squeezed on board, a striking blonde woman in her mid-forties, dressed in a trouser suit. She carried a clutch bag and steadied herself as the train left the station tumultuously.

Her name was Caroline Kirk, and she was Manson's go-to "fixer" for jobs that required the utmost discretion. As the tube train disappeared into a tunnel, Kirk briefly faced the door, concealing the swift retrieval of a small gun with a silencer added, which she moved from her bag to the pocket of her coat. The carriage was filled with warm dry air as she walked down the car, smiling flirtatiously with each of the passengers one by one as she moved closer to her prey.

After a while, she found Lord Hagley, buried in the stocks and shares pages of his newspaper.

'Do you mind?' she asked, pointing at the seat beside him.

'Be my guest,' he said, not even registering to look at her.

'Funny sort of weather out there, isn't it?' she said. 'Too warm for a coat. Too cold to go without.'

Hagley made the most basic of human acknowledgements. Part grunt, part murmur. A sound that clearly meant "shut up and leave me to my newspaper".

Kirk enjoyed this reaction. It pleased her enormously to know that her target showed such contempt for her very existence. Even though, unbeknownst to him, she would soon join his mother in becoming one of the two most important characters in his story here on Earth. A tale that began with one woman bringing him into this world and would shortly end with another removing him from it. She did absolutely nothing to conceal her face because she was already invisible to the vast majority of her targets. And an object of fantasy for the rest. Hagley never once stopped to look at her, which made it all the easier. In fact, he was so disinterested, Manson might as well have carried out the hit himself and saved himself some money, but he liked others to do his dirty work.

Kirk wasn't a psychopath, or a sadist – at least they weren't labels that she would have identified with. She was a gun for hire, she was paid to do a job and it was a job she did well. Mostly that didn't include taking lives, more often it involved ruining them. She'd never had to take out someone in government before though. That was something new, and it had inflated the price by fifty per cent. Not least because although they said they'd abolished capital punishment, anything was possible with *this* government.

As the familiar screech of brakes began their discordant symphony, Kirk knew what had to be done. Had Lord Hagley been the gentlemanly sort that let ladies step through the door before him, he may have given himself a fighting chance. Instead, by darting for the exit the second the carriage doors opened, Kirk seized her opportunity, quietly withdrawing her gun and firing it into Hagley's leg just as he was stepping onto the platform. Unseen, she stowed the gun back in her bag and took a seat on the train, disappearing a few seconds later into the tunnels as inconspicuously as she had arrived.

Hagley noticed a sharp sting but thought nothing of it, instinctively feeling the puncture site and inadvertently knocking the tiny dart away from his flesh as if swatting an insect after a bite. It took a few minutes for the effects of the vial to properly kick in. He managed the steps to the surface with relative ease, although he was feeling a little more breathless by the time he reached sunlight. But by the time he'd walked across Parliament Street and towards the Cenotaph, he was feeling decidedly unwell. The world was starting to spin, he was sweating profusely, and it finally dawned on him that something was amiss.

Fortunately, he'd just taken a left onto Downing Street and Number 10 was in sight. A cold towel, a stiff drink and a sit down were sure to perk him up. Or so he thought. But as he made his way down the famous street, things went from bad to worse. Once he'd cleared Number 9, his knees were starting to buckle, and by the time he reached blackened bricks, his hands had gone numb. Once he called out to the policeman on duty, he knew his time was up; he could barely manage a breath, let alone a sound. As he collapsed at the doorstep of his final destination, his hands slid down the polished black door he'd pledged his life to serve, smudging the finish and making a final mark on this world. The door opened at the exact moment his life slipped away, his limp body crossed the threshold and collapsed onto the black and white tiles beneath. In his last moment of consciousness, he reasoned he was having a heart attack. He had lost his faith in recent years, but now – at the end – he implored his maker to be his salvation. Oblivious to the fact that his fate had been decided by a far more prosaic source.

15

STEED AND MRS Peel had spent more time in mortuaries than either would have liked. Having examined the body, Steed pulled the white cloth back over Lord Hagley's face, leaving the man to rest on the cold steel table surrounded by fellow cadavers.

'Well at least we know what motivated them to target the Prime Minister,' said Steed.

'The Common Market?' Mrs Peel replied.

'Has to be,' said Steed. 'What I don't understand is *how* they knew Hagley was taking over. *He* was only informed this morning.'

'You think there's a leak?' asked Mrs Peel.

'Something's not adding up.'

'Did you find EUTOPIA?' she asked.

'You mean this isn't it?' Steed replied playfully.

'Not unless you happen to be at ease in the company of the dead,' she replied.

'You *more* than compensate, Mrs Peel.'

She grimaced, telling him this wasn't the time.

'Mad as hatters,' Steed continued, 'but killers? Unlikely.'

'I wish I could say the same about the EUNOCs,' said Mrs Peel. 'My lot felt positively dystopian. And I have the bruises to prove it.'

Steed looked worried when Mrs Peel rubbed her wrists.

'Nothing I couldn't handle,' she said, sensing his concern.

'Which is more than we can say for our late lord,' said Steed, glancing at his wristwatch. 'Did she say how much longer she'd be?' said Steed, noting it was already past eight o'clock.

'It's the toxicology reports,' Mrs Peel replied. 'It takes time for the blood tests to come back.'

She could sense Steed was anxious to get back out there and solve the case.

'Patience is a virtue,' she said witheringly.

'You of all people should know my virtues are beyond reproach, Mrs Peel,' he replied,

'Hmmm,' she replied, unconvinced.

Eventually the mortician, a frizzy-haired woman with skin as pale as her "patients", entered the room. She sported gigantic eyeglasses, each lens as thick as a slice of toast. Steed and Mrs Peel exchanged glances.

'Sorry to keep you waiting,' said the doctor, Elizabeth Phelps. 'I 'spect you want to know what offed the poor bugger?' she said glancing at the notes on her clipboard, and squinting to read the small print, despite the telescopic magnification of her eyewear. 'Let's see what this Steed fellow died of then, shall we?' she said pulling back the blanket to reveal Lord Hagley's leg.

Steed went to correct her, but Mrs Peel stopped him.

'Please do,' she replied.

'Well, it looks like Steed was past his physical prime certainly,' said the doctor, 'that much is clear.'

'Indubitably,' said Mrs Peel, loving every minute.

'He was overweight, smoked too much, drank too much, a fairly idle fellow I should wager.'

Mrs Peel was in her element.

'Signs of a philanderer too, I shouldn't wonder,' Phelps continued. 'Look at those scars, classic venereal disease if I'm not mistaken.'

'Sounds about right,' said Mrs Peel. Steed rolled his eyes playfully.

'That's why it took effect so quickly,' said Dr Phelps.

'It?' Steed asked.

'The poison,' she replied. 'I'm still waiting on some final tests, but probably something like a barbiturate. Burned his heart out. Delivered *here* most likely,' she said, pointing to a tiny pinprick on Hagley's right calf.

'Someone injected him?' asked Steed. 'Were there signs of a struggle?'

'Absolutely none whatsoever,' said the doctor, 'something this small… it was probably an automatic delivery system.'

'Like a dart?' asked Mrs Peel.

'Exactly like a dart, Mrs Peel. Poor sod probably never knew what hit him. Quite literally.'

Steed considered this information carefully. 'He left the house around 5 p.m. and collapsed at Downing Street less than an hour later,' he said. 'Any idea how long it would take for something like that to take effect?'

'It's very hard to say, depends a lot on his metabolism,' the doctor answered.

'Are we talking seconds, minutes, hours, days?'

'Certainly not days. If he'd been jabbed the night before, he'd never have woken up. If he left the house feeling well enough to commute, I'd say they got to him en route most likely.'

'The London Underground?' said Steed, checking if Mrs Peel was on the same wavelength.

'Has to be,' she answered, 'it's the perfect cover. There must have been hundreds of people around, given it was rush hour.'

'There are at least a couple of stops between his house and Westminster,' said Steed. 'The odds of finding the perpetrator are astronomical.'

Mrs Peel agreed. 'They'd have been gone within seconds most likely, hiding in plain sight.'

'So, we come at it from a different direction,' said Steed.

'A fresh mound of earth?' asked Mrs Peel, knowing exactly what he was thinking.

'Precisely,' said Steed. 'I'll get my torch!'

The mortician was looking between them like a spectator at Wimbledon, utterly confused by the whole conversation. Mrs Peel decided to translate.

'He's going to catch a mole.'

16

'**ORDER,' ROY JENKINS** shouted, 'I must call you all to order.'

This morning's emergency Cabinet meeting had been even rowdier than the last, now that word of Lord Hagley's untimely demise had spread through the front bench like dry rot.

'What on Earth are we going to tell the press?' said Jim Callaghan.

'We're lurching from one disaster to another,' added Barbara Castle.

'I don't see we've any choice but to put things on ice, until we can get this situation under control,' said Callaghan.

'Well, you would say that,' said Jenkins, noting Callaghan's innate Euroscepticism.

'Absolutely not,' said Castle. 'Whatever some of us think about the Common Market – and you know perfectly well where I stand – our course should *not* be dictated by extremists. We don't give in to intimidation, gentlemen. It's simply not British.'

'We're barely managing to cover up the Prime Minster's absence,' said the government's Press Secretary, Trevor Lloyd-Hughes. 'I can probably eke that out another day at most. After that, it's untenable.'

'Then pull in some favours,' said Callaghan.

'Favours? How exactly do you think we've got this far?' Lloyd-Hughes replied. 'I owe so many hacks quid pro quos, we'll be leaking more than my Morris Minor – if they find out about Hagley, we've had it. The public interest angle will trump anything I can do to shut it down.'

'So we make sure they *don't* find out,' said Castle.

'What if it's already too late?' asked Jenkins. 'Surely someone will have seen something?'

'Such as?' asked Callaghan.

'Well, off the top of my head… a death in Downing Street might do it. I know the Upper House try to keep their distance from this lowly place, but Lords of the Realm don't usually perish upon setting foot in it.'

'He was there for barely a second,' said Castle. 'The doorman closed the door almost immediately. Nobody spotted any photographers lurking, so even if anyone saw anything, it's our word against theirs. We'll just say he tripped.'

'And the Underground?' Jenkins asked. 'The station master said he was seen staggering across the platform. That can't have gone unnoticed.'

'Relax,' said Castle. 'If the public noted every man in a suit that's started a night out on the tiles a little early, they'd do little else.'

'Surely he'll have been recognised?' came a voice from the far end of the table.

'Hagley?' said Castle. 'Not a chance. I *barely* recognised him, and I've played doubles with him and his wife! The only Lords that make headlines are infamous for their ambitions or their indiscretions. Hagley never had the former, and never got caught for the latter. That's why we gave him the job. He was a safe pair of hands.'

'Dispensable, you mean?' said another voice from the back of the room.

'I said no such thing,' she replied.

'You didn't have to,' the unseen man said. 'We all know why Jim gave the negotiations over to an also-ran.'

'Nonsense,' Callaghan protested.

'Well one thing's for sure,' said Jenkins, keen to move the conversation on in a different direction, 'the security services are going to want to sweep through every department like a dog with a scent for meat. Outside of this room, barely anyone knew Hagley was our man!'

'What are you suggesting?' said Callaghan, apparently wounded.

'Oh simmer down, Jim,' said Jenkins, 'I'm not insinuating, I'm summarising. The security services are going to rightly ask how exactly Hagley was promoted, briefed and assassinated all in the space of a day. And it doesn't take Hercule Poirot to conclude someone in this room's been careless or…'

'Or?' Callaghan asked.

'Or somebody's sold us up the Thames.'

Eyes darted around the room, each trying to read the other before Callaghan asked the question on everyone's lips, 'But who?'

17

STEED HAD NEVER really had an office. Certainly not one as grand as this. He'd been assigned room number twenty-two in Downing Street, a space favoured – or so he'd been told – by William Pitt the Younger. An appropriately named man who served as Britian's youngest prime minister and, legend had it, had written the order to establish a penal colony in Australia from that very office.

As Steed sat in his Eames chair, spinning impatiently on the swivelled base, he liked to imagine that if walls could talk, the room would have had quite a story to tell. He was sure the panelled room must have hosted its fair share of liaisons between spies and spivs, heroes and heretics, liars and lovers. Steed felt in good company on all counts.

He didn't relish the task in hand. He'd already seen four Ministers of State and had many more still to go. This wasn't really his purview. The Ministry was full of security personnel that could get a confessional out of a turncoat minister faster than they could say Geneva Convention, but if there was a traitor amongst the pack, their vetting procedures had obviously failed to spot the usurper. After a short respite from his last conversation, candidate number five was shown in.

'Minister,' said Steed, standing to greet his visitor and

instantly transforming his manner from ever-so-slightly bored to earnestly engaged. 'Do sit down,' he continued, as if greeting an old friend, 'we appreciate you clearing some time, especially on a Saturday.'

'Not at all,' the man replied. 'Time and tide wait for no man and all that.'

'With that in mind, do you mind me cutting to the chase, Minister?' said Steed.

'Goodenough.'

'I'm sorry?' said Steed, pondering what exactly was so mediocre about his delivery.

'Eric Goodenough, MP,' he repeated. 'You can call me Eric.'

'Capital, Eric,' said Steed, 'thing is, there's quite a flap on upstairs about all this business with Europe in light of, well, you know what...'

'Upstairs?' asked Eric, knowing full well they were on the top floor, in the attic rooms at Downing Street.

'The powers that be,' Steed clarified.

Goodenough looked up to the clouds through the dormer window.

Steed shook his head. 'Too high,' he said, flattening his hands and using a "go lower" sign. 'The situation is... delicate,' said Steed. 'I need someone I can trust. And your name came *highly* recommended.'

'It did?' asked Eric, somewhat incredulously.

'It did,' echoed Steed. 'They said Eric...' Steed struggled to remember his name.

'Goodenough,' he added.

'That's right,' said Steed, 'Goodenough by name, outstanding by nature, that's what they said.'

'Who?'

'All of them,' said Steed, 'quite the consensus let me tell you.'

Goodenough wasn't convinced by what Steed was saying, but life had taught him never to look a gift horse in the mouth. 'Well how about that!'

'I'm putting together a crack team of insiders,' Steed explained, 'people who can stay under the radar until called upon.'

'Called upon by whom?' Goodenough asked.

It was a good question. Steed looked around and saw a portrait hanging on the wall that did the job. 'By Her Majesty,' he said, lifting the dusty portrait of Queen Elizabeth II off the wall and handing it to Eric.

Eric's face swelled with pride, 'I suppose I could…'

Steed interjected, 'Good man.'

'I'm flattered and all, Mr Steed,' Goodenough said, 'but I'm astonished the Undersecretary for Farming and Rural Affairs would make your cut.'

'Not at all, Minister,' said Steed, 'I mean Eric. You've been getting *a lot* of positive attention in Number 10 let me tell you. And your…' Steed glanced at his notes on the desk, trying to find the file on Goodenough '… paper on the natural acidity of soil and its effects on arable land is turning heads.'

Goodenough smiled. Pleasantly surprised to hear that his work was being noticed. 'Well then,' he said, 'you can absolutely count on my support. What do you need me to do?'

Steed shook the man's hand. 'On behalf of your country… thank you,' he said melodramatically. Then he dropped a labelled package into the man's lap. 'That's the name and address of the minister taking over from Lord Hagley on the negotiations to join the Common Market. I need you to take this over to him at three o'clock this afternoon. Can you do that for me, Eric?'

Goodenough glanced at the label. It was the other side of Greenwich, and it meant losing even more of his Saturday, but when Queen and Country summoned, Goodenoughs answered the call.

'Of course,' said Goodenough, 'and the rest?'

'Just that for now please, Minister,' said Steed, 'then await further instructions.'

'Right you are,' said Goodenough walking towards the door.

'Don't forget your package,' said Steed, foisting the parcel into the absent-minded man's hands.

Well, thank you… I suppose,' said Goodenough, unsure quite whether this was an honour or a liability.

'No, *thank you,'* said Steed. 'We'll be in touch.'

'Good day,' said Goodenough, closing the door.

Steed retrieved a fountain pen from his jacket pocket and handwrote the name JACK DEETS next to Goodenough's name and ticked him off the list. Then he leant back in his chair, pulled his bowler over his eyes and counted down the fifteen minutes till the next minister was due – staggering his appointments to make sure nobody knew quite how many people had been invited to Steed's inner circle. As he tried his best to steal forty winks, he knew it was going to be one of those days.

18

MRS PEEL WAS tuning her piano when the phone rang. A ridiculously difficult task that required her to manually adjust 230 individual strings in equal temperament. This wasn't a task for an everyday pianist, especially one that practised the craft as seldom as Mrs Peel was wont to do. However, every time she'd paid someone to tune the instrument, she'd been tempted to give it a go herself, just for the sheer challenge of it.

She'd made a good go at it, and the left hand of the keyboard now sounded passable. She was working her way up to middle C before she'd planned to give herself a well-earned break. The telephone rang while she was wrenching the piano hammer on a particularly stubborn E string, hitting the note repeatedly as the tone yo-yoed from low to high, trying to settle on the correct frequency. Mrs Peel thought about letting the phone ring, but it was probably Steed and she'd promised him she'd be available over the coming days to do everything she could on the case.

As the third ring chimed, Mrs Peel was seconds away from settling on the right note. She reckoned it would only take one more turn of the peg and it would be done. But in her haste, she overcompensated, and the string snapped abruptly – sending her hand flying back at breakneck speed, to protect her digits. The sound of the metal wire snapping left her ears ringing from the high-pitched implosion as she rushed over to the phone.

'You snapped my E string,' she said, thoroughly expecting Steed to be on the other end of the line, 'and before you say anything, that's E as in elephant.'

'Come again?' came a meek and nasal response.

'I'm sorry,' said Mrs Peel. 'I thought you might have been somebody else.'

'Is this Mrs Peel?'

'Yes,' she replied.

'My name is Jeffrey Lamb,' said the caller. 'I'm with the *Gazette*. Can I ask you a few questions about the Harold Wilson case?'

Mrs Peel made no attempt to conceal her annoyance.

'No comment,' she replied, 'and how did you get this number?'

'Nothing happens in Westminster without me knowing, Mrs Peel,' he said.

'Is that so?' she asked, despising arrogance. 'In that case, you don't need anything from me.'

'I think you misunderstand, Mrs Peel,' he said. 'I'm not looking for information, I'm looking to cut a deal.'

'A deal?' she asked.

'I'm in possession of a number of photographs which I suspect Her Majesty's Government wouldn't like the great unwashed to see. My editor's meeting with me in three hours, and the information I have would make his day... *and* his front page.'

'What's that got to do with me?' asked Mrs Peel.

'Well, under the right circumstances,' he explained, 'I *might* be amenable to... er... adjusting my priorities – just a little you understand. Do my bit. A civic service you might call it.'

'Would I now?' she replied.

'Dark rooms are dangerous places,' he continued, 'negatives don't like to be exposed to light and sometimes you end up spilling the wrong sort of chemical all over them! Then they'd be quite useless wouldn't they, Mrs Peel? If you catch my drift.'

Mrs Peel knew this man's sort all too well. 'What exactly is it you want, Mr Lamb?' she asked, pondering whether he was wearing his wolf's clothing on the other end of the line.

'Money, Mrs Peel, and lots of it.'

'And why exactly would *I* care if you've caught some politician with his trousers…'

'Downing Street, Mrs Peel,' said Lamb. 'This particular information pertains to what's been going on down there over the past few days. I haven't a clue what errands they've got you running for them, but I think it's probably not going to help your cause to have the entire population of Fleet Street outside your flat come the morning papers.'

'That sounds like a threat,' she replied.

'It was intended to,' said Lamb. 'Sadly, these days, it's the only way people like me ever make a living. It's Profumos, not Pulitzers that pay the bills you see.'

'Inspirational,' said Mrs Peel, 'I'll speak to the powers that be. *If* they're interested in cutting a deal, how do I contact you?'

'Superb,' said Lamb. 'I'm in Mayfair, got a studio above the flower shop in Shepherd Market. You can't miss it, you'll smell the lilies from a mile away.'

'I can hardly wait,' she said.

'I don't expect something for nothing, Mrs Peel. I'm sure we can arrange a broker's fee.'

'No thank you,' said Mrs Peel.

'Suit yourself,' he said.

'And if they won't pay?' she asked.

'Then you can read all about it in tomorrow's *Sunday Gazette*.'

'I don't have a cat I'm afraid, Mr Lamb,' Mrs Peel replied, 'so I've no need to line a litter tray.'

'We could use your acerbic wit over at Fleet Street,' said Lamb.

'A job offer and a bribe all in one morning. I must be popular.'

'Here's what I'll do, Mrs Peel,' Lamb said. 'In the spirit of goodwill, what say we forego the Sunday splash and I'll stall my editor for – say – twenty-four hours? After that, I'll presume your employers aren't interested.'

'They're *not* my employers,' Mrs Peel said emphatically, 'and frankly it's no business of mine whether they pay you, arrest you, or ignore you. But I'll do them the courtesy of allowing them to choose.'

'I'm pleased to hear it,' he said, 'I've no doubt I'll be seeing you at ten o'clock tomorrow morning. Good day, Mrs Peel. Please make sure to remember to bring the Government's pocketbook… I do so enjoy autographs.'

With that the line went dead.

Mrs Peel grabbed her coat and headed for the door. She had no intention of paying a bribe – whether or not the Government sanctioned it – though she fully intended to bill Lamb for her broken E string. Instead, she had another plan which would include playing her ignominious photographer at his own game.

19

THE HONOURABLE ERIC Goodenough, Member of Parliament for the Brentwood East constituency, was ready and waiting for his afternoon pick up. As the black Humber Imperial rolled up to collect him, the driver, Mrs Emma Peel, slid out the car, opened the door for her passenger and returned to the driver's seat in a seamless motion that suggested she must have racked up an ungodly number of hours picking up the great and the good and moving them around the country, like pawns on a chess board. Despite never having chauffeured a day in her life.

Goodenough didn't feel particularly great or good. But he was a hard worker and loyal to the Government. In truth, it was nice to know that all those long days burning the candles at both ends had finally been noticed. It was an honour to have been invited inside the tent by Steed, and – as a paid-up Europhile – it pleased him enormously to think he was playing a part, however small, in writing history. Not that his wife would be too pleased about it of course. She'd always been wary of him pursuing politics. She feared at best, some angry constituent would put their windows through, and at worst, someone might take a pot shot at her husband. Once she inevitably found out about Wilson, and now Hagley, she'd command him to keep a healthy distance from Westminster. And that meant appeasing local people's moans and gripes about dog fouling, noise abatement and potholes. If she knew he was setting off to meet a man who was wearing dead man's shoes, she'd have had a heart attack. Especially when the feet in question were barely cold. But he rationalised that politics was about service. And that meant, from time to time, having to step up and put your country first. That and the fact it probably wouldn't hurt his chances with the electorate when they returned to the polls to be seen to be shmoozing with the big boys. Voters liked to see their MPs moving in important circles, because they felt it meant their local needs would get airtime with the powers that be. But it was a delicate balance, because they were also perfectly capable of lambasting him for abandoning his constituency. As so often occurred to him in the job, some days it wasn't just a case of pleasing everyone, but *anyone*.

'Straight home?' asked Mrs Peel, swivelling her chauffeur's hat so she could see him in the rear-view mirror.

'No, I have a quick errand to run if you don't mind, driver. Could you take me to Greenwich please? It's an office block over on Salt Lake Wharf.'

'Right you are,' Mrs Peel replied.

The drive was uneventful but for the return of the heavy rain that had plagued the day. It was barely a fifteen-minute journey to the location that Steed had bid Goodenough visit and as they approached the gates to the complex, Mrs Peel's passenger could see it was a drab white box with a dozen or so floors. A "futuristic" monstrosity they said was called brutalism – from the French for "raw concrete", which just about summed up the charm of the place. In front of the imposing building were chain-linked fences and an intercom system.

'Who shall I ask for?' Mrs Peel asked.

‘Mr Jack Deets, please,’ Goodenough replied, ‘Floor eight.’

Mrs Peel wound down her window and pressed the buzzer, just as she’d done half a dozen times already that day for everyone else on Steed’s hit list.

‘Good afternoon. How may I help you?’ asked an all-too-familiar voice. This time, Steed was affecting either a terrible Liverpudlian accent, or else a Scottish brogue.

She parroted the information Goodenough had given her and after a few seconds, there was a bleep and the gates slid open by themselves.

Mrs Peel drove the car all the way up to the entrance canopy, to spare her passenger from the drizzle as best she could, and Goodenough used his attaché case as an impromptu umbrella to bridge the short gap from the vehicle to the porch. As he stepped into the revolving doorway, he took a moment to glance behind him, to check he hadn’t been followed. As far as he was concerned, he’d been entrusted with national secrets of the utmost importance and if there was one thing Goodenoughs excelled at, it was following instructions.

20

THE FACILITIES AT PP&P Automobile couldn't have been more different from Jacobs' own. Where his factory was coming to the end of its working life, this one was born of a "new world" of modernity and automation, and was positively gleaming. As the workers flooded out of the building with the ringing of the 5.30 p.m. bell, ready for a day of rest after a gruelling six-day week, Jacobs waited from afar until the coast was clear.

He'd travelled to the garage on foot. It wasn't far from his factory, just on the other side of the water in fact. But now that he knew the Government were sniffing around, he didn't want to take any chances. That's why he'd come through the old exhaust tunnels that vented waste water into the Thames back in the day. The bleeding heart liberals had stopped all that years back to protect the fish. Only for fishermen to go and kill the blighters. It made no sense to Jacobs, but then neither did most things when it came to Britain's post-war decline. At the other end of the pipe, he kept a small wooden boat – capable of getting him and maybe three or four of his men to safety if things ever got too hot. And he had friends on the other side of the river that could do the rest. In other words, Bill Jacobs could disappear from the world completely at a moment's notice.

Fortunately for Jacobs, today wasn't the day to execute that plan. The situation was tepid at most. Mrs Peel may have had her suspicions, but she had no hard evidence. That said, the next few days were going to be make or break. He hoped to get out of it unscathed, but deep down he knew it *might* end badly, and he'd made peace with that. Maybe a small part of him even *hoped* it might be his last stand. His hadn't exactly been a happy life. His achievements amounted to a failed marriage, a son he wasn't entirely sure was his, who he hadn't even seen for over ten years, and a business that had been thriving until he'd taken it over. Maybe on some level, he really was ready to call time. But that was by the by. His focus was on the mission. His determination – whatever the odds – to keep Britain out of Europe. That was all that mattered. It was a cause that, after years of coasting through life in neutral, had finally revved him up and got his blood boiling. It had finally given him purpose.

The journey from the boat to Henderson's garage was around twenty minutes by foot. Ideally it wouldn't have been raining, but his hooded anorak had serendipitously afforded him greater anonymity, so it proved to be a blessing. To all intents and purposes, Jacobs looked like any other punter arriving to settle their account and pay Henderson's exorbitant fees.

After a few minutes, things looked like they'd calmed down enough for Jacobs to make his move. So he jogged up to the building and headed round the back. There he let himself in through the solid metal door, using his own key. Inside, he made himself at home in a break room. He grabbed a tea towel and used it to dry off as best he could. Henderson kept the place in immaculate condition and the room had all the mod cons, including a dishwasher. Jacobs thought about lighting up but thought better of it in case Henderson threw a hissy fit. He could just imagine him arguing that the smoke would stain his lead-white walls.

Eventually, Charlie Henderson, a very tall, middle-aged

man, walked in wearing overalls that looked like they'd been freshly laundered, and with barely an oil stain on them.

'You sure you weren't followed?' he asked, removing his gloves and giving his hands a wash in the sink.

'Obviously. What do you take me for?' Jacob asked.

'Trouble,' he replied.

'Money,' Jacobs said, flashing the wedge of notes that was burning a hole in his jacket pocket. Money he had every intention of holding onto until he'd received what he'd come for.

'Both,' said the man.

'The trouble with you, Henderson, is that you never know when you're onto a good thing.'

Henderson didn't reply at first. He didn't have the time or energy to spar with Jacobs.

'Is that right?' he said eventually as he dried his hands.

Henderson was a handsome man who looked like he'd have been more at home as a sportsman or actor than a glorified mechanic. He'd first met Jacobs decades ago. Henderson's father had been drinking buddies with Jacobs' old man, and their social circles had overlapped. But he didn't much like Jacobs. Nor did he agree with his politics. If anything, Henderson thought a monetary union with Europe was exactly what his country needed to escape the doldrums of post-war Britain's industrial decline. Granted, it wouldn't do much for him personally, as his business was London based – refitting cars and vans for specialised use. His bread and butter involved turning Morris LDs into ambulances, adding the decals to panda cars and the odd kit out for a hearse for good measure. But about a year ago, he'd won the contract for a very profitable new line – installing security features for Government motors, thirty-two cars in total. And a three-year contract to maintain them. Jacobs had been onto that like a fly on dung, and despite Henderson's best efforts to swat the blighter, it was impossible to stop him buzzing around.

'Let's get on with it,' said Jacobs, itching to get business done.

'Not yet,' said Henderson, 'people are still finishing up on the floor.'

'Who's going to know me from Adam?' said Jacobs impatiently.

'We wait. I'm taking no chances,' Henderson responded. 'Anyone connects the two of us and we're buggered.'

Jacobs rolled his eyes, but there wasn't much that he could do. It was Henderson's gaff, Henderson's rules, so the two men sat there in awkward silence waiting. Neither said barely a word for fifteen minutes, until at last, Jacobs heard the sound of shutters clanging down, footsteps walking across concrete, and finally a car starting its engine. Henderson walked to the window to check the coast was clear.

'Right,' he said, 'let's make this quick.'

Henderson led Jacobs through his set-up. A series of self-contained units, containing a whole fleet of vehicles, from emergency service transport, to vans, trucks and cars. Sometimes, Jacobs wondered why exactly Henderson was so keen to take dirty money – his business looked like a veritable gold mine. He liked to imagine that Henderson had some kind of expensive hobby that ate up cash like it was going out of fashion – maybe girls, cards or Dexamyl. Not that he was one to judge. In fact, it amused him to think there may be a vice-riddled partygoer hidden beneath the insipid mask that Henderson wore for the world. Either that, or maybe the business wasn't going as well as he liked to let on. Jacobs certainly knew a thing or two about that too. And he knew it couldn't be cheap to maintain a facility like this.

Eventually, they arrived at the Government compound.

Henderson led Jacobs to the Prime Minister's dark blue Rover P5, where the key was already in the lock.

'It's in for repair,' Henderson said, simultaneously smiling and raising an eyebrow. 'Apparently it was involved in a skirmish. Word is, some terrorists tried to drive our illustrious premier off the road.'

'How unfortunate,' said Jacobs, 'let's hope nobody was hurt.'

'I knew you'd be concerned,' said Henderson. 'Being the patriot you are.'

'I'll pray for him,' said Jacobs.

'Lucky Wilson,' Henderson replied as he opened the back door of the car and lifted the leather seat, using a hidden catch beneath. He retrieved a small listening device, no bigger than a golf ball which he placed into his visitor's palm. Jacobs quickly dropped it into one pocket, and retrieved a fresh bug from the other which Henderson installed in exactly the same spot. They repeated this procedure on another four cars – two Jaguars, a Vauxhall Viva and a Humber Imperial that had only just been brought in not an hour before. Each time exchanging devices like school kids swapping cigarette cards.

After locking up the last of the vehicles, Jacobs counted his bounty. 'Hang on,' he said, 'I was expecting six.'

'We couldn't get the Daimler back here,' said Henderson. 'I tried, but they said they needed it in service.'

Jacobs was displeased. 'You should have insisted.'

'Listen,' said Henderson, 'there's only so many oil changes a car needs before people start to get suspicious. These motors have picked up more belts than Cassius Clay. I need to keep things inconspicuous. If they so much as get a whiff I'm on the take, I'm done for. And that's not going to happen, Jacobs. I promise you that much.'

'It'll do.' Jacobs snatched the last of the tiny devices from Henderson's hand.

‘That’s gratitude for you,’ said Henderson.

‘Here’s your gratitude,’ said Jacobs, retrieving the stack of blue five pound notes from his coat and throwing a bundle on the bonnet of the Imperial.

Henderson turned to retrieve the money, counting it to check whether his perfidious friend had short-changed him given he was one bug short.

‘Same time tomorrow,’ said Jacobs, but when Henderson span round to protest that he couldn’t keep up with the ever-increasing regularity that Jacobs demanded, he realised his associate had scarpered. It was then he realised it hadn’t been a question, but an instruction.

Henderson knew his alliance with Jacobs couldn’t last much longer. Otherwise, he risked losing everything. He’d made a mistake doing the deal with Jacobs in the first place. It was a rash decision born of a desire to pay down the enormous mortgage he’d taken out to get his operation up and running. And another factor was that Jacobs had threatened Henderson that if *he* wasn’t going to play ball, he’d find someone else inside Henderson’s business that would. And as much as he liked and trusted his boys, they had mouths to feed like everyone else, and he was confident one of them – at least – would have taken Jacobs up on the offer. So, agreeing to Jacobs’ proposition seemed the lesser of two evils. And he much preferred his chances if he, and he alone, was in control of executing the plan. Jacobs was becoming a liability, but extricating himself from the arrangement would require careful thought. After all, if he felt Jacobs was dangerous when he was inside the tent, he knew full well he’d be positively lethal outside of it. But one thing felt certain, Jacobs was heading for a downfall and Henderson had absolutely no intention of being connected to him when he tumbled over the precipice.

21

STANLEY MICHAELS WAITED patiently outside the office block on Salt Lake Wharf just as Jacobs had instructed. The light was starting to go, and he began to catch a chill inside his Ford Transit van. He rolled a cigarette and lit up to keep out the cold as he waited tight for the call to come. It took around four and a half fags before Jacobs' gruff voice came through on the two-way radio they'd rigged up in Michaels' van.

'The name's Jack Deets,' Jacobs said, through the radio. 'Juliet, Alpha, Charlie, Kilo, Delta, Echo, Echo, Tango, Sierra. He'll be there from nine thirty.'

Michaels pulled the microphone to his bearded mouth. The plastic was a little melted from years of sharing his lips with his rollups, and today was no exception. 'Never heard of him,' said Michaels.

'Nor me,' said Jacobs. 'But he won't be around for long enough for it to matter.'

'Leave it with me,' said Michaels.

'Call me when it's done,' came the reply.

'Will do. Out.'

Michaels switched off the radio. His conversations with Jacobs over the air were always purposely brief just in case they were intercepted. Though they took the obvious precautions like adopting a little used wavelength to receive and transmit, never using names over the air and keeping the range to no more than five miles, it paid to be cautious in Michaels' line of work.

While Michaels was finishing the last embers of his "oily rag", he retrieved a loaded magazine for his Welrod gun, which he skilfully managed to insert with one hand. Stubbing out the smoke, he climbed out of the van and closed the door without making a sound.

The first challenge was to gain entry to the building. By now, it was nearly nine fifteen and darkness had fallen. That allowed him just enough time to do a quick recce around the perimeter to see what was what. There were three doors in all, each electronically locked with one of those state-of-the-art keypads that were cropping up all over the place in new build industrial units. They looked the part and allowed people to easily allow entry to large workforces, without cutting new keys, meaning entry could be rescinded with a code change when someone moved on. But they were a godsend for people like Michaels. Unlike the best traditional deadlocks on the market, which could take a good few minutes to pick by hand, electronic locks could be disarmed in seconds if you knew what you were doing. There were lots of methods to effect this, and Michaels considered each before settling on simply cutting the power, using the breaker he'd seen at the side of the building. Most of these boxes could be breached easily enough when the electricity was off because they relied on basic electronic circuits. The very worst models on the market were rendered entirely useless in this event, and even the best could be easily circumvented without power being fed to the unit. Michaels chose this particular method because it also had another fringe benefit – it tripped the alarms, if there were any. If he was going to set them off, it was better to do it now while he was still in the shadows, rather than once he had made his way inside.

He glanced the time on his watch and cut the power. Then he listened. No alarm. Next, he checked the keypad was immobilised – which it was – and propped the side door open with a plant pot. Then he went back to the meter and restored the power, rebooting the system and sliding inside the office block, all in under forty-five seconds. Even by his standards, he'd impressed himself, but he'd learned never to get cocky. That was the easiest way to find a bullet between your eyes and the pin money he collected from Jacobs to supplement his lacklustre old age pension wasn't worth that.

From his vantage point, Michaels could see one nightwatchman. It looked like most of the workers had long since left for the evening. All except – he hoped – his target, the mysterious Jack Deets. Michaels didn't have a clue how Jacobs knew Deets was going to be working late into the evening, but he hoped the information was accurate – though it usually was where Jacobs was concerned – because he was only ever paid fifty per cent upfront for kills. The other half came when the body was lying on a slab. He'd given up another good job over in the East End to fit this in at late notice, so he had absolutely no intention of walking away light.

It took a while for the nightwatchman to finally turn his back to retrieve something from a cupboard under the desk. When he did, Michaels seized his chance and scuttled across the lobby like a spider diving for cover behind a chest of drawers. Arriving at the lift, there was a long list of names attached to each of the twelve floors. On floor eight, he saw the listing for "The Honourable Jack Deets, Member of Parliament, Tykes Water Constituency Office." Summoning the elevators would signal the guard quicker than the sound of gunfire, so he'd have to do it the old-fashioned way, if his aging knees were up to it.

The first three or four floors hurt, the next half dozen killed, but by the time he was at the twelfth floor, his calves were positively burning. He took a moment to catch his breath and felt embarrassed. He was glad his old battalion couldn't see him now, but most of his old brothers-in-arms hadn't even made it past forty, having been picked off one by one in their youth, when their joints still worked, and their reactions were still sharp. Not that any of them wouldn't have gladly traded places in an instance. Despite the indignity of old age, he often reminded himself that it was undeniably better than the alternative.

Michaels paused at the top of the stairs to get his breath. A second for each of his seventy years on this Earth. No good bungling the job because he sounded like a wheezing train. After a little over a minute, Michaels' heartbeat started to slow and the oxygen began to flow back into his lungs. As it did, he opened the door from the stairwell to the corridor and began moving his way through the landing. Deets' office was the tenth one on the right, the corner office – easily recognisable because it was the only one glowing from an artificial yellow light. He grabbed his gun, removed the safety and peered through the glass, which was obscured by metal blinds on the inside. Through the gaps in between powder-coated metal slats, he could see the outline of a man at his desk. Deets had his back to the door, which made it all the easier for Michaels. He'd be dead before he even knew what, and especially who, had hit him.

He counted down from five to prepare himself and then it was time. The assassin quietly turned the doorknob to make sure the catch was unlatched, then he kicked the door open and raised his shooter to fire the fatal round. But before he could aim, let along pull the trigger, the gun was kicked out of his hand by Mrs Peel who pounced from behind the door as Steed spun round in his chair to inspect his would-be killer. Michaels reached down to retrieve the gun, but Steed was already out of the chair, hurling himself across the room to step on Michaels' right wrist. The putative assassin grabbed Steed's ankle with his left hand, pulling him to the ground whereupon they both tussled, neither managing to land a killer blow. Mrs Peel interceded but was knocked flying, winding her in the process.

Michaels was the bigger of the two men, but Steed was by far the younger and more agile. Michaels had always feared this: the risk of continuing in this line of work long after retirement age. You didn't need to have youth on your side to fire a gun, but if you failed to eliminate the target, and a scuffle ensued, your chances of getting out of there in one piece were greatly diminished. Michaels hadn't a clue how a Member of Parliament was such a good fighter. Even so, he knew that in his prime he'd have dispatched the man with ease, but this wasn't his prime. Back on his feet, Michaels grabbed Steed around the waist in a desperate attempt to immobilise him, but "the Honourable Jack Deets" contorted himself at such speed that he evaded Michaels' grip. As Steed recovered his balance and dusted himself down, Mrs Peel had recovered her breath and knocked Michaels back down to the floor in the entrance to the office and placed the sharp edge of her blue knee-high boots onto his sternum, aborting any attempt for him to climb back up.

'Start talking,' she commanded.

'About what?'

'Who put you up to this would be a start.'

'My jacket,' he mumbled, her boot clearly causing him some distress. 'Let me reach inside. You'll find what you need.'

He knew she wouldn't let him retrieve the object himself, for fear he'd grab a weapon. Instead, she reached inside just like he'd hoped, which allowed him just enough time to grab her ankles and launch her into the corridor. As Mrs Peel came crashing down to the floor, Michaels pulled himself up, then seized his opportunity. He kicked the door closed with his foot, turning the brass key inside the lock to prevent Mrs Peel from re-entering.

Immediately Steed had a choice to make: cross the floor to go to Mrs Peel's aid – potentially allowing Michaels enough time to grab his gun – or try for the weapon himself. Steed ran both scenarios in his mind, a process that felt like it had taken a lifetime but was only a fraction of a second. Steed didn't like guns, and he rarely carried them, relying on other means of protection. But as the old saying went, nobody wants to bring a knife – or in Steed's case a bunch of fives – to a gunfight.

After what felt like a lifetime of indecision from both men, they simultaneously rushed for the weapon, both electing to fall to the ground for a hand-to-hand battle for control of the gun. But neither could grip it as they pummelled one another relentlessly. At last, Steed got the upper hand and managed to curl his fingers around the trigger and get a clear line of sight. At that point, Michaels conceded. He knew he'd been bested, and both men slowly got to their feet.

'Enough,' said Steed, gesturing with the gun for the man to take a seat. Michaels complied because his aching frame needed the respite. 'I believe my partner asked you a question. Who do you work for?'

Steed could hear Mrs Peel putting her shoulder to the door to try to break it down, so he walked across the room to the door to let her in. But the key was gone, knocked to the floor in the fight. Steed glanced downwards, but he couldn't see it. 'Well?' Steed prompted.

'We both know I'm a gun for hire,' said Michaels calmly, 'and that you'll get nothing from me.'

'We do?' said Steed.

'I spill...' said Michaels, 'word gets out and I never work again.'

Steed pointed the gun at him. 'Some would argue a bullet isn't great for your career prospects either.'

'True,' said Michaels. 'I suppose I'm counting on you *not* pulling the trigger.'

'And why's that?' asked Steed.

'It doesn't feel very...' Michaels thought for a moment, 'parliamentary.' The man smiled. 'Or perhaps you're a gun for hire too!'

Once again, their conversation was interrupted by a loud thump from Mrs Peel which made the wall shake, but the solid wood door remained intact. This time Steed knocked on the door and shouted to his partner, 'It's okay, Mrs Peel. Everything's under control. We're just looking for the key.' He couldn't quite hear her muffled reply, but she fell silent, so he presumed she'd got the message.

'Well?' said Steed. Pointing at the floor, he added, 'Down you get. You heard what I said to Mrs Peel.' Michaels picked up on the cue and began searching the floor for the brass key. It was a somewhat demeaning picture, but Steed hadn't intended it to be, that wasn't really his style. It was sheer practicality – Steed couldn't afford to take his eyes off the assassin.

'Got it,' said Michaels, but as he passed it to his captor, Steed had no choice but to drop his guard and Michaels took full advantage and rugby tackled Steed, which sent him careering into the window panel behind. As the glass splintered into countless shards, the gun hurtled into the night sky, and there was an audible clang as it hit the concrete a dozen floors beneath.

Steed was left precariously hanging out of the window: his bottom half still inside the room, his chest exposed to the wind and his hands hanging onto the aluminium frame for dear life. Now Michaels had *all* the cards. The assassin walked slowly over to Steed and extended a flat palm – the only weapon he'd need to end John Steed's life – and reached over to finish the job. Moments from death, Steed saw the office door burst open, and splinters of wood fly across the room. Mrs Peel ran inside, wielding a fire extinguisher, which she'd used as a makeshift battering ram. As she spotted what was going on, she operated the device and doused Michaels in foam. With a hand from Mrs Peel, Steed pulled himself back inside and the two of them turned to face their attacker.

Michaels knew his only advantage was his physical size, so he ran towards his targets with all his might, hoping to overpower them. But Steed and Mrs Peel were quicker on their feet. As they spotted their ageing assassin charging towards them, they dropped to the floor, leaving Michaels hurtling towards the broken window. With nothing to break his momentum, he accelerated towards the glass like a tennis player hitting the net when they couldn't find their footing. Disorientated from the struggle, and with the floor wet from the fire extinguisher, there was nothing Michaels could seemingly do to avoid his fate. Before he knew what was happening, he felt his body colliding with glass shards and experienced the sensation of falling. It had all happened slowly enough to process what was going on, but too quickly to send the signal to his body to abort the manoeuvre. As he was thrown from the building, Michaels knew his fate before he hit the concrete. One final thought ran through his mind. It wasn't fear, it wasn't peace, just incredulity that he'd managed to survive two world wars in active service, yet he was finally about to meet his maker in an industrial park in Greenwich. As his final synapses fired, he knew he'd been right about one thing: it would be a politician that killed him.

Steed and Mrs Peel looked down at the scene that lay beneath.

'Something tells me that *wasn't* meant to happen,' said Mrs Peel, dusting herself down.

Steed came away from the window and retrieved the package marked "Top Secret" that the traitor was *supposed* to have stolen. He threw it on the desk. 'Best laid plans and all that.'

'So our informant isn't just on the take...'

Steed picked up the assassin's gun. 'Apparently not.'

'I'm guessing our dear departed visitor wasn't one of your canaries?'

'Well it certainly didn't look like he could fly,' said Steed, his face grimacing at the thought.

'So I'm guessing this room means something?'

'Twelve names, twelve floors Mrs Peel. Pity for him his paymaster wasn't one of the names on the bottom levels...'

'So who do we have to thank for this evening's escapades?'

Steed instantly knew who'd sold them out, but that was tomorrow's problem. Right now, he was simply grateful to be alive.

22

STEED'S EYES WERE heavy as he wended his way along the country lanes of Buckinghamshire in his open-top Bentley. The breeze helped to revive him after a night of tossing and turning. He'd learned years ago to never let the job get to him, but last night's events weighed heavy. But for a chance of fate, it could easily have been Steed kissing the pavement and some days he did wonder if he was getting a bit old for it all. He reckoned the mystery assassin must have easily been in his late sixties, maybe his seventies, and he hoped to goodness that when he was a septuagenarian he'd have his feet up with a brandy in one hand and a newspaper in the other by eight o'clock. But with his insatiable appetite for keeping busy and seeking adrenaline wherever it could be found, he knew life might have other ideas. Thankfully, Steed wasn't one to dwell. After a while, his introspection started to grate, and he snapped himself out of it. Frankly, he didn't have the time or energy to feel sorry for himself or his attacker, and he remembered Sir Winston Churchill's sage advice: "keep buggering on."

As the Bentley began to climb a sharp hill, Steed winced as his freshly sprained wrist pulled hard at the gear stick. The Bentley was a magnificent car to look at, and her engine sounded sublime, but she was an absolute pig to drive, given she was built for the racetrack not the road. As Steed slipped the car into first gear, the magnificent six litre engine rumbled to life. What the bulky car lacked in manoeuvrability, it more than made up for in sheer power and Steed could suddenly see how the Speed Six had won the 24 Hours of Le Mans two years running.

At the top of the hill, Steed arrived at Viscount Manse, the country pile of Eric Goodenough MP. A home that couldn't have been more different from the average two up, two down enjoyed – or not as the case may well have been – by the politician's constituents.

Steed dropped the car in the courtyard of the old Elizabethan mansion and saw Goodenough in the distance, playing bowls on the lawn with a few chums. He suspected Goodenough would neither be expecting nor excited by his arrival.

Goodenough spotted him immediately and removed his sunhat. Steed did not reciprocate. 'Do excuse me for a moment,' Goodenough said to his companions. 'Dorothy will fix you some breakfast on the veranda.' As his guests retired, he walked across the lawn to meet Steed, bemused but in no way hostile. 'To what do we owe the pleasure at this early hour?' asked Goodenough.

'Pleasure's in rather short supply I'm afraid, my *honourable* friend,' said Steed, lacing the penultimate word with sardonicism.

'I don't follow?' Goodenough replied.

Steed walked over to the bowling green, which was freshly cut to regulation height.

'May I?' said Steed.

'Please,' said Goodenough.

Steed picked up a dark blue bowl and rolled it forward. It came to a stop no more than six inches away from the jack.

Goodenough was impressed. 'You enjoy tickling the kitty I see, Mr Steed?' he observed.

Steed raised an eyebrow.

'It's what we call the jack,' Goodenough clarified.

'I dabble,' said Steed.

'Are you here to brief me on another mission?' asked Goodenough, who launched his own bowl, which collided with Steed's, taking the lead. 'I must say, I find all this cloak and dagger stuff awfully invigorating.'

'Well, you certainly seem to have mastered the dagger,' said Steed, sending another bowl into battle and recovering his pole position, 'but your cloak leaves a lot to be desired.'

'I don't follow?' said Goodenough.

'The information I gave you?'

'Yes? About Deets?'

'Yes. Jack Deets,' said Steed.

'There's a problem?'

'You could say that.'

'I did as you asked, Steed,' said Goodenough, starting to feel uneasy. 'I delivered the package as instructed, and I told no one.'

'What about the information your driver slipped you?' Steed asked.

'You know about that?'

'She was *my* driver.' Steed's expression changed, from jovial to deadly serious. 'She told you – and only you – that there was going to be a very important meeting on the eighth floor at nine thirty last night.'

'And I haven't spoken a word of it.'

Given how uncomfortable Goodenough looked, his guests, who'd been hovering a few yards away from their host, took the hint and headed inside. Goodenough gave them an appreciative nod.

'Look here, Steed. Will you tell me what all this is about exactly?'

'Moles,' said Steed, running his umbrella across a mound of earth that had recently been disturbed. Half a dozen blemishes on an otherwise beautifully kept lawn.

'Inundated with them, I'm afraid,' said Goodenough. 'My groundskeeper's tried everything.'

'You need to smoke them out,' said Steed. 'Suppose there was a mole in Government?'

Goodenough looked blank.

'It's what the Russians call a sleeper agent. Someone selling us out to the other side. How would you solve a problem like that?'

'Impossible,' said Goodenough. 'In Cabinet? I won't hear a word of it. I've worked with those men for years. I'll grant you there's probably a bad penny or two in there, like any group, but defection? Treason? Never!'

'But someone *did*, I'm afraid. And it proved fatal.'

'Another death?' Goodenough asked, his face ashen.

'Extinguished. Snuffed out. Cut down in the prime of his life,' said Steed, 'taken before his time. Practically a bairn. A true man of the people.'

'But who?' asked Goodenough.

'I wonder if you can guess?' Steed said, 'Everyone with even an ounce of suspicion on them was asked to deliver the same package to the same building. And everyone was fed the same line from my associate, Mrs Peel, that there was going to be a top secret meeting that very evening regarding the Prime Minister and the Common Market. Guess who arrived at the eighth floor at nine thirty?'

Goodenough knew where this was going. 'Jack Deets is dead?' he asked under his breath, trying to make sense of the information.

'Exactly. So you see why I'm so very, very disappointed, Mr Goodenough. Because I really didn't think it would be *you*.'

'But it wasn't! Believe me Steed, I didn't tell a soul,' he whimpered, 'I got in my car at Westminster, delivered the package, and was then driven straight home. And I haven't left the house since last night. I haven't even told my wife, Dot. You can ask her yourself if you don't believe me...'

Steed grabbed Goodenough by the lapels, about to shake some sense into him, but as the two men made eye contact, Steed could see the fear in the man's eyes. His gut told him Goodenough was telling the truth. And Steed's gut was seldom wrong – except for where Mrs Peel's camembert was concerned. Steed had collared hundreds of ne'er-do-wells and traitors in his time, and Goodenough didn't fit the bill. He released his grip on the man's jacket and dusted him down, straightening Goodenough's tie with renewed affection. He picked up another bowl and launched it across the green. This time it clipped the jack itself. 'You'd better not be lying to me,' said Steed.

'I swear it, Steed,' said Goodenough.

'Then I need you to tell me who knew where you were going,' said Steed. The precise details. Someone you told. Anyone that might have been in ear shot. Perhaps you wrote it down, and someone found it? I need you to rack your brains.'

'That's what I've been telling you. I'm not a fool, Steed. I didn't write it down. I told nobody. The only person who knew was the driver. A pretty thing she was too. That Peel woman who gave Cabinet a good dressing down.'

Steed didn't like the sound of that one little bit. It meant leaving Goodenough's estate none the wiser. 'Then our business is concluded...' said Steed, 'for now.'

He picked up the final bowl and placed it in Goodenough's hands. 'Good luck.' And then he was gone.

His guests poked their heads around the corner when they heard the Bentley drive off, each nursing a slice of Victoria sponge. Goodenough tried to shake off the experience off as best he could and assembled the perfect faux smile, the one he'd perfected over a long career visiting factories, meeting dignitaries and begging voters. As the game resumed, his mind was elsewhere – helpless to avoid turning the problem over again and again in his head. He didn't know how these villains had got hold of the information, but he hadn't been lying to Steed. Whoever betrayed the country it certainly wasn't him. But his Dorothy's face said it all. Things were getting too hot in Westminster and working in government had suddenly become a whole lot more dangerous.

23

MRS PEEL ARRIVED at Jeffrey Lamb's Mayfair flat thirty minutes late. It was a small act of defiance, but she was nobody's lap dog – least of all a blackmailer of Lamb's calibre.

She dug her finger into the buzzer, frustrated by the amount of time this had all taken. At a time when she and Steed had plenty to be getting on with already.

'Come on up, Mrs Peel,' came the reply over the intercom.

Lamb's studio was everything she'd have expected. A bohemian flat full of the latest furniture from Terence Conran. Peeling walls and mottled paint completed the "struggling artisan" aesthetic, despite the man's evident wealth.

'Fashionably late I see, Mrs Peel,' said Lamb, extending his arms to take her black and white coat. 'Never mind, won't you come on through to my dark room?'

Mrs Peel slapped his hand away.

'Just get on with it,' she said. She was in no mood to be schmoozed.

Lamb led her to his workplace, which was filled with a smorgasbord of photographic ephemera including chemicals, trays and other apparatus. Dozens of photos were hanging from pegs, each more salacious than the last.

'Is that…?' Mrs Peel asked.

'It is indeed, Mrs Peel,' he replied.

'That's not his…?' She tilted her head.

'I'm afraid so.'

'Hardly David Bailey, is it?' she said scornfully.

'Perhaps not. But it pays the bills. And rather handsomely at that.'

'Yes, I can see,' she replied.

'I see you've brought my remuneration?' said Lamb, eyeballing the brown paper package that Mrs Peel was carrying in her hand.

'First, perhaps you'd like to show me your leverage?' she asked.

'Certainly,' said Lamb. 'It won't surprise you that my editors like me to tail the Prime Minister. Nothing sells headlines like a naughty premier.'

'And…?' Mrs Peel was growing impatient.

'And the man's thoroughly dull, I'm afraid. Or very diligent… Not so much as a snifter in over two years of following him on and off. And you know the irony?'

'Clearly,' said Mrs Peel.

'The one time something happens to dearest Harold. And I'm guessing you know precisely *what* that is, I wasn't there to snap it. How's that for divine inspiration?'

'The world's loss, I'm sure,' said Mrs Peel.

'Yes. The *News of the World*!' he replied, 'I'd have made a small fortune on something like that – no questions asked.'

'So, you're turning to extortion to make up the difference?' she enquired.

'A man's got to live, Mrs Peel.' He tossed her some photographic prints. 'Think of it as a side hustle…'

Even with the artificial red light, Mrs Peel could see the images were long lens snaps of the Prime Minister being treated by doctors through a window. Probably at Chequers. In the photographs he looked bewildered and scared. One particularly incriminating photograph showed Mr Wilson seemingly desperate to get out of the window, while men in white coats pulled him back and tried to inject him with a needle.

'Not definitive by themselves…' said Lamb, 'but given the Prime Minister hasn't been seen since Thursday and all his appointments have been cancelled, it could be… unsettling for the electorate, wouldn't you say?'

'Oh believe me, Mr Lamb, I've got plenty to say,' said Mrs Peel.

'I'm quite sure you have. But before you do, I've got something else to show you. After all, I'm a businessman, Mrs Peel. And I don't expect something for nothing.'

'Oh?' enquired Mrs Peel.

Lamb cleared his throat twice in quick succession – the universal sign for "not before you've given me what I want."

Mrs Peel passed the brown envelope she'd been carrying across to Lamb. He opened the package and instead of the money he was expecting, he retrieved some photographs. As he glanced at them, his smile turned to instant dread. His eyes bulged, as he vividly remembered the event depicted and feelings of shame, fear and perhaps a little forbidden excitement flowed through his veins.

'You're not the only one that's done a little bit of digging, Mr Lamb…' said Mrs Peel, looking particularly pleased with herself. 'Looks like we both have friends in *low* places. And somebody's been a *very* naughty boy.'

Lamb put the photographs back in the envelope and returned it to her. 'Touché, Mrs Peel,' he conceded. He retrieved a cardboard folder from the desk and offered it to her. 'Even Stevens?' he asked.

'It depends…' Tucking her own envelope beneath one arm, she opened the file he'd given her. Inside were a number of pedestrian photographs of politicians going about their normal business.

'And...?' asked Mrs Peel, failing to see anything remarkable.

'Ask yourself what they all have in common, Mrs Peel,' Lamb suggested.

She scrutinised the photographs once more, which wasn't easy given the red light, which illuminated the room. This time, she spotted a hidden detail. Every photograph depicted a different member of the Cabinet. There were images of the Prime Minister coming and going from Buckingham Palace, the Chancellor outside Number 11 and a handful of ministers that Mrs Peel couldn't have identified in a line-up making their way here and there. But one face popped up in *every* image. A man in his early forties with a long gaunt face.

It was the Prime Minister's chauffeur.

'Do you have a name?' asked Mrs Peel.

'Kilpatrick,' said Lamb, 'and that's about *all* I can find out about him. Government personnel files are hush-hush as you'd expect. And I couldn't find anyone in the department I could lean on. But I did put the word out to some of my chums over on the Continent and...'

'And...?'

Lamb was smiling. 'You'll like this.' He walked over to a filing cabinet and retrieved a much bigger file. He scattered over two dozen photographs of the same man onto his bench – this time the chauffeur was standing alongside other European leaders. There was de Gaulle from France, Kiesinger from West Germany, and Aldo Moro from Italy along with lots of other dignitaries that Mrs Peel didn't quite recognise.

'He has been around, hasn't he?' said Mrs Peel as she reluctantly handed her leverage over to Lamb.

'I presume there aren't any copies?' he asked.

She shook her head. 'Negatives are in there with the prints,' she answered. 'The positives – well I'll leave them to your imagination.'

'An honourable woman, Mrs Peel,' he said, 'refreshing in this day and age.'

Lamb retrieved all the photographs of Wilson from pegs on his line and added them to the Kilpatrick envelope.

'Aren't you going to ask if I made any copies?' said Lamb.

'Did you?'

'Well, surely it's a risk. After all, I might *still* sell the story to my editor, mightn't I? Given the Government aren't going to play ball. I've still got a good few hours to make the Monday morning papers…'

'You won't do that,' said Mrs Peel.

'You seem very sure.' Lamb stated.

'I am,' she said, 'for two simple reasons. One: I know who helped you… *make* those photographs.'

Lamb blushed. 'And two?'

Emma smiled as she walked towards the door, never looking back. 'Keep your word, Mr Lamb… and you'll never need to find out.'

24

GERALD EASTMAN HAD spent over two decades in politics. His first cabinet post had come in the final months of Clement Attlee's premiership, before the country booted out the Labour Party and returned Churchill to power. He'd spent thirteen long years in the political wilderness as a shadow minister and, by the end of his exile, a shadow of a man. In retrospect, if he'd have known it was going to take so long for the Labour party to get back into office, he'd have called it quits years ago, but time had crept up on him, as it always does.

Eastman waited inside Number 10, ready to be given the nod that his car had arrived. It was always an awkward encounter, held back by the doorman like a teacher restraining a student until their parents arrived to collect him. When the door opened, Eastman launched himself into the Daimler, eager to get home.

'Morning,' said Kilpatrick, suited and booted with a freshly shaved face and slicked back hair. 'How was Cabinet?'

Eastman barely registered his existence, mumbling a reply that sounded like a guttural regurgitation of the same greeting.

'They got us both working on Sundays now then I see,' observed the chauffeur.

'More's the pity,' said Eastman. 'There's a hoo-ha on at the moment.'

'Yes, I'd heard something about it, sir. Is it true what they're saying about the Prime Minister?'

Eastman glanced at the chauffeur's eyes in the rear-view mirror. Surprised word had got out, he said firmly, 'I'm not at liberty to say, I'm afraid.'

'Of course, sir,' the driver replied, 'I'm sure whatever it is will sort itself out. Usually does.'

'I expect so,' said Eastman.

'Well sit back and relax, sir,' said the chauffeur, 'we'll have you home in no time.'

As Eastman whipped out a copy of the *Sunday Telegraph*, his driver pulled out of Downing Street and headed south towards Battersea. Checking that his passenger was entrenched in his newspaper, he began his work.

'Is it me…' asked the chauffeur, 'or is the temperature in the lake hotter than the postmaster?'

Eastman looked bemused.

'Sorry,' the chauffeur continued, 'what I mean to say is, how long will it take to get to Westminster if we left through the open gate?'

'What are you talking about, man?' said Eastman.

The chauffeur didn't reply directly, or even take his eyes off the road; he just kept firing absurd sentences at Eastman, ten to the dozen.

'And you'll remember that the ocean has no memory if it's left alone by the Secretary General.'

Eastman's mind was racing.

'Tin cars are only as good as the width of the continent.'

'Stop it,' said Eastman.

'And a graveyard can only accommodate the number of penguins that live in the field,' he continued.

'I said stop it!'

'How can there ever be respite if there's nobody to tune the engine?' the chauffeur insisted.

'You're a maniac, man,' said Eastman, checking to see if the doors were unlocked. They weren't and he was speeding through the streets.

'Cattle raised in space never develop paperwork. Did you know that?' the chauffeur added.

'Stop this car at *once*!' shouted Eastman.

'Milk is only ever the colour of envelopes, except when using a thermometer.'

The sheer bombardment of inanity was sending Eastman giddy and his heart was racing – unsure what the madman was going to do to him.

Sensing his subject was very nearly primed, the chauffeur issued one final statement, informing Eastman that, 'nobody in East Cheam can ever deny the existence of the Loch Ness Monster,' before moving onto the next stage. He checked ahead to make sure the road was straight and clear, to buy him a few seconds to take his eyes off the road and – without warning – he turned round and slammed the glass partition between him and Eastman. As he did so, he issued a single command: 'Sleep.'

With that, Eastman's head slumped to the ground and the chauffeur pulled the car into a layby. There he withdrew a small needle from his jacket pocket, removed Eastman's watch and administered a clear fluid into a prominent vein in the man's wrist. Then he wiped it clean and replaced the watch. He retrieved Eastman's newspaper, which had fallen to the floor and propped it in his limp arms. After a moment, the chauffeur climbed back into the driver's seat, turned the ignition and pulled back onto the road as if nothing had happened.

About five minutes later, the chauffeur began speaking again. This time in a very slow and dominant voice, like a strict father lecturing his child. The chauffeur had a thick accent – but his command of the English language was exemplary.

'It's time to wake up in a moment, Mr Eastman,' the chauffeur said. 'When you hear the sound of my car's horn strike twice, you'll be up and about. You'll have absolutely no memory of the last few minutes, you'll merely be engrossed in your newspaper as you were before. But you'll still feel tired. Like the pull to return to slumber is never far away. The feeling you get when you're looking out of a train window and the warm, golden sunlight is hitting your face after a long day. The feeling that you're at peace with the world, and a daydream is more appealing than the real world. When you hear my voice, it'll feel calm and relaxing. It'll elicit a feeling of trust and relaxation. You'll open up to me like you would a confidant. Only too happy to unshackle yourself from the burden of the secrets you hold. And better still, when you've finished this journey, and I sound the horn a third and final time, you won't remember *anything* that's been said inside this car. As far as you're concerned, you'll have taken your secrets to the grave. If you understand me, Mr Eastman, raise a finger.'

It took a few seconds, but eventually Eastman's pinkie twitched and shot up.

After that, the chauffeur honked his horn twice in quick succession, causing another driver to flip him the bird angrily.

When he heard the sound, Eastman's eyes snapped open, exactly as the chauffeur said they should.

'Sorry about that,' said Eastman, 'must have nodded off.'

'Not at all, sir,' said the chauffeur, 'I'd do the same in your shoes.'

'Too many late nights in a row, I shouldn't wonder,' said Eastman.

'We never finished our conversation, sir. You were telling me about Cabinet.'

'Was I?' Eastman asked, somewhat surprised.

'Something or other about Europe? The ECC was it?'

'The E*E*C? Well, yes. That did rather dominate Cabinet.' Somewhere in Eastman's brain, he knew he shouldn't be talking about this, but his gut told him he could trust this man. He didn't know why, but somehow it didn't just feel okay to divulge his secrets, it felt positively apposite.

'What's been going on over there then?' said the chauffeur.

Eastman put down his paper to spend time with his "friend." 'Well,' he said, 'where do I start…'

25

'THOMAS KILPATRICK,' SAID Steed, handing the file over to Mrs Peel who was sitting on his Chesterfield-style burgundy settee. 'He's been on the Government's books for six months. Full security clearance. Came highly recommended from the chauffeuring agency.'

'Hmm,' was all Mrs Peel could muster.

'Apparently,' Steed continued, 'he can parallel park blindfolded, do a *two*-point turn, and has the reaction speed of a cat. He's worked for six European governments, so he sailed through the vetting process.'

Mrs Peel looked at his photograph. 'It's a promising lead,' she said.

'Why do I sense there's a but?'

'*But* we're missing something, aren't we?' said Mrs Peel, 'Kilpatrick wasn't driving when Goodenough paid his visit to Deets. I was! And Lord Hagley was murdered on the Tube.'

'Maybe so,' said Steed, 'but there were only two people inside that car when the Prime Minister went…'

'Doolally tap?' ventured Mrs Peel.

Steed smiled. 'One is Wilson.'

Mrs Peel nodded. 'The other is Kilpatrick.'

'Which at the very least,' said Steed, 'means he warrants a visit.'

'Agreed.'

'Now we just need to find him.'

'Surely his address is on file?'

'An address was on file, but not *the* address.'

'Ahh,' said Mrs Peel.'

'I've got some people digging, but it probably warrants a visit to the chauffeuring agency.

Mrs Peel nodded, while glancing over at the jigsaw they'd been working on previously. Since she'd last seen it, Steed had completed the red brick structure that depicted a bridge across a lake. The crossing was decorated with a parapet that was decorated with diamond shaped holes.

'Any idea what this is all about yet?' asked Emma.

'Haven't a clue,' Steed replied.

'So no inheritance for you!'

Mrs Peel looked at the handwritten note sitting alongside the jigsaw. As instructed, she tried to identify the car. 'What is it? A Bugatti?'

'Yes. A Type 35,' Steed replied.

'Does that mean anything to you?'

'Thirty-five million pounds?' said Steed optimistically.

'Perhaps he left you the car.'

'He didn't drive a Bugatti,' said Steed. 'He had a Ford Popular with a rusted chassis. You could see the road beneath your feet whenever he took you for a spin.'

'Who was Uncle Robert anyway?' Mrs Peel asked.

'Aunt Irene's husband,' said Steed.

'Very informative,' she replied. 'Did he own anything of value?'

'The only thing I remember old Bobby collecting was wives,' Steed replied. 'Aunt Irene was his sixth wife.'

'Like Henry the Eighth,' said Mrs Peel. 'Let me guess? Divorced, beheaded, died, divorced, beheaded, survived?'

'Not quite,' said Steed, 'from memory it was more like adultery, inadequacy, divorce, virility, banality, remorse.'

Emma smiled. 'Quite a catch. I can see the family resemblance.'

Steed placed another piece of lake down on the puzzle – a segment of lily pads by the look of it. 'Not sure how painting in the scenery will help us identify the car, but we can but try,' he said.

'How about we concentrate on a problem we *can* solve?' said Mrs Peel.

'Okay,' said Steed, 'what will it be then, Mrs Peel? The chauffeuring agency or Kilpatrick? A driving school or schooling a driver?'

'You take the chauffeur,' she said. 'I'm the better driver.' Steed didn't argue.

Mrs Peel spotted another two pieces of the lake and attached them to the lily pads to produce an image of a duck. 'Maybe the number plate is a clue,' she said, getting up and walking towards the door. 'I have a hunch.'

'Not from where I'm standing,' Steed said playfully.

'I'll let you know what I find.'

'About my inheritance?' Steed asked, expectantly.

'About our demon driver.'

'Likewise,' said Steed. 'Let's hope he doesn't offer me a lift.'

26

HORATIO GRAINGER HAD only just woken up by midday. He'd been up half the night, reading every book he could find in his collection. Page by page, under the light of a green banker's lamp, he looked for any reference to an episode like Wilson's, but nothing was forthcoming. He'd found references to hypnosis-led psychosis, whereby subjects had emerged from a trance and become violent and aggressive. And the literature frequently talked about people whose personalities had changed post-hypnosis, but this tended to be in small and relatively insubstantial ways – like hating coffee after a lifetime of caffeine addiction, or becoming a night owl when they'd formerly been a morning lark. But he hadn't seen *anything* that could explain, let alone fix, what had happened to Wilson. And that profoundly worried him.

It had been four o'clock in the morning before he'd even noticed the time and conceded he was on a hiding to nothing. Whatever he'd done, inadvertent or otherwise, nobody was coming to his rescue. He'd have to find his own way out of this, or else all of his hard work would be for absolutely nothing. As exhaustion set in, he allowed himself to tune out and grab a few hours rest, even though his mind was racing. It was a skill he'd long since mastered and was particularly helpful in times of stress.

As he got himself up and dressed, Grainger attached his identification badge and smiled at the label. Thomas Kilpatrick was merely the latest in a long line of pseudonyms. His real name was Horatio, named after Nelson – the famous British naval commander who triumphed at the Battle of Trafalgar over the French. This had sparked a lifelong fascination with European history that had – in a roundabout sort of way – led him towards this very moment.

In the past couple of years, Grainger had been Louis Janssens from Belgium who'd managed to wheedle his way into the Paleis der Natie, as well as Joseph Schmit who drove cars for the Grand Duchy of Luxembourg, and Hans Klein who worked security for the Bonn Republic. Grainger's reason for wanting European unity was simple. At the outset of war, Horatio's family had been living in Austria, his birthplace. The Anschluss of 1938 had driven him out of his country and the War had ravaged his family every bit as much as it had devastated Europe, driving a wedge between his German father, Karl and his French mother, Lise.

A teenager during the War, still dependent on his parents for shelter and sustenance, Grainger had been pulled from pillar to post, moving to a whole host of Axis and Allied countries when his parents divorced, and neither seemed keen to hold onto him. By the time the War ended in '45, it had claimed both of them. His father had been killed in a bombing raid by the British and Americans on Dresden only a matter of months before Germany surrendered and his mother had died in the sinking of the HMHS *Newfoundland* – a hospital ship that she was serving on as a nurse in September '43, despite such vessels being protected under international law.

As Horatio began to rebuild his life, he became obsessed by the War, and the senseless suffering it had delivered to mankind. Worse still, it was the second such conflict in just over twenty years, and he was determined it would be the last. In his opinion, it was foolhardy to put humanity's fate in the hands of atomic weapons.

Commentators believed they would ensure peace because slowly but surely more and more countries were getting the A-Bomb. But Grainger foresaw a time when everyone had armed themselves to the back teeth and conflict became the norm, not the exception. To him, the *only* way peace would prevail in Europe was if the Continent stopped concentrating on its differences and instead came together and recognised its common values.

By the mid 1950s, he'd got himself a job as a negotiator and later a diplomat working on the accord that would become the Treaty of Rome in 1957, which laid the foundations for a European Union. But ten peaceful years after its formation, the fledgling alliance had still not expanded beyond its six founder members, despite many countries, including the United Kingdom, trying and failing to accede during that time. That's when he'd resolved to travel, country to country, in his capacity as a diplomat, to remove the barriers to the EEC fulfilling its potential.

At first, Grainger relied on conventional methods to effect change. He met with negotiating committees, provided assurances about issues of national sovereignty and economic protectionism. He navigated issues around agricultural policies and immigration, but he found himself forever hitting a brick wall. Despite his best efforts, he could never seem to get in front of decision makers, only ever civil servants who were often wet behind the ears and buried his requests inside a sea of red tape. That's when he'd decided to deploy his other skill set to advance his work.

Ever since he'd been a boy, Grainger had been aware

of his natural – almost effortless – ability to encourage, persuade and even cajole people into doing things. Even if it went against their best interests. He vividly remembered inciting his classmates to get themselves in trouble for his own amusement, prompting them to do naughty things to get a laugh, while safely staying in the shadows during the ensuing chaos. And he was struck by how easy it was. Through a simple combination of flattery, confidence and a fair bit of charm, he could get his own way more often than not, and this set of skills served him well in a myriad of ways.

When he was eighteen years old, he'd attended a cabaret act where a stage hypnotist had invited him, and a select few other audience members, up to the stage. He'd sat there and watched each participant succumb to the hypnotist's trance through the eyes of a sceptic, presuming his fellow stage buddies were either in on the act, or were faking it to please the audience. That was until he awoke, some twenty minutes later, back in his chair. His girlfriend at the time told him that he had indeed been hypnotised, and had performed a "hilarious" farmyard routine, which had apparently brought the house down. Grainger was utterly astonished, not least because he wouldn't have believed it was possible to control another human being in this fashion – least of all him – and because he was, and always had been up until this point, an introvert who could never imagine performing in front of a group of people, let alone barking, oinking and making whatever other animal noises he'd somehow recited against his better judgement.

Grainger had met the hypnotist backstage after the show and been given a crash course in the basics of the craft. The performer – Monsieur Mesmo – had recommended a number of books on the subject of hypnotism for him to read, many of which he still owned to this day.

His technique had also been fine-tuned by the work of the American psychiatrist Milton H. Erickson, who posited that hypnosis could be a powerful tool to effect change and that by using a combination of verbal commands designed to interrupt, confuse, provoke memories and tell stories, he could heal trauma and allow people to open up their psyches to another.

At first, Grainger had used these new skills sparingly – to nudge, rather than change other people's opinions. But the more he encountered resistance to ideas and ideals that he cared about, the more he turned to the "dark arts" of hypnotism – the aspect of the discipline that reputable hypnotists advised nobody to tread – in order to get his own way and, as he saw it, to further his mission.

But in all his years of practice, he'd never come across anything like Wilson's case. And if he hadn't had his eyes on the Prime Minister throughout their encounter, he'd have suspected a simple head injury was the cause.

He did find one paper from the previous year that was published in the *International Journal of Clinical and Experimental Hypnosis* that identified two types of post-hypnotic amnesia: one state which the authors, Evans and Thorn, called "Recall Amnesia" occurred when people who had been hypnotised couldn't remember anything about their trance, which was perfectly normal. The other, dubbed "Source Amnesia", meant subjects had no memory of being hypnotised, but did recall any ideas, skills or information gained while under the influence, oblivious to how they acquired said knowledge. However, he struggled to see how that helped him with Wilson's case. He found an article on age regression, which seemed to fit the bill, but this seemed to be more of a therapeutic tool, and nobody gave credence to the idea that it could induce a permanent state, even allowing for the fact he hadn't even performed such a benign incantation. But it did illuminate some new techniques to help people get in – and indeed out – of such a mental state, which was something at least. *If*, he was ever allowed within a hundred feet of the Prime Minister, that was – which in itself seemed dubious right now.

Grainger knew the next forty-eight hours were going to be critical. Not only did he have to find a way to get close to Wilson, he also knew there was another – arguably bigger – problem to consider: *How long before the authorities started asking questions about Grainger himself?* And that meant tying up some loose ends.

27

THE HEADQUARTERS OF The Mastering Motoring Institute was an exquisite example of Art Deco architecture. An imperious building, rendered in ivory, surrounded by a mile or two of private roads, winding round the building like a snake swallowing its prey.

Mrs Peel spotted the left turn to the building at the last minute and pulled onto the tarmacked slip road that led up to the main office. As she did so, a handful of attendants scrambled to greet her. When she drove past the first, a man held up a large metal sign from a collection which sat at the side of the road. It read TOO FAST in large, government-issue font on a white circular background. As she hit the next marker, a few yards down the road, a woman displayed a sign which read LOWER YOUR GEAR. And as she pulled into the parking space outside the entrance, a final employee, this time a parking attendant, reviewed her efforts to reverse into the visitors' space with a pained expression before choosing a final sign which read REAR ASKEW. Mrs Peel frowned, displeased by this brazen review of her driving ability – which she considered to be more than serviceable, and the impertinence of reviewing the efforts of unwitting drivers, whether by their rear or otherwise.

Mrs Peel got out of her car and slammed the door, making

her feelings about the situation quite clear. Instead of greeting her to enquire about the nature of her visit, the attendants were nowhere to be seen, so she made her own way from the car park to the reception. Now she could see just how peculiar this place was. Half a dozen cars were on manoeuvres around the tracks that criss-crossed the building.

Suddenly, she saw a car careering towards a mother crossing the road with her baby in a pram. Instinctively, she cried out to give warning, but it was too late. As the car was about to strike the pram, the driver slammed on his brakes and came to a stop no more than an inch away from the pedestrians. As Mrs Peel dashed over to check they were okay, the "mother" whipped off a brown curly wig to reveal a middle-aged balding man's head beneath. He retrieved a doll from the pram, to reassure her.

'Don't worry my dear,' he said, 'just manoeuvres. See yourself in, and I'll be with you in a moment.'

As she made her way towards the entrance, Mrs Peel spotted the man rummaging in the pram and retrieving a flat cap, brown overcoat and a cane as he dashed across to a different driver, this time feigning a decrepit pensioner, walking across a makeshift zebra crossing and forcing another driver to an abrupt stop. As Mrs Peel looked around, she could see similar eccentrics posing as other road users – from cyclists, to delivery men, and window cleaners to workmen.

Arriving at the entrance, she found an engraved brass plaque which bore the company's motto: DRIVING UP AUTOMOTIVE STANDARDS. Amused, she stepped inside a modest waiting room, which was every bit as quirky as the exterior. Rather than characterless plastic chairs like every doctor's surgery and dentist up and down the country, the room sported leather benches and reclining seats which looked like they'd been ripped straight out of a wide assortment of cars, vans and even buses.

Perhaps most bizarre of all was the receptionist's screen, which was shaped like a car window, complete with one half of a pair of wing mirrors.

'Good afternoon,' said Mrs Peel, greeting the fair-haired receptionist on the other side of the glass. Her response was audibly distorted by the glass, but she made a gesture that Mrs Peel initially mistook for a fishing mime. But when she subsequently pointed to a poster beneath the glass, Mrs Peel saw what she had to do. As instructed, she reached for the handle beneath the glass and duly wound the window down, as you would a car's.

'Afternoon,' said the receptionist at last.

'My name is Mrs Emma Peel. I'm here to see the proprietor,' said Mrs Peel. 'I believe he's been informed.'

'Yes indeed,' said the lady, 'Mr Feldon will be with you shortly.'

'Thank you.'

'Something to read while you're waiting?' asked the receptionist.

'Please,' said Mrs Peel, never one to turn away an out-of-date magazine. Instead, she received a pocket-sized copy of the Highway Code. Mrs Peel handed it back. 'No thank you,' she replied, still unimpressed by the uninvited appraisal of her driving skills earlier, 'I prefer something a little more intellectually challenging.'

The receptionist smiled. 'It's a weird place, isn't it?' she said, looking around to check she wasn't being overheard.

'Decidedly odd,' Mrs Peel agreed. 'What exactly is it you do here?'

'Advanced motoring skills,' said the receptionist, 'for policemen, ambulance drivers, chauffeurs – those kind of folks.'

'And politicians?' asked Mrs Peel, 'do you train government drivers?'

'Perhaps,' said the receptionist, who looked like she wanted to be working anywhere but here, 'but you didn't hear that from me.'

Mrs Peel smiled. Sensing she'd got all she was going to get from her new acquaintance, she gestured to the handle. 'Shall I?'

'Oh yes please,' the woman said, her voice pleasant if a little squeaky.

Mrs Peel rolled back the window and as she did so, she heard a loud car horn honking in the distance. At first Mrs Peel ignored it but when it went again, this time in more regular, almost aggressive bursts, she mimed the question, "Is that for me?" to the receptionist by pointing at her own chest. The woman nodded through the glass and pointed towards the back door. As Mrs Peel opened it, she saw a Rolls Royce waiting, passenger door already open. Mrs Peel climbed into the vehicle and saw the same balding gentleman she'd encountered earlier, this time wearing a chauffeur's outfit and hat. He extended his hand and proffered something she passionately despised in a man – a limp handshake. His skin was smooth, as if he'd never done a day's manual work in his life, but his tired eyes betrayed a stressful existence.

'Giles Feldon,' he said.

'Emma Peel,' she replied.

'To what do we owe the pleasure, Miss Peel?'

'Mrs,' she corrected.

'Another one of the good ones taken then,' he said fawningly.

'I'm here from the Ministry,' she told him as he slipped into first gear and began driving around the course.

'The Ministry? I trust everything's okay? I hope none of our drivers has been letting the side down?'

Mrs Peel drew breath to answer but was suddenly catapulted towards the dashboard as Felton effected an emergency stop. He wound down his window and greeted one of his assistants who flashed a "10" card at him.

'Top marks, sir. Impeccable reaction speed.'

Mrs Peel couldn't see what the supposed hazard was meant to be, but the officer knelt down and retrieved a small radio-controlled tortoise made of plastic. As Felton continued the journey, a bemused Mrs Peel continued, 'It's about a driver who graduated from here. His name was Thomas Kilpatrick. Does that name ring any bells?'

'It certainly does,' said Felton, eyes firmly fixed on the road. 'One of our best students. Nearly up to my standard, you know?'

As if to prove the point, he narrowly avoided careering into a brick wall by executing a perfectly timed "bootlegger's" turn. Again a "10" score card was flashed.

'You don't say,' said Mrs Peel.

'You can't possibly have a problem with dear old Thomas, surely?' said Felton. 'What is it? Speeding offence? He was a bit keen perhaps. I used to tell him, "better late than never." I remember telling him once, don't let Thomas *Kill* Patrick,' he laughed remembering the terrible pun. Mrs Peel's face remained stoic. 'No, he didn't laugh either,' said Felton.

'We've got reason to believe he might be involved in some nefarious activity against the Government.' she said.

'Nefarious?' asked Felton. 'Oh I very much doubt it, Mrs Peel. He seemed harmless enough to me. He came to us with very good references. Our training was entirely a formality. He already had what it takes. Just needed the piece of paper really.'

'When did you last see him?' asked Mrs Peel, suddenly aware they were now travelling backwards, at speed, towards an open garage.

'In the past few days,' he answered. 'He's a regular here.'

'Oh?'

'All our members have access to the clubhouse, Mrs Peel. A kind of gentlemen's club for car enthusiasts and liquor lovers. At least until this wretched "Road Safety Bill" gets passed.'

'Will he be here tonight?' she asked.

'Not on a Sunday dear girl,' he replied. 'Though tomorrow's snooker night and he won't want to miss that – the man has an incredible double kiss.'

'I'm sure he does,' said Mrs Peel.

'Mind if I join you?'

'Oh, I'm not sure about that. Gentlemen only, I'm afraid.'

She expected the answer but felt she'd extend him the courtesy of asking before attempting entry by more covert means the following day.

'We'd be happy to take you on as a client though, Mrs Peel, if you ever fancy becoming a certified driver. I'd love to see you behind a wheel.'

'Thank you for the offer, Mr Felton,' said Mrs Peel, 'but I'm perfectly happy with my abilities. Meagre as they may be.'

'I meant no offence,' said Felton.

'It's quite alright,' she replied, keen to move on. 'Perhaps you'd be good enough to walk me to my car?' The ruse offered her a chance to clock the many entrances and exits to the building, which Felton showed off proudly. 'Is the business yours?' Mrs Peel asked, passing the time.

'Oh yes,' he replied. 'I'm the third generation of Feltons to run the Motoring Institute. Can you believe we were one of the very first driving schools in the country, back when all you needed to hit the road was a cheque book and a pair of eyes. Back when people could *really* drive. These days, it's all seat belts and radios. Thank goodness neither is mandatory is all I can say.'

After the small talk had long expired, they arrived at Mrs Peel's car and Felton opened the door for her.

'A nice motor,' he said.

'Thank you. It gets me around.'

'Four speed, I'm guessing?'

'Yes, that's right.'

'May I? Felton asked, gesturing to the passenger seat, keen to see the car for himself.

'Why not?' she said unenthusiastically.

He marvelled at the dash and the controls.

'A lovely bit of engineering,' he said, 'steel backbone, but a fibreglass body you know – first of its kind. No need to worry about rust.'

'So I understand,' said Mrs Peel, 'but if you don't mind, Mr Felton, I really must be on my way.'

'Oh of course,' replied Felton, realising he'd overstayed his welcome. 'I'll leave you to it.'

But as he half opened the door to leave, Mrs Peel spotted a car parked opposite. She sensed she recognised the driver when he'd first pulled up, but as he stepped out of his car into plain sight, her suspicions were confirmed. It was Thomas Kilpatrick.

Mrs Peel stuck her head out of the car and called out, 'Excuse me,' but he took one look at her and dived back in his car, slamming it into reverse at breakneck speed.

Mrs Peel did the same thing, realising too late that a reluctant Mr Felton was still in the passenger seat, door akimbo.

'Sorry about this,' she said, 'but you did say you wanted to see my driving.'

Felton pulled the door back in and appeared invigorated by the chase. By the time they'd both got out of the car park, Kilpatrick had a head start of around twenty yards. They both pulled onto a B road and Mrs Peel put her foot down to make up lost time. From his rearview mirror, Kilpatrick could see that his pursuer's lightweight Elan was more than a match for his ageing Triumph Herald, so he tried the age-old trick of pulling a handbrake turn at the very last second, into a single-track road, in the hope the Lotus wouldn't have time to react. But Mrs Peel was too long in the tooth to fall for the ruse and managed to follow him effortlessly onto the narrow country lane, and was now practically tailgating him. This made the chase all the more dangerous, as both drivers realised *anything* could be ahead of them, from a bicycle to a tractor. But this favoured Mrs Peel, as Kilpatrick was the first in line for a head-on collision if they did happen to meet any oncoming traffic.

'I say, Mrs Peel,' said Felton, becoming unnerved when he saw her speedometer spin well past the sixty miles an hour speed limit – itself ludicrously fast considering the narrowness of the road. The velocity caused both cars to decapitate hundreds of berries that were hanging off the bramble bushes that lined both sides of the enclosed lane. As Mrs Peel's needle passed ninety miles per hour to keep up, Felton gripped the dash, prepared for an imminent crash.

'Is this strictly necessary?' he asked.

'I'm afraid so,' she said, unflinching as she navigated every twist and turn with ease.

'Very impressive though Mrs Peel,' he said, realising that despite his aversion to her speed, she really *was* a very accomplished driver. 'Crazy but impressive. Ten out of ten and no mistake.'

Mrs Peel kept pace with the car ahead but realised that, short of ramming him from behind, there was little she could do to force him to stop, so she took the only course of action available to her. A shortcut.

'Hold on Mr Felton,' she said, 'this manoeuvre *definitely* isn't in the Highway Code.'

With that, she locked the steering wheel to the left and sent the car flying through a small opening in a hedge and into a farmer's field.

'Heavens,' said Felton, terrified and excited in equal measure.

As Mrs Peel picked up speed again, the car began to shake violently as it flattened a farmer's crop and took her parallel to Kilpatrick's car, which she could still see through the thicket that divided them. Ahead of her was a wide stream and absolutely no sign of a bridge, so she knew her window of opportunity was closing. That's when she slammed the car into a lower gear and pushed the accelerator pedal as far down as it would go, reaching speeds of nearly one hundred miles per hour. This was enough to clear Kilpatrick's Herald with ease.

'Mrs Peel!' screamed Felton as the obstacle came closer and closer. 'Mrs Peeeeeeeel!' But at the last minute, she found another gap in the shrubbery, this time wider than a person, but not *quite* wide enough for a car.

'Hands in,' she commanded as the Lotus squeezed through, branches scraping both of their arms as they pulled back onto the road. This time, Mrs Peel hammered the brakes and turned the car 180 degrees to block the road. Unless he was suicidal, she hoped this would be enough to stop Kilpatrick and thankfully it was.

Mrs Peel suspected Kilpatrick might have tried to reverse the car, as a three-point turn was impossible given the width of the road, but he didn't even *try* to escape. Instead, as his car came to a stop, he calmly exited the vehicle and walked straight up to her Elan.

'Stay here,' Mrs Peel instructed Felton. He looked only too happy to oblige.

She walked over to Kilpatrick slowly, gearing up for a scuffle. But instead of attacking her – which in Mrs Peel's line of work was the standard order of play – he greeted her warmly and extended his hand.

'You must be the resourceful Mrs Peel that I've heard so much about.'

She refused the shake.

'The diameter of an astronaut is deliberately encouraged by the mother hen.' he said.

'I don't remember Patrick Moore mentioning it,' said Mrs Peel incredulously.

'The time of year dictates the restaurateurs' choice of asphalt,' he added, trying again.

'You really need to work on your chat up lines,' said Mrs Peel.

Kilpatrick placed his hand firmly on Mrs Peel's shoulder and told her how tired she was supposedly feeling, but Mrs Peel grabbed it and practically twisted his arm halfway out of its socket.

'Try that again,' she said, 'and I'll break it.'

Then Kilpatrick threw out a few more nonsensical phrases, as a look of desperation descended upon his face.

Was the poor fool trying to *hypnotise* her, Mrs Peel pondered? Was this how he was able to extract information from witless government ministers? If so, it was entirely wasted on her. She was utterly impervious to his charms.

'Better men have tried,' she told him.

'Can't blame a man for trying,' he said.

'I most certainly can,' she replied, still awaiting an altercation.

Instead, he walked over to her and placed his wrists in front of her as a mark of surrender.

'What? No struggle?' asked Mrs Peel.

'Words are my weapon,' he told her. 'If they hold no sway, then I am truly at your mercy.'

'I told you,' Felton said, piping up from the car, 'he's harmless. Just a case of mistaken identity that's all. Tell him, Thomas.'

Kilpatrick smiled. 'Thank you for your advocacy, Mr Felton. I do admire loyalty. But this impressive woman must do what she feels is right of course. Shall I?' He gestured towards her car. Arms still outstretched.

'Be my guest,' she said.

'No cuffs?'

Mrs Peel shook her head.

'Pity,' he smiled.

'I'm not the police,' she replied, 'and it's unusual for a fugitive to surrender!'

'A fugitive?' he asked, as if offended.

'You're a wanted man, Mr Kilpatrick.'

'What every man wants to hear,' he replied.

'By the authorities,' she clarified, 'it seems you're a suspect in the attempted murder of the Prime Minister.'

'Errant nonsense,' said Kilpatrick, 'I'm the one who *saved* him.'

'Perhaps,' she said, 'not me you've got to convince.' She opened and closed her right palm twice in quick succession. 'Keys?'

Kilpatrick passed them to Mrs Peel, and she tossed them to Felton.

'Mr Felton. Sorry for disrupting your day. Would you be

so kind as to drive Mr Kilpatrick's car back to the Institute please?'

Felton nodded, still somewhat shell-shocked from the encounter.

Mrs Peel frog-marched Kilpatrick into her Elan. 'I'll take it from here.'

28

KILPATRICK'S APARTMENT DOOR put up relatively little resistance to Steed's shoulder. An instrument that had become adept at breaking hinges through decades of experience.

Inside, Steed found a minimalist space more reminiscent of a holiday rental than somebody's home. The walls were white, the furniture was sparse, and the plastic floor looked like it had come from a hospital waiting room. It was always a mixed blessing when digging for dirt in a half empty building. It kept it quick and easy to search, but it usually meant the really good stuff was hidden elsewhere, away from prying eyes.

Steed turned the place over in under ten minutes, constantly checking that Kilpatrick hadn't returned. He'd found copies of half a dozen books about hypnotism, more than twenty books about politics – including a number written in other European languages – and most telling of all, he'd discovered the man's papers, taped onto the underside of his bed. Steed was disappointed by this singular lack of imagination. Whoever "Horatio Grainger" was, two things were clear: he looked the spitting image of Thomas Kilpatrick and he was *not* a master criminal.

Steed took one final look around and checked the window once more for any signs of Kilpatrick, or Grainger, or whatever the chauffeur's *real* name might actually be, but there was nothing. Steed was a little disappointed. He operated by reading people. Charming them, amusing them, angering them or choosing to ignore them. He wanted – or rather needed – to see the whites of a person's eyes to know what made him or her tick. To understand their motives, and to keep one step ahead. Otherwise, he was just another government stooge being paid to rifle through someone's belongings. And there were a lot of people better up to that task – and far less conspicuous doing it – by Steed's very own admission.

As Steed took a final glance out of the window before leaving, he spotted a large white van pulling round the corner and parking up outside the apartment building. His smile quickly turned sour when he saw that it wasn't Grainger, but a man he didn't recognise behind the driver's seat. By the time the driver opened the back doors of the van and eight burly men tumbled out, Steed's expression transformed into a veritable frown as the armed men rushed into the entrance way that he'd come through not a quarter of an hour before.

What did they want? Were they looking for him? Or Grainger? Either way, he couldn't imagine things ending well. Steed was a fighter, and a good one at that. He wasn't as fit as he had been back in his army days, but his right hook was still effective, and he had zero scruples about fighting dirty. He'd taken on the unenviable role of the underdog more times than he'd care to admit and still come out on top, but overcoming nine heavily armed men would have been challenging even for him. This left him two options, and he only had a split second to choose: run or hide. The latter wasn't an option – there was barely anywhere to hide incriminating paperwork in the spartan flat, let alone a six-foot man with broad shoulders, an umbrella and a bowler hat. Steed knew there wasn't an elevator in the building, and there were approximately nine sets of stairs between him and his pursuers, which probably gave him a minute's head start. Two if he was lucky and they were particularly unfit.

Steed dashed over to Kilpatrick's grey rotary phone and dialled a seven-digit number – his index finger rotating clockwise as quickly as it possibly could, accompanied by the sound of a cheerful chime which belied the seriousness of the situation. At last, a voice answered.

'It's Steed. Security clearance 37689,' he said. 'Passcode, Aubergine. You know how you offered me *unlimited* resources? I'm going to have to take you up on your offer…'

29

'GO ON THEN,' said Kilpatrick. 'Ask me whatever it is that you're dying to know. I can tell you're curious.'

Mrs Peel didn't bother taking her eyes off the road. 'All in good time,' she said calmly.

'I have a question,' he asked.

'Do you?' she replied, disinterested.

'What's your name? I've seen your face, but none of my associates seem to know who you are. Or why you keep popping up.'

'Never mind me,' she said, 'why don't you start by telling me *your* name.'

'Kilpatrick. Thomas Kilpatrick,' he said.

'Then my name is Veronica Phillips.'

'Is it?' he replied, struggling to see her as a Veronica.

'No,' she replied looking him in the eyes, 'I thought we were both giving pseudonyms.'

Kilpatrick smiled. 'I see you're shrewd, whoever you are, "Veronica". My name is Horatio Grainger. I was born in Austria, schooled in Switzerland and *forged* in Italy. Just in case you're trying to place my accent.'

She turned to look at him. 'Mrs Peel,' she volunteered, now that she felt he was finally telling the truth.

'So, tell me,' Grainger replied, 'who *is* Mrs Peel?'

‘Like I said. I’m not important,’ she replied.

‘Oh but you are,’ he snapped back, ‘to me you’re very important. The person standing between me and a decade’s work.’

‘Ten years to stop an economic union?’ she replied. ‘You need a hobby.’

‘Stop it?’ said Grainger, genuinely shocked. ‘Why on Earth would you think that I’d want to stop it? I’ve spent my life orchestrating it.’

‘Well, you’re not doing a very good job so far,’ Mrs Peel said. ‘By my reckoning, you’ve incapacitated the man who’s supposed to be signing off on joining the Common Market in a matter of hours, killed his replacement, and attempted to murder his replacement’s replacement who, admittedly, never existed in the first place.’

‘I haven’t killed *anybody*, Mrs Peel,’ said Grainger, ‘it is not in my nature.’

‘A likely story,’ she replied.

‘Likely or otherwise, it happens to be true! I am, as you English would say, a lover not a fighter.’

‘Well, you’re not much of a fighter,’ she said, glancing witheringly at Grainger, ‘I’ll have to take your word on the other.’

‘I’ve no idea who’s been causing such carnage and chaos, but I assure you they’re not acting on my instructions,’ he said.

‘Go on…’ she replied, ‘I’ll bite.’

‘I’ve already said more than enough without a lawyer present,’ he said. ‘I have no intention of incriminating myself.’

‘Mr Grainger,’ said Mrs Peel, ‘let me do you a favour and explain how this works… At the moment you’re suspected of plotting to bring down the Government of the United Kingdom of Great Britain and Northern Ireland. Things aren’t going to go well for you unless you co-operate.’

'I *saved* the Government,' protested Grainger. 'Wilson would be dead if it wasn't for me!'

'He was in your care,' said Mrs Peel, 'and you drove him straight into an ambush.'

'Poppycock,' said Grainger, using one of his very favourite British words.

'You falsified your identification to secure a position of trust,' said Mrs Peel. 'You've driven several members of Cabinet who themselves have fallen under suspicion for supposedly leaking information, even though they point-blank deny it, and you ran a mile when I tried to speak to you. You don't need to be Perry Mason to know that doesn't look good.'

'And how did *you* find out about me?' Grainger asked. 'It looks to me like you've been surveilling me unlawfully. And having the audacity to stalk me at my gentlemen's club to pursue you and your partner's personal vendetta? It sounds to me like entrapment by government agents.'

'I'm *not* a government agent, Mr Grainger. And you're not a chauffeur.'

'Then I ask again, Mrs Peel. Who *are* you?'

'I'm an interested party,' she answered, 'and at the moment, I'm particularly interested in whether you're going to help me.'

Grainger's demeanour softened a little, as if he was considering whether or not to trust Mrs Peel.

'I don't much care what happens to you frankly,' said Mrs Peel, 'but it will be a shame if you end up at the end of a hangman's noose for the sake of a misunderstanding that we can clear up here and now.'

'You can't spook me quite so easily, Mrs Peel,' he replied. 'I don't have to be a native Englishman to know Britain abandoned the death penalty a decade ago. It made headlines around the world.'

'Not for treason,' she replied.

'You haven't the evidence,' he insisted.

'Who do you think you're dealing with here?' she said. 'You'll be interrogated by the security services. Not the average bobby on the beat. It may surprise you to know, Mr Grainger, that when someone attempts to assassinate our prime minister, it doesn't tend to end too well for them. With or without a lawyer.'

Grainger thought it over. 'I'm behind the Prime Minister's…' he searched for the right word, '… *predicament*. But I had absolutely nothing to do with the gunmen, or anything that's happened since, I swear it. Like I told you – I'm a pacifist. I want Britain to take her place in our union to prevent another war ever descending on Europe. I've done everything I possibly can to persuade other world leaders likewise. So, believe me when I say, there's absolutely nothing in it for me if the Prime Minister dies!'

Mrs Peel took a read of the man. She was inclined to believe him.

'So help me understand why our dear prime minister is currently learning his alphabet.'

'Hypnosis,' Grainger replied. 'I've been "encouraging" Mr Wilson – along with a select few of his inner circle – to follow their instinct to take Britain into Europe. Despite the opposition, despite the political fallout, despite the doom and gloom-mongers' best efforts. And I'd been rather successful in the endeavour.'

'Until?' said Mrs Peel.

'Until we were ambushed. Just after I'd done an induction. My process is meticulous and achieved after weeks – sometimes months – of work with a target. It's a delicate moment for the psyche, and any kind of interruption, especially a violent or especially stressful one, can – it seems – be utterly catastrophic.'

Mrs Peel was beginning to understand. And if it wasn't Grainger who orchestrated a Prime Ministerial shoot out, she had a pretty good idea who had.

'You could say I opened a door, Mrs Peel, a particularly dangerous one, that I never had a chance to close. Believe it or not, I've made several attempts to see Mr Wilson, to put things right, but I've been met by a wall of security.'

'Hardly surprising,' said Mrs Peel.

'Indeed. But you will appreciate that if there's even a hope of reversing the process, I *must* be granted access.'

'A tall ask given what you've just told me,' said Mrs Peel.

'Nevertheless, it must be done,' Grainger replied.

'Will it even work?' she asked.

'I've no idea. But unless you've got a better idea, I suggest we find out.'

30

JACOBS AND HIS associates couldn't believe their luck. He'd been trying to find out where the damned chauffeur lived for weeks. And after getting the address from an informant – invariably a civil servant who he'd been able to extort courtesy of months of covert recordings – he'd raced over there with over half a dozen of his men, armed to the teeth and ready to capture the man that had caused them such a headache. And when they pulled up outside, they saw a racing-green Bentley. According to his information, that fit the description of the man Mrs Peel was working for – someone by the name of Steed. He didn't know for sure it was one and the same, but it was a fair guess. After all, how many people drove a 1930s racing car in this day and age? That meant Jacobs still had a chance of pulling this thing off. It was as if it was written in the stars.

'I need Steed alive,' said Jacobs briefing his men who were piled up like sardines in the back of his Transit. 'The chauffeur can be eliminated.'

'Why not fix both of them?' asked Manson. 'It'd be cleaner.'

'Because I said so,' Jacobs replied, 'you pay the bills, you call the shots.'

Jacobs had been bugging government cars for the better

part of a year. Ever since the rumour mill began to sound the klaxon that the United Kingdom was trying – for a second time – to join Europe's club, after the idea had been resolutely rejected by the French back in '61. First time round, Jacobs had sniped from the sidelines and written a handful of letters to his MP and the Foreign Secretary to no avail, but he hadn't done much to actively thwart it besides attend the odd protest. Back then, he was too busy trying to keep his business in the black and navigate the breakup of his marriage.

He'd never liked Europe. The British had spent centuries fighting their continental neighbours and Jacobs felt strongly that the cultural gulf between his homeland and the land of the Franks was far wider than the English Channel. Jacobs had been born just before the first war, which had claimed his grandfather, and devastated every community in Britain. Growing up, he barely knew a single family that hadn't lost a brother, a son, a father, or a friend. Granted, he'd made a pretty penny once the spectre of war had once more fallen upon the British Isles in '39, but even that was a poisoned chalice.

The strain of commerce had torpedoed his marriage. That and his self-proclaimed obsession with Europe, which his wife had described as the "other woman" in their relationship. And it was Europe that finally delivered the killer blow to his business, flooding the market with their "superior and more affordable" product lines, which to Jacobs' mind equated to cheap crap procured via back-handers.

He could still remember where he was, about twelve months to the day, when he'd heard that the idea was back on the table. It was a throwaway line in the fish and chip wrappers from some godforsaken rag. It read: PM TO USE HIS MAJORITY TO JOIN THE EEC. No debate. No referendum. A unilateral action to dictate the future of the country. It was abhorrent to Jacobs.

He'd forged a deal with Henderson to install recording equipment in as many government cars as could practically be bugged, in return for settling an old debt that had hung like the Sword of Damocles over Henderson's family for decades. The recordings had been intended to help Jacobs establish whether the rumours about the Common Market were true. And, if so, what the Government's plans were.

Instead, they mostly recorded party tittle-tattle, Whitehall gossip that helped him blackmail a few loose-lipped junior ministers into spilling the beans, but nothing profoundly useful. That was until, around three months prior, he settled down with a beer and a Woodbine to listen to the day's tapes and heard a voice he'd never forget.

Accented dulcet tones that belonged to a new driver who'd joined the government's books. Jacobs had burned his hand that evening, too distracted to note the alight tobacco spilling onto his skin, such was his disbelief about what he was hearing. It was a series of bizarre instructions that seemed to put his passengers in some sort of trance, subsequently making them sing like canaries and – best of all – be none the wiser afterwards.

Although it was clear immediately that the driver was busy masterminding the very outcome Jacobs was sworn to stop, he'd kept him in play until now because he was being fed more intelligence than he could ever have imagined. The man's subjects told the mysterious Thomas Kilpatrick what they were doing, and when they were doing it, allowing Jacobs to stay one step ahead. In fact, he'd even considered buying the chauffeur off, but it was clear that his adversary was as hell bent on forcing the EEC application through as Jacobs was on stopping it. He could have tried to force him to comply, but he couldn't work out how that would even work logistically.

But that was then, and this was now. Things were getting too hot to maintain the status quo. There was less than a handful of hours to go until the application deadline and Jacobs was none the wiser about who was now leading the negotiations inside Number 10, or whether or not it was even still going ahead. What he did know – courtesy of his contact at the Motoring Institute which had certified the chauffeur – was that the security services *had* twigged Kilpatrick's involvement and had tried to apprehend him. That meant the chauffeur was of no further use to him, except as the perfect fall guy for recent events. Especially if Kilpatrick wasn't around to offer a defence. Plus, it stood to reason that if the chauffeur had got Wilson into this mess, he might be able to get him out of it. And that was the last thing he needed. Any way Jacobs looked at it, it was time for the hypnotic chauffeur to shuttle off this mortal coil.

But contrary to his foreman, Manson's advice, he needed to keep Steed alive, for now. Albeit safely locked away. He knew only too well that if both turned up dead, it would only add fuel to the fire and indicate a third party was in play. Steed and Mrs Peel would have to go, but later, and in a way that couldn't possibly implicate Jacobs.

Jacobs' men entered the building first, and he followed a few minutes behind. A few hundred steps – and two aching hip joints – later, he joined his men, berating himself for being so out of shape.

'Empty,' said Manson. Jacobs ducked his head into the chauffeur's ransacked flat to see for himself.

'No way they could be hiding?' asked Jacobs

'Not a chance.'

'Fire escape?'

'Nothing,' said Manson, 'this place is old. Georgian I reckon. They'd rather keep listed buildings like this pretty than safe.'

Jacobs realised he'd have seen Steed and the chauffeur if they'd come down the stairs, so there weren't many possibilities.

'The other apartments?' Manson asked, as if asking for tacit permission to smash down every door with the butt of a gun.

Jacobs paused, trying to get inside Steed's mind. He shook his head. 'If he's as squeaky clean as we're led to believe, he wouldn't risk involving civilians.' Jacobs looked up to the ceiling. 'The roof,' he declared, as if sensing his opponent through a sixth sense.

'That'd be madness,' argued Manson, 'there's no way down from there. They'd have boxed themselves in.'

Jacobs took a second glance in the chauffeur's apartment and saw a telephone, hanging on its wire off the hook. 'That phone. Was it like that when you got here?'

Manson looked confused. 'What do you mean?'

'It's a simple enough question,' snapped Jacobs. 'Was it or wasn't it off the hook when you arrived?'

Manson wasn't sure, but he turned to his boys. 'Anyone touch the phone?'

There were mumbles but nothing definitive.

'Think!' shouted Manson, emulating his employer.

'No, boss,' they seemed to shout in unison.

That was all Jacobs needed to know. 'Get up there *now*!' he screamed, as eight out-of-shape men hauled themselves up another four flights of stairs.

Steed knew he'd rolled the dice. If his punt didn't come off, there'd be no second chances. By his reckoning, he had about thirty seconds before his navy-blue suit was blasted with a dozen holes, which was frankly a travesty for him and his Bond Street tailor.

He could hear salvation in the near distance, but it would be touch and go as to whether the helicopter would manage to land before the inevitable shoot out. He needed to buy himself some more time. Not long. Maybe less than a minute. Even if he managed to just about climb on board in time, that was only half the battle. He'd need to be out of firing range to make good their escape, otherwise the chopper would be shot out of the sky.

Steed looked around him for inspiration. The heavy steel door that led to the roof space had a hole for a lock, but no sign of a key. At the side of the door, there were two welded hooks that looked like they held a crossbar that was also missing in action. The roof itself was empty. Just a felted floor, a three foot wall around the perimeter and the odd vent. There was nothing else for it, Steed *had* to make the ultimate sacrifice for Queen and Country. He lifted his umbrella and clicked a button near the handle. This caused the fabric to slide off to reveal a metal core which, in times of extremis, could be used as an improvised weapon. That would be no good right now, because he was facing insurmountable odds, but as he laid the umbrella horizontally across the door, he hoped to goodness that it would hold long enough to get the job done.

It felt like it took an eternity for the pilot to land atop the building, and when the small two-seater helicopter began its descent, Steed knew there could be no more than a handful of steps left between him and his attackers. As the chopper's legs touched the bitumen, they clipped an extraction outlet and Steed couldn't help but think that when this building had been designed in the eighteenth century, helicopter landing pads might not have been top of the architect's priorities. The second the aircraft touched down, Steed practically threw himself inside, as if diving for cover from an explosion. And as the chopper's engines lifted him back into the sky, he saw his beloved brolly snap in two as the door swung open and Jacobs' motley crew burst through like ants escaping a disturbed nest.

The pilot was twenty yards away from the building by the time Jacobs and his men reached the edge of the roofline. They didn't even try to shoot at the helicopter. Perhaps because they knew, just as Steed had hoped, that it would be futile, or maybe because they didn't want to explain how a government helicopter had been brought down in the middle of London. Either way, Steed was safe, at least for now.

Inside the fuselage, the pilot tossed Steed some headphones to shield his ears from the bombastic dirge of engines and propellers, and to allow him to communicate through the in-built microphone.

'I can't thank you enough,' Steed said, realising how rare it was to be able to call on the big guns – at least there were some perks of working with the top brass.

'Where do you want us to drop you off, sir?' said the pilot.

'Anywhere that serves cellar temperature Moet & Chandon,' said Steed, 'I need a glass.'

31

DR IAN SUMMERS had never seen a case quite like Harold Wilson's in his forty-odd-years of general practice. He'd come across schizophrenics, drug addicts and sociopaths of course, and taken more than his fair share of bizarre consultations. Like the woman who was utterly convinced she was shrinking at a rate of several inches per week, whom he diagnosed with a rare condition called "Alice in Wonderland Syndrome". Or the man who was convinced he didn't exist and was simply a figment of Dr Summers' imagination – a disorder coined "Cotard's Delusion". He'd even seen – and smelled – a case of "Spontaneous Human Combustion" which would stay with him until his dying days. But in every instance – from "Foreign Accent Syndrome" to "Stone Man's Disease" – there had *always* been a clinical cause. The result of complex biological, neurological or psychosomatic processes. Or else the random act of sitting too close to an open fireplace after you'd nodded off and spilled your tipple.

But Summers had *never* encountered a fully grown man who believed inexplicably – to his very core – that he was an eight-year-old boy. The doctor's vocation still had the knack of throwing up new and oftentimes ridiculous cases to puzzle and frustrate him. He'd been staying at Chequers ever since the Prime Minister had been moved there, and the housekeepers were being delightful hosts, providing him with cooked breakfasts, an endless quantity of Earl Grey and an errand boy to fetch his morning newspaper, *the Daily Mail*.

As one might have deduced from his choice of rag, Dr Summers wasn't of the "left persuasion" and was counting down the days until Wilson was ceremoniously booted out of office for – as he saw it – highway robbery, having imposed a ninety-five per cent income tax rate on Britain's most prosperous captains of industry.

He didn't know if Tory Ted had it in him to govern either quite frankly – the country clearly hadn't believed it in last year's general election – but he couldn't *possibly* do a worse job of it than Labour were managing right now.

However, above all, Summers was a professional. He'd been on the government's books for over two decades and it didn't matter whether he was treating red rosettes or blue, he'd *always* done everything in his power to care for his patients – whether parliamentarian or pauper. That wasn't just his Hippocratic Oath speaking, it was his Christian upbringing that preached the sanctity of life.

For Summers, one of the most interesting things about being inside the great and powerfuls' tent was that you realised *everyon*e was human. While he profoundly disagreed with Wilson ideologically, as a man, he found him perfectly pleasant and very down-to-earth. Wilson had never treated Summers with anything other than courtesy and professionalism, so he'd gladly afforded him the same respect.

If he was being completely honest, since he'd been stationed at Wilson's bedside, Summers had actually found himself liking the "eight-year-old" Harold more and more. Beneath the seriousness and pomposity that all premiers wear like armour, Wilson had a vulnerable side. He'd *occasionally* see it in Wilson's everyday dealings – for instance, he distinctly remembered a particularly endearing interview with Wilson when he'd won the election where he'd remarked that he simply couldn't believe that a lad from behind "lace curtains in Huddersfield" was about to see the Queen and become Prime Minister – but these windows into the soul were few and far between.

Stripped of his mask, it made it easier to not only respect Wilson, but to like him as well. They'd played the odd board game together, including a Chequers favourite called "Diplomacy", a wargame set in pre-First-World-War Europe. And he'd even been persuaded to bring his own son's Subbuteo football game over to keep Wilson entertained.

Summers wished his stay had been more productive. He was, at best, monitoring the Prime Minister's vitals, which seemed perfectly normal, except – unsurprisingly – that his blood pressure was elevated. And he was periodically sedating him to make sure he was getting a good night's sleep. But as the days passed by with no sign of improvements, he felt more like a childminder than a doctor.

He'd been out that morning, just for a roam around the 1,500-acre grounds at Chequers to stretch his feet and try to get some perspective. Was there another avenue he should be exploring? The doctor had been busy phoning every specialist he could think of night and day, including the very top American physicians, but the possible remedies he was getting back were as diverse as the people he was canvassing. He'd been advised to do everything from electroshock treatment, to pumping his anonymous patient full of every drug under the sun – some of which were highly experimental. Other practitioners insisted his subject was faking it, or in some kind of "fugue" state. Any way Summers looked at it, things were coming to a head. Not just because the Government was in some kind of flap about

European negotiations, which to be blunt he wasn't remotely interested in, but because he was becoming more and more convinced by the day that the longer Wilson remained in this state, the greater the chances it would likely be irreversible. Sooner or later, as unpalatable as it would be for the Prime Minister's Cabinet colleagues to accept – and indeed for the electorate to hear – everyone concerned might have to concede that "their" Harold Wilson, was gone. And despite Summers' own political affiliations, that was a pyrrhic victory at best, not only because he wouldn't wish this on his worst enemy, but because he could well see the Chancellor, Mr Callaghan, stepping into his shoes, which didn't feel like much of an improvement.

As Summers returned to the sixteenth century manor house, he kept his coat on. There was a chill in the May air and the building was always kept a little bit cooler than he'd have liked. Realising he'd been out for longer than expected, he decided to check on Wilson before he got himself cleaned up for the best fry-up he'd ever tasted.

He walked into Wilson's favourite room and was surprised to find it empty. No matter, he thought, presuming Harold had been caught short, or was in his bedroom. But when the Prime Minister hadn't returned after ten minutes, he checked both locations and was left wanting.

So, he checked the dining room, and the kitchens, the bedrooms and the hallways. He walked around the perimeter and asked the house staff, but no matter how loud he called or how hard he looked, Harold Wilson was nowhere to be seen.

32

'WHAT DO YOU mean "VANISHED"?' asked Tully.

Peter Walburg-Smith knew he was going to have to take responsibility for this foul-up, as head of security at Chequers. 'We've searched the building and the grounds. We can't find hide nor hair of him.'

'That's utterly absurd, man,' Tully ranted. 'He's the Prime Minister for heaven's sake. Didn't we have someone watching him?'

'No, sir,' said Walburg-Smith, 'he's a guest, not a prisoner.'

'He's a patient is what he is, Peter, and a particularly confused one at that.'

'What do you want us to do?' Walburg-Smith asked.

'Find him!' Tully instructed.

'But we've…'

Tully didn't want to hear the end of that sentence. 'I don't care. Search again. And then when you've finished, do it a third time.'

Walburg-Smith nodded timidly.

Tully turned to another aide, a young lad called Myers who couldn't have been much older than his early twenties. 'Take a drive around the local streets,' Tully said, 'he can't have got far. It's a mile or two to the nearest… *anything*.'

As Myers was about to leave, they spotted one of the

Government's cars pulling up to the house. 'Hang fire,' said Tully as they dashed through the corridors to check if it was the Prime Minister returning.

Outside was a bewildered Government driver called Hoskins, a red-faced well-built chap who barely squeezed into his uniform and was struggling to conceal his baldness with the last few strands of his comb-over.

'Is the PM with you?' Tully demanded as Hoskins stepped out of the car.

'I've just dropped him off, sir,' said Hoskins nonchalantly. 'He was up with the birds this morning. Reckoned I'd come back here in case a few of you were heading back to London now Mr Wilson's concluded his business.'

Tully was dumbfounded.

'What do you mean, you've "dropped him off", he said. 'On whose orders?'

Hoskins was confused. 'He called me himself. Asked me to take him to the train station.'

Tully's heart sank as he remembered the stack of calling cards in the sitting room helpfully positioned next to the telephone.

'Let me guess,' said Tully, addressing Myers. 'We haven't told the drivers about the Prime Minister's condition?'

'No, sir,' Myers confirmed, 'I was told it was on a need-to-know basis.'

'Of course it is,' said Tully, rolling his eyes – while recognising the blame was his as much as anyone else's. 'Did you not think there might have been something wrong by the way Mr Wilson was acting?' Tully said to the driver, keen to assuage at least some of the responsibility.

'He *was* a bit quieter than usual I suppose,' said Hoskins, 'but they're like that sometimes aren't they?' he continued, 'when they want to zone us out, I mean.'

'Where did you take him?' asked Tully.

'Princes Risborough. Said he needed to go back home. I offered to drive him all the way to London o'course, but he seemed adamant on using the railway. I wasn't gonna argue.'

'How long ago was this?' asked Tully.

'Not thirty minutes ago,' Hoskins replied.

'Myers, phone the station right now and find out if he's still there,' said Tully.

'And if he is?' asked Myers. 'Sorry – I don't mean to be rude, sir. It's just… well, we can't exactly ask them to detain the Prime Minister can we?'

Tully conceded that his young aide made a fair point.

'Look, am I missing something?' asked Hoskins, failing to understand why it was a problem if Mr Wilson wanted to get on a train.

'Plenty,' said Tully, 'and I'd remind you that you've signed the Official Secrets Act. So, anything I share is strictly confidential. Do you understand?'

Hoskins duly nodded, sorry he'd asked the question.

Tully turned to Myers. 'If the train's already left, ask the station master where it was going!'

'No need,' said Hoskins.

Tully and Myers both stared at Hoskins the driver.

'This time on a Monday morning, only train that's running will be going to London. Marylebone if I'm not mistaken. Like I said, he was heading *home*.'

'Then why not accept a lift?' said Tully. 'It doesn't make any sense.'

'Beats me?' said Hoskins.

'Maybe he's getting better?' said Myers.

'That's the kind of miracle I could do with about now,' said Tully, 'but if that's the case, surely he'd have come and spoken to one of us?'

'I s'pose,' said Myers.

'How long will the train journey take?' asked Tully.

'Forty-five minutes,' said Hoskins, 'maybe an hour, tops.'

'Forget about the station,' Tully told Myers, 'he's probably long gone by now. Call Downing Street and tell them to get someone to Marylebone *before* Wilson does. And for heaven's sake get them to close the platform. Lord alone knows what the passengers will think if he tries to speak to any of them en route. But we can at least contain things at the station.'

Myers nodded his agreement.

'Hoskins, get me back to London as quickly as you can please,' asked Tully.

'Right you are, sir,' Hoskins replied.

'Let's just hope for all of our sakes nothing's happened to him,' Tully said, 'otherwise, Steed will kill me.'

33

FROM THE MINUTE they'd started feeding him all this guff about being the Prime Minister, Harold knew someone was either playing a rotten joke on him or meant him very real harm. Either way, there was only one place he wanted to be, and that was back home with his mum. Wilson's mother, Ethel, had always told him not to talk to strangers, and he distinctly remembered her telling him that if he ever found himself in danger, he should come home as fast as his legs would carry him. So that was precisely what he was planning to do.

It hadn't been hard to slip past the toffs at Chequers. They'd been far too busy worrying about running the country to notice him making the call. He'd told the driver to meet him outside the front gates, away from the house, to make sure nobody spotted the car. He knew he wasn't *that* far away from London, so figured there'd be a railway to the capital from the nearest station. And he remembered there was a train from London to Huddersfield because he'd made that very trip with his father.

He thought about asking the driver to take him all the way back home – or at least to London – but he reckoned the longer he stayed with these people, the higher the chances they'd cotton on to him and drag him back to Downing Street kicking and screaming. But if they were going to insist on keeping up this charade, he might as well profit from it, and sure enough, the driver, a friendly grown-up called Mr Hoskins, had taken him there, no questions asked. He just kept his head down and muttered, "absolutely" whenever a question was posed.

The whole situation really was terribly confusing. Harold hadn't any idea what they were hoping to achieve with all this silliness. But his mum would know. She *always* knew.

When he'd arrived at London Marylebone station, just after ten o'clock, the scary people in the ticket office said there weren't any trains direct to Huddersfield, but they told him to get into one of the black cabs outside the station and ask to be taken to a place called King's Cross. This he did, and the train was waiting for him at the platform when he'd arrived.

Money wasn't a problem because there was a wallet full of notes already stuffed in the pocket of the coat he was wearing. He had more than enough to cover travel, and he'd even helped himself to a serving of lardy cake at the station, which certainly attracted a few glares from onlookers. Clearly, they weren't used to proper baking down south. In fairness, it was a bit naughty to steal someone else's money to buy a ticket, especially one in the posh end of the train, but he reasoned that it was the price his abductors would have to pay for bringing him here against his will.

The journey was long, and he couldn't help but think he must have had pen on his face or food around his mouth, because everyone was staring at him any chance they got. In the end, he'd locked himself in one of the toilets for a good half an hour, just to get some respite from the feeling that he was an animal in a zoo. And fortunately, the train thinned out as they headed further north, so for the last leg of the journey, he ended up with a first-class compartment all to himself. Eventually, he saw the Pennines coming into view on the horizon and he knew he was nearly home. It called to him like a siren, embracing him when he was at his most vulnerable.

His house on Warneford Road in Cowlersley was a three mile walk from the train station, but he was used to that and the fresh air would do him good. He suddenly wondered what his mum and dad would think when he walked through the front door. They must have been frantic with worry, he'd been gone at least a couple of days. Maybe even a week, though it felt much longer, as if he hadn't seen his dear parents for a lifetime.

Harold found his house with ease and it looked more or less like it always did – a simple terraced house built from yellow Yorkshire stone that reflected the family's working-class roots. Though the trees and shrubs that lined the road seemed a lot bigger than Harold remembered and the front door looked like it had seen a new lick of paint, which seemed an odd sort of thing for his parents to prioritise while their son had been kidnapped. Realising the keys that were jangling in his pocket didn't fit the lock, Harold gave the door a solid knock.

'It's me, Mum,' he shouted from the doorstep. 'I'm back.' But there was no reply, so he knocked again. This time, the net curtains in the living room window twitched and a few minutes later, a woman in her sixties or seventies came to the door. He didn't know who this woman was, but one thing was for sure, it was *not* his mother.

'Well, look what the cat dragged in,' she gnarled, before calling up the stairs to her husband. 'Terry, you'll never believe who's at our door.'

Harold stood shell-shocked. 'What are you doing here?' he asked.

'It's my bloody house,' Sheila snapped, 'though you lot have done the best to turf us out of it.'

The woman's husband came down the steps and did a second take when he saw the Prime Minister on his doorstep. 'Crikey,' he exclaimed, instinctively shaking the man's hand.

'Never mind her,' he said dismissing his wife. 'She didn't vote Labour. I did though. Come on in, out of the cold.'

Harold didn't know what to say. 'Where are my mum and dad?' he asked. 'What are you two doing in our house? I don't understand?'

Sheila and Terry looked at each other as if to say, "has he been on the cans?"

'That's right,' said Terry. They told us you used to live here. We didn't believe 'em, but here you are.'

'*Used* to live here?' said Harold. 'I *do* live here.'

'Are you feeling okay, lad?' said Terry, popping his head out the door to see if there was anyone with Wilson. 'Where are all your people?' he asked, 'security, lackies, that sort of thing?'

'I came here on my own,' said Harold, 'to find Mum and Dad.'

'Can't help you there, Mr Wilson,' said Sheila, softening to the man a little, despite her opposition to his policies. 'They moved out years back I expect. We didn't even buy the house from your lot. It had already passed hands long before we moved in.'

Harold stepped inside the property, and – inexplicably – the woman seemed to be telling the truth. It wasn't his house. The wallpaper was different, the carpet had been changed. He recognised none of the furniture, and there was electrical apparatus everywhere that he couldn't even begin to comprehend. Without asking, he darted up the stairs to find his old bedroom.

'Hang on,' said Sheila, 'you can't just barge into someone's house without asking. I don't care if you are the bloody Prime Minister.' And there it was, the same title, over and over again. But now it wasn't just cranks in London spouting this nonsense. Even his fellow Yorkshiremen and women were at it. Seeing that his childhood bedroom was full of posters of teenage boys with floppy haircuts and awkward fringes, he dashed back down the stairs and ran out of the house and down the street. Shaking his head as if trying to wake himself from a nightmare.

'Hang on, lad,' Terry shouted after him, but it was no use. Harold wouldn't look back.

After half a mile or so, Harold's knees packed in, and he found a bench to plop himself down on. Tears were welling up in his eyes. He was afraid and baffled and he hadn't a clue what to do next. That's when he heard a familiar voice.

'Harold? Is that you, chuck?'

Harold turned to see an elderly lady crossing the street to greet him.

'Do I know you?' Harold asked.

'Well, you used to,' she said, 'a long, long time ago. I were friends with your mum.'

Harold looked at her, and when he squinted his eyes, he could see it.

'Mrs Winters?' he asked.

'That's right love,' she said, 'the very same.'

'But you look so old!' he said, bluntly.

'Cheeky sod,' replied Mrs Winters, laughing, 'you always did have a way with words.'

'Where are me mum and dad?' he asked the lady who, despite looking like she'd somehow stepped through a time machine and come out looking grey and pruned, was the only person he recognised in the whole world.

'Well they left love, years ago didn't they? Went over Liverpool way if memory serves. Or was it the Wirral?'

'But why?' asked Harold.

'How should I know, Harry,' she replied. 'I must say it's nice to see you back here though. We're all incredibly proud of you! You're my claim to fame you are.'

Harold said nothing.

'Listen,' said Mrs Winters, 'is everything alright love? You seem very out of sorts, is there someone I can call?'

'My mum!' said Harold, a single tear running down his face.

'Oh deary. Now you mustn't cry,' she said, placing a hand on his shoulder. 'Why don't you come with me and I'll get you a cup of tea, and we can phone the operator. Maybe they'll know how to reach your folks. How does that sound?'

Frankly, it sounded like the best offer he'd heard all day.

34

'GONE?' SAID MRS Peel. 'Gone where exactly?'

'Well if we knew that, he wouldn't be missing,' said Steed drolly. 'How exactly the most famous man in the country *can* disappear though is anyone's guess!'

'Oops,' said Emma, finishing the last few pieces of sky in Steed's jigsaw.

Steed paced anxiously around his apartment. 'Said he was going home apparently. On the *train* would you believe?'

Mrs Peel instantly made the connection, remembering the plot to kill the Prime Minister onboard a train, which she and Steed had thwarted last time they were roped into protecting Her Majesty's Government.

'That was first thing this morning,' said Steed. 'So, unless he's decided to walk, he should have been back in Downing Street hours ago.'

'Not exactly a surprise is it?' Mrs Peel asked.

Steed looked at her. 'Well, it's certainly come as a surprise to the Cabinet. And not a particularly happy one,' he replied.

'That's because you're looking at it wrong,' said Mrs Peel, still slotting the final pieces of the puzzle together and adding a small biplane to the painted cumulo-nimbus clouds.

'We are?' said Steed.

'What year is it?' asked Mrs Peel.

'1967,' said Steed, happy to play along.

'Wrong,' said Mrs Peel. 'It's 1924.'

'It is?' said Steed, humouring her. 'That means I'm a babe in arms. And you. Well, you're barely a twinkle in your mother and father's eyes.'

'And a certain prime minister is eight years old,' she said.

Steed's proverbial penny began to drop. 'He's going *home*... Where *was* home back then?' asked Steed.

'Beats me,' said Mrs Peel. 'He's a Yorkshireman, isn't he?'

'Hang on', said Steed, looking through his collection of books in the corner of the flat. On the third row from the bottom, he found a huge red hardback book called *Who's Who* which was at least double the width of every other volume that neighboured it. Dropping it on the table, atop the jigsaw puzzle – much to Mrs Peel's chagrin – it made a weighty thud. 'A directory of the great and the good,' said Steed, leafing through the pages to find the letter "W".

They found the Prime Minister's entry, listed as: "WILSON, Rt. Hon. (James) Harold" and his address was given as 10 Downing Street, SW1. The short entry noted he'd received an OBE in 1945, been the Member of Parliament for Huyton since 1950, Leader of the Labour Party since 1963, and Prime Minister and First Lord of the Treasury since October 1964.

'He went to school in Huddersfield,' said Steed, 'a place called Milnsbridge apparently.'

'Then my guess is that's where you'll find him.'

'Right,' said Steed. 'I'm off to visit the grand old Duke of York.'

'Are you taking ten thousand men?' Mrs Peel asked.

'Even better,' said Steed. 'I'm taking one *formidable* woman!'

'Is that an invitation?'

'Just think of it, Mrs Peel,' he said, attempting to persuade her. 'We can blow away the cobwebs, get out of London for a few hours and – if we're lucky – bring home the Prime Minister in time for tea…'

'Two's company, three's a crowd,' said Mrs Peel.

He looked at her pleadingly.

'Go on then,' she said, 'but don't you want to know what you've inherited before we go?'

Steed's eyes lit up. 'Oh sorry,' he said, removing the book from the puzzle. The painted landscape was now complete. As suspected, it showed an idyllic British countryside lake, with a brick-built bridge.

'Is it riches beyond my imaginings?' he asked.

'No,' she replied.

'How very disappointing,' said Steed. 'Is it something I can show off at dinner parties?'

'It depends on the party,' Mrs Peel answered.

He stared at the image for a good thirty seconds, but nothing was forthcoming. 'Go on then, you'll have to point it out.'

'It's the number plate,' said Mrs Peel.

Steed had to get close to the painting to even read it: M0RT NST03.

Mrs Peel smiled. 'Mean anything?'

'Mort? As in death?' Steed looked worried.

'Worse,' said Mrs Peel playfully, 'take off your shoe.'

'I beg your pardon?'

'You heard,' said Mrs Peel, 'your inheritance is located inside your sock.'

'Now steady on, Mrs Peel,' he said. 'I know Uncle Robert was part of the village Magic Circle, but I think it might be pushing it a bit to fill my boots with gold from beyond the grave.'

Mrs Peel delivered a glance that told him "if you want to find out, do as I say." So, he reluctantly complied, sitting down on the settee and removing his right shoe.

'Socks off,' she said.

'Really, Mrs Peel, if this is your idea of foreplay, I…'

'Eyes on the prize,' she said, interrupting him.

With Steed's foot out on the floor, Mrs Peel's suspicions were confirmed. 'Well?' she said.

'It's my foot,' he said glibly, 'and unless I've been told some terrible fibs about my parentage, he most definitely *didn't* give me those.'

'And what do you notice about said foot,' she asked, 'in particular, your toes?"

'They're an exceptional example of the male appendage?' said Steed.

'Sorry to burst your bubble', said Mrs Peel, 'but you have a deformity.'

'A deformity?'

'Your second toe is *longer* than your big toe.'

Steed looked again, aghast. 'Is it not *supposed* to be like that?'

'Not in most people,' she answered, always pleased to put her scientific knowledge to good use. 'It's a fairly rare but harmless condition called Morton's Toe.'

Steed looked perplexed by how she'd deduced that.

'M. 0. R. T. N. S. T. 0. 3,' she said, reminding him of the number plate, but reading out the zeroes as O's. 'It's your *genetic* inheritance.'

Steed thought about this for a moment. 'I shall have to see yours, Mrs Peel,' he said, chancing his arm. 'Strictly for comparison, you understand.'

'Down, boy,' she replied.

Steed shrugged. 'Well at least I won't have to pay death

duties. I can't see even the Chancellor coming for these digits.'

'Speaking of which,' said Mrs Peel, 'this little piggy needs to go to market.'

Steed nodded, 'Then let's go Wee! Wee! Wee! and find Wilson's home.'

35

THE JOURNEY TO Huddersfield took over five long hours by car. It would have been quicker to go by train, but the last thing Steed and Mrs Peel wanted was for the Prime Minister to be paraded in front of anyone else. Steed had even raised the seldom used retractable roof on his Bentley for discretion – should Mr Wilson be found and brought back to London – and to drown out the sound of the newly built M1 motorway that took them out of London towards the North.

When they arrived in the pleasant district of Milnsbridge, which was notable for its clothing mills, they asked around and discovered that Wilson hailed from the small village of Cowlersley nearby. A pretty little village set against rolling hills, farmland and industrialisation.

Retracing Wilson's steps, they found Sheila and Terry, who were only too happy to recount their adventure, and they spoke to a couple of local villagers who remembered the Wilsons but didn't know what happened to the Prime Minister's parents once they moved away.

Sat atop Castle Hill in Huddersfield, an Iron Age forge with breathtaking views of the villages – including Cowlersley – beneath, Mrs Peel was eating a sandwich from a picnic basket which lay atop a woven blanket. Making the most of a moment's peace after the long drive, she poured herself a cup of lukewarm tea from the flask. She couldn't take her eyes off the vistas all around her, as if somehow, she might see Wilson from miles away. He was down there *somewhere*. But where?

She'd been relieved to hear from the villagers that Wilson *had* been seen in Cowlersley, as it would have been terribly embarrassing if Wilson had turned up in Islington, having led Steed on a wild goose chase. But Mrs Peel knew better than to doubt her instinct. Her gut had saved her bacon countless times before and should be ignored at her peril. She knew that when an eight-year-old boy was scared, there was only one place he'd want to be: tucked into his mother's loving arms. As she took a bite out of a particularly lacklustre cheese and pickle sandwich, she saw Steed marching back up to the top of the hill from the red telephone box beneath.

'Any joy?' she asked as he made it to the summit.

'They're concerned,' said Steed.

'They're *always* concerned,' Mrs Peel replied.

'Apparently we've got two hours to find him, or they're sending in the army.'

'Subtle,' said Mrs Peel.

'The press are gossiping,' said Steed. 'They don't think they can keep it under wraps for much longer.'

'What about his parents?' asked Mrs Peel.

'His mother died a decade ago,' said Steed, 'though we may be best keeping that to ourselves until he's a little less... fragile. They've telephoned his father. Hasn't seen him for weeks apparently.'

'So what do we do?' Mrs Peel enquired, handing Steed his ham and lettuce sandwich.

'We wait for divine inspiration,' Steed answered, turning his mouth up at the stale bread sandwich, 'and it's not to be found here.'

'We've just got to put ourselves in his head,' said Mrs Peel. 'What are his interests?'

'I don't know,' said Steed. 'The economy, health, transport.'

'That's his portfolio,' said Mrs Peel. 'For once you're *not* thinking like a child.'

'I was a late bloomer,' Steed agreed.

'What three things do all men love?' said Mrs Peel.

'The fairer sex,' Steed answered.

'Hasn't hit puberty,' she replied.

'A drink?'

'He's under the legal age.'

'Football?' said Steed.

'Bingo!'

Harold Wilson sat in the humble terraces at Leeds Road watching the empty pitch, lost and alone. His stomach suggested it was teatime, and his goosebumps told him he was ill-dressed for a cold May evening in God's Own Country. His rendezvous with dear Mrs Winters hadn't exactly gone to plan. He'd been grateful for her hospitality: a chance to use the John, eat a slice of tea cake and chug down a glass of lemonade – the pink stuff. But then she'd started harping on about how she never thought she'd live to see the day a Tyke became prime minister and she even had the brass neck to say his beloved mum was dead. That's when he made his excuses and legged it.

He hadn't a clue how the London lot had managed to rope his mum's friends into this great big lie, but one thing was certain: they had eyes and ears *everywhere*. Wherever he went, those two words followed him like a bad smell: prime minster. Could what they were saying possibly be true? How else could he explain what was happening?

Harold had been a passionate supporter of Huddersfield Town Football Club all his life along with his dad. As he closed his eyes, the empty seats and silent stands transformed in his memories. He could see the greatest team in England duking it out on the grass under the direction of their legendary manager Herbert Chapman. Harold could hardly remember the legendary defenders missing a tackle – uniquely able to transform defence into attack with quick silky passes from the lion-hearted Clem Stephenson. He might not have been the fastest thing on two legs, but he had a prodigious footballing brain. Like all his schoolmates, Harold's hero had been the centre-forward George Brown, who had an unrivalled ability to leave his markers for dead and find the net with unerring accuracy.

As with everything Harold had experienced over the past few days, nothing was as it had been. Archibald Leitch's famous ground had gained huge spotlights, and it looked bigger than it ever had. How he longed for his father to be sitting next to him now. Harold had never found it easy to make friends and had always been a bit of a loner. His mum regularly encouraged him to go and play out with the local boys, but he preferred his own company, and a boy could never be truly alone when he had his team.

Lost in his thoughts, Harold saw two people walking across the pitch in the distance. A man wearing a hat and carrying an umbrella, and a woman wearing a blue catsuit. As they came nearer, he recognised the man from Chequers. *They'd found him.* He thought about running, but he didn't know what he was running from, nor what he'd be running to. It felt like the end of the road. At least at Chequers he'd had a roof over his head, a warm fire to keep out the cold, and an endless supply of food and drink, which had been in short supply over the past few hours. So, he waited for the man, who he remembered was called Steed, to approach and capture him, like a deer snared by a lion because it's run out of energy to run or to fight.

'How did you find me?' asked Harold meekly.

'Mrs Peel,' said Steed. 'She's here to help you, Harold.'

'How about we make a deal?' Mrs Peel said. 'Come with us back to London and we'll have your father brought down to meet you there. How does that sound?'

Harold nodded. Resigned to his fate, and hoping beyond hope that he could trust them.

'I know this has all been very strange, and very scary,' said Mrs Peel, 'but we've found somebody we think can help you. Would you be happy to meet him?'

Again, Harold nodded. 'I don't want to feel like this anymore,' he said.

'I know,' Mrs Peel replied. 'Come along,' she said offering him a hand up from the stands, 'it's a long journey back, but you can tell me all about your favourite team on the way.'

Steed marvelled at his partner, admiring her abilities to move between her many personas: scientist, fighter, dark comic, outrageous flirt and extraordinary empath. As they headed back to the Bentley to return to the capital, he felt proud to have her by his side.

36

THE LATEST RECORDINGS Jacobs had accessed were a veritable goldmine of information. A loose-lipped civil servant at Downing Street had told an aide *everything*, including that the chauffeur – who he now knew was called Horatio Grainger – had been detained by Emma Peel and taken to "Box 500" which he knew was an old wartime name for military intelligence – based on the old post office box number for MI5. His inadvertent informant had also let slip that he was being transferred to a prison cell later that afternoon. Jacobs didn't yet have a location or a time, but at least now he had a plan. Or the bare bones of one at any rate.

He felt like an abject fool when he learned that Grainger wasn't even with Steed last night on the rooftop, but it amused him to uncover the full details of the Prime Minister's condition. Given his economic policy felt like it was drawn up by a child, it was a fitting punishment for the man who would shackle us to Europe.

It was obvious that now Grainger was in custody, they'd use him to reverse the Prime Minister's condition. If, indeed that was even possible. That afforded Jacobs one final chance to intercept the hypnotist. At first, he began to plan another roadside heist. Ambush the car, eliminate Grainger and his driver and be away. But it was risky. Now he was under suspicion, it would be next to impossible to pull off the same kind of operation as Thursday's heist. It also required people and detailed planning, which would take time.

Instead, he'd decided on another plan. One inspired by Horatio Grainger himself.

Becoming a Government driver had been a stroke of pure genius on the chauffeur's part. And with a bit of effort, Jacobs realised he might be able to emulate it. True, he couldn't hypnotise his subjects, nor was he a registered driver on the Government's books, but he did have one recourse. He could access the cars themselves.

Henderson would never have gone for it. He'd given him an earful for stopping by for *another* collection of bugging devices, but Jacobs knew time was running out and he couldn't afford to be kept out of the loop. Especially, because his intel suggested Steed and Peel had disappeared, destination: unknown. Commandeering one of the Government's vehicles was essential, but looping in Henderson wasn't an option. After all, if a dead man turned up in an abandoned Government car with no driver, it wouldn't take long for Henderson to become a person of interest for the authorities.

Jacobs had no great desire to drop his old partner in the proverbial. By and large, he'd done right by him, but the two men were not in any way what you might call friends. If the price for completing his work was razing Henderson's life to the ground, it was a price he'd have to pay. The mission could not be allowed to fail.

That's why he'd enlisted a safety net. One of Henderson's crew who loved the smell of cold hard cash and knew a friend of a friend who had served time with Jacobs when he'd done thirty days for tax evasion of all things. Mitchell was only too happy to pocket the cash in return for two simple favours. First, a check on the vehicle rota to find out where

Grainger was being taken: Pentonville; and what time he was being moved: eight o'clock. Next, he needed access to *two* Government vans – a pair of Black Marias, the name given to prisoner transports, which would be dispatched from the garage when the call came. The first would be driven by Jacobs and would have a valid security pass and duplicate plates to allow him to pick up Grainger as planned. The second, driven by a Government driver, would arrive some minutes later to find Grainger had already been transferred. By the time they worked out what had happened – and that it wasn't just an administrative cock-up – he'd have been long gone.

At least that's how it was supposed to go down, but as he parked up just around the corner from MI5's headquarters in Mayfair, his nerves bubbled below the surface. There was still a lot that could go wrong. First of all, there was a chance they might insist on sending a security detail to accompany Grainger, either inside the vehicle or trailing alongside as an escort. That's why he'd brought Manson with him, dressed as a security guard, to convince them that Grainger – and his driver – would be well protected en route. Worst case, they'd have to kill both of them, but that was best avoided if at all possible, especially as it wasn't impossible they'd send an armed guard, and the last thing he wanted was a shoot-out inside the vehicle! The plan wasn't perfect, but right now, it was all he had.

When the signal came, he drove around the corner to Leconfield House and found the rear entrance to the building off Chesterfield Gardens where Jacobs' security pass was checked and his registration was verified. As soon as the car pulled up alongside a door, Grainger was led out by two guards. Jacobs wound down his window.

'Evening, gents,' Jacobs said. 'I'm taking a prison by the name of Grainger to "The Ville".'

'Right you are,' said one of the guards, glancing into the car and clocking the size of Manson. 'Looks like you can take it from here,' he said. 'Need one of us to ride in the back with him?'

'No need,' said Jacobs, getting out the door and opening up the back of the van. 'I'm sure you've got better things to be doing with your time than slumming it in this oven with a crazy geezer.'

The guards laughed. 'You're not wrong, mate,' said one of them.

'Appreciate it,' said the other.

'Don't mention it,' Jacobs said, 'stick him in here and we'll see he gets there in one piece.'

The guards led Grainger to the car with his hands cuffed, helping him to take the step up to the van and avoid banging his head. Inside was a metal cage, with two basic plinths to sit on. The guards dropped him down on one of them, and jumped back down to the ground, slamming the doors shut.

'Follow this road down,' said a guard, 'and you'll come to a boom gate. They'll let you straight through.'

'Top man,' said Jacobs. 'No doubt they'll call you when he's arrived. Have a good'n.'

'You too, guv'nor,' said the guard, 'and these are for you,' he dropped the keys to Grainger's handcuffs into Jacobs' palm while the other guard handed over Grainger's briefcase to ride up front with the two men.

And with a cheerful bang on the back of the van to send them on their way, Jacobs was gone. He and Manson glanced at each other as the van cleared the second barrier, a look that expressed their mutual delight – and surprise – as to how well that had gone.

They waited until they'd cleared London and were nearly

in Buckinghamshire before they opened the hatch to speak to Grainger. It was much easier for someone to disappear in the vast open countryside of England than it was in the city, and they didn't want Grainger to become disruptive. As far as he was concerned, he'd been picked up by a legitimate driver, which Jacobs considered deliciously ironic.

Eventually, Jacobs spotted a turn-off that looked like it would do nicely. He saw an old, abandoned barn up ahead which – given it had no roof – was certainly uninhabited, and it was far enough off the beaten path to conceal their activities. Their prisoner probably wondered why the road was so uneven as they pulled onto muddy paths to hide the van out of sight, but if he did, he didn't say anything. They hadn't heard a squeak from him since they arrived. As Jacobs flicked the engine off, he and Manson exited the van in unison and opened up the rear doors.

Inside, Grainger was already suspicious. He knew Pentonville was only a hop, skip and a jump away, yet they'd been driving at full speed for not far off an hour. Surely he should have arrived in half that time?

'Don't mind us,' said Jacobs, climbing into the van with Manson and shutting the doors behind them. 'We just want a little talk before we go any further.' They took a seat on the bench opposite, making quite the intimidating pair in the battery-powered lighting that cast ominous shadows across their faces. In the second or two he had to glimpse outside while the doors were open, his fears were confirmed. Even though he wasn't a native Londoner, he knew enough about the city to know there weren't any sheep in central London.

'Let me guess,' said Grainger. 'Passing yourself off as Government drivers to extract information from an unwitting passenger? Not a very original tribute act.'

Jacobs laughed. Despite their ideological differences, he

still grudgingly liked the man. 'Sorry to disappoint,' he said. 'Let's just say you inspired us.'

'I'm honoured,' said Grainger.

'If it's any consolation,' said Jacobs, 'we're not wholly unoriginal. You could say we've mixed up the ending a little.'

When he heard this, Grainger's nonchalant act dropped as it dawned on him these men weren't here to make him talk. Their intentions were to do precisely the opposite.

'So who sent you?' asked Grainger, stalling for time while he could work out the best play.

'I sent myself,' said Jacobs, 'you don't know me, but I know you.'

'Very cryptic, Mr…?'

Jacobs ignored the prompt.

'I'm guessing you were the men firing at me on Thursday?'

'That'd be Manson and a few of my best men,' said Jacobs. Manson smiled, happy to take the credit.

'I imagine it didn't play out the way you'd hoped?' said Grainger. As he spoke, he was gently tapping his hand, crossing his legs, and wetting his lips, to see if either man would pick up on his non-verbal cues and inadvertently emulate them.

'It seems we have a shared interest,' said Jacobs.

'Oh?' said Grainger. 'I find that hard to believe.'

'We both have something of an…' he looked for the right word, '*obsession*, when it comes to Europe.'

Noting that Jacobs and Manson were both now sitting cross-legged, Grainger twigged, 'So *that's* what this is all about. You're trying to scupper the negotiations. May I ask to what end?'

'The liberty of Europe,' Jacobs said. And curiously he was now wetting his lips, while Manson was tapping his finger.

'Then you *were* right to say we are alike,' said Grainger. 'That's exactly what *I'm* trying to achieve also.'

That's when Jacobs launched into a diatribe about the evils of European unification. Grainger could have anticipated each and every one of Jacobs' arguments because they were the antithesis of his own beliefs. From his perspective the Common Market equalled economic security, to his antagonist it was an economic disaster. Where one saw hope, commonality and partnership, the other saw fear, division and competition. Perhaps neither was implicitly wrong or right, they were just opinions – two voices amongst millions – but Grainger recognised he did have one thing in common with the scruffy man sitting opposite. They were both *fanatics*, willing to stop at almost nothing to get their own way. But as Grainger looked into Jacobs' eyes to see whether he'd really be prepared to take a life over a political union, he realised – perhaps for the first time – that he himself could never go *that* far.

He sensed that as soon as the man's rant was over, he'd move against him, so if he was going to try to defend himself – and he was – it had to be quick. By now, both men were copying most of Grainger's non-verbal cues. That gave him a good indicator that they might be susceptible to hypnotism – the ringleader probably a little more so than his lackey by Grainger's estimation. It was a risky strategy of course, but he didn't really have a backup plan. Even if he hadn't have been cuffed, the chances of him overpowering a couple of muscleheads was slim to none. No, if he was going to have any chance of getting out of this alive, it would be through his words, not his fists.

'Sorry to interrupt,' said Grainger, sensing the moment was right. 'But can I ask you something?'

This threw Jacobs who was midstream. 'What?' he snarled.

'I just wondered if you knew why pigeons don't drive space tractors…?'

37

MERCIFULLY, HAROLD WILSON had fallen asleep after less than fifteen minutes into their long journey back to London, which was hardly surprising, given the poor man had been roaming Huddersfield like a lost puppy for who knows how long and they were losing the light. This gave Steed and Mrs Peel some breathing space to plan their next move, out of earshot of the man formerly known as the Prime Minister.

It was clear Harold was becoming a little more lucid – insomuch as it seemed he was starting to believe that *his* version of events wasn't quite right. He didn't need his university degree to know that the cars he was seeing on the roads weren't Model T Fords or Clynos. Or that he'd travelled the railway on a diesel locomotive, not a steam train. He'd seen people he knew age before his eyes, trees grow from saplings to mighty oaks, and it was clear – even to him – that there wasn't a logical explanation. But to everyone's great frustration, he still couldn't accept the truth. He couldn't see the fifty-something man in the reflection of a mirror, and he couldn't access his life beyond 1924.

'You can't quite imagine this happening to Churchill, can you?' said Mrs Peel, turning around to check on the poor soul that Harold had become. Lying prone in the back of the Bentley, a blanket over him to keep him warm.

'Oh, I don't know,' said Steed, 'I'd have quite liked to have seen the British Bulldog as a child.'

'A Bullpuppy,' said Mrs Peel.

'Quite.'

'Question is, what are we going to do with our own First Lord of the Treasury?' she asked.

'Can this Grainger be trusted?' asked Steed.

'Not for a moment,' she replied, 'but…'

'He's our only chance?'

'Well, yes,' said Mrs Peel, 'and… I'm pretty sure he means it when he says it's in his best interests too.'

'What's in *our* best interests?' said Steed.

'To drop the Prime Minister off at the nearest police station. Drive down to Kent and head for the South of France to savour a glass of Châteauneuf-du-Pape in the Rhône.'

Steed glanced over to his old friend. 'Thanks for getting involved with this one. I know we try and avoid the top, *top* brass where at all possible.'

'Just make sure we get a medal,' said Mrs Peel, jovially. 'I want a very, very big one, made of gold. And I'll be biting it to check.'

'I'm sure that can be arranged,' said Steed. 'I'll ask the Palace.'

'Speaking of which,' she said, 'what's Her Majesty's take on all this?'

'Her Majesty has a soft spot for the old boy, from what I can tell,' said Steed. 'She'll have been kept informed no doubt. Not least because Wilson would have had to cancel his weekly audience.' This was a regular ritual that prime ministers past and present had all agreed was a godsend in times of trouble. Not just because the Queen possessed a great deal of wisdom that belied her years, but because they knew they were talking to the one person in politics – perhaps the entire world – to whom they could speak freely, with every confidence that their secrets would go with her to the grave, such was her dedication to duty.

'What a mess,' said Mrs Peel. 'The papers are getting more vocal.'

'Yes, I read some of today's headlines,' said Steed. 'The *Mail* said the Prime Minister is dead, and we're parading a body double around town.'

Mrs Peel smiled, 'Yesterday's *News of the World* said he'd run off with his mistress.'

'The *Guardian* said it was a crying shame for the unions,' Steed added.

'The *Telegraph* said it was a national embarrassment for the country,' Mrs Peel replied.

'And it's anyone's guess what the BBC thinks,' said Steed.

'Well, it's a frustration for Emma Peel.'

'And it's a positive disaster for the Bentley,' Steed said, noting the steam slowly gathering pace beneath the hood of the car, as it far exceeded the mileage it was used to these days.

'I wonder if Horatio is behaving himself?' asked Mrs Peel.

'Probably hypnotised the lot of them by now. I did tell them to avoid any swinging pocket watches. Though I notice *you* were impervious to his charms,' said Steed.

Mrs Peel patted Steed gently, 'I'd have thought you – of all people – would know I'm impervious to *any* man's charms.'

'But still we try, Mrs Peel,' said Steed, 'but still we try.'

38

HORATIO GRAINGER KNEW it was risky to drive to Downing Street. This time, behind the wheel of the prisoner transport, instead of in the back, but he didn't know where else to go. He'd momentarily thought about doing a moonlight flit, given someone was actively trying to kill him, but that only made handing himself in more attractive as he figured the worst the authorities would do would be to lock him up, rather than execute him – whatever Mrs Peel may have intimated. Not to mention, his number one objective continued to be treating the Prime Minister and that could only happen if they were in the same room. So, reluctantly, his objectives and the Government's were uncomfortably aligned.

Before setting off back to London, Grainger had stopped at the nearest telephone box to call the police and let them know there were two would-be assassins dazed and confused lying in a barn near Borehamwood, but he was fairly sure that by the time they arrived, Grainger's hold on his attackers would have faded and they'd have scarpered. That was *if* the police even believed his tall tale, which frankly, was a big if.

It hadn't been easy to hypnotise Jacobs and Manson. They were both susceptible to basic manipulation, but neither were prime candidates. Having worked with people for over a decade in the field, Grainger had a pretty good feel for who could and who couldn't be hypnotised. And who fell somewhere between. The two men he'd left snuggling up to one another in a damp cold barn in Buckinghamshire weren't at either end of the continuum. And without access to his concoctions, it's unlikely he'd have been able to have extracted information from them, as he had his unwitting political canaries. But getting subjects to "sleep" was amongst the easiest command one could give, as it relied on a simple "glitch" in most people's minds, whereby the brain, when overwhelmed with information, could fairly easily be instructed to simply "reboot" itself to bring an end to the discomfort, which usually took five to ten minutes to wear off. More than enough time to retrieve the keys to his cuffs, roll the two henchmen out of the van, and hotfoot it out of there as if his life depended on it, because it very much did.

Before the day was out, Grainger had handed himself in at Number 10 and been detained by the security services, while they waited for Mrs Peel – and this inimitable John Steed character he'd heard so much about – to arrive. He used the time wisely, practicing over and over again what he was going to say and do if he got another chance to see the Prime Minister. He knew he'd only get one chance, and he was canny enough to know it wasn't only the Common Market that was at stake if he messed up, his own fate hung in the balance.

39

JACOBS' EGO HADN'T just been bruised by the encounter with Horatio Grainger, it had been hung, drawn and quartered. The walk of shame to the nearest village was filled with silence. Neither Jacobs nor Manson said a single word to each other about what had just gone down. Geiger had tried his best not to take the Michael when he'd received the call to come and pick them up from the middle of nowhere, but Jacobs sensed the contempt in his vocal cords, buried just below the surface. That's why he told him, in no uncertain terms, to send Cynthia to pick them up.

It was bloody embarrassing to think that they'd fallen for Grainger's schtick, not least because he'd been listening to the very same chicanery for months. He was also furious with Manson, for being of absolutely no use whatsoever. Not that he was surprised Manson had fallen under the influence. After all, Jacobs knew his number two wasn't first in line when brain cells were being given out, but he was there for the muscle, and he should have clobbered Grainger long before he even had a chance to open his big mouth. That said, it would have been cold comfort if he'd been hypnotised and Manson hadn't. That might have been better for the mission, but he'd have never lived it down amongst his men nor been able to look at himself in the mirror ever again.

The two men cut a pathetic figure outside The Black Mountain pub while they waited for Cynthia to arrive, nursing their stout as if it were medicine, their bedraggled faces illuminated by a moth-infested outdoor light that barely gave them enough light to see their drinks.

'When I get my hands on him,' said Manson, 'he won't know what's hit him.'

'Really?' said Jacobs, 'because you just had your hands on him, and – if I remember rightly – his were in cuffs, yet we're the ones stranded in the back of beyond, and he's driven off into the sunset.'

'We are going after him though, *right*? When she arrives, I mean?' Manson asked, 'I can have twenty men hunting for him by sundown.'

Jacobs didn't say a thing.

'You hear me, boss?' Manson asked. 'We're going to make him pay, yeah?'

Jacobs shook his head. 'He's not worth it.'

'You kiddin' me?' said Manson, outraged. 'After what he pulled?'

'We were about to kill him,' said Jacobs, ever the only voice of sanity amongst his merry band of men. 'It was hardly personal, was it?'

'But still,' said Manson, 'don't we need to send a message?'

'To who?' Jacobs asked. 'I think you've got me mistaken for Al Capone, my friend. I'm a businessman.'

'Hmm,' said Manson, unconvinced. 'Clyde maybe?'

'Aye?' asked Jacobs.

Manson's head and eyes pointed behind Jacobs, 'Bonnie's arrived.'

Jacobs was pleased to see Cynthia pulling up alongside the pub in her Vespa 150 Super Combination, even if she'd taken her own sweet time to get there. He'd hoped she'd have had the good sense to bring one of the cars, not one of her *four* motorbikes – this one complete with its own sidecar. She walked straight up to them, removed her helmet and took a huge swig of Jacobs' stout, finishing it in a single glug.

'You ready?' she asked.

'More than,' he replied.

Manson chugged the rest of his pint, and they set off.

'Sidecar,' said Jacobs, instructing his number two where to travel, while he hopped on the bike itself, behind Cynthia to ride pillion.

As she started the bike and began flying round the country lanes a good deal faster than she safely should, Jacobs enjoyed feeling the warmth of her body, even through the leathers, and it was good to hold her again. He wrapped his arms around her – as much to show her he'd missed her as for safety. She rubbed her foot against his shin to communicate the feeling was mutual.

After a thirty-minute ride, they dropped Manson off back home. Jacobs would have gladly stayed up all night long to progress the cause, but as he'd told Manson, there was nothing *to* do right now. Just wait. With Grainger gone – and if he had any sense he'd be across the Channel by midnight – there was little hope of Wilson recovering, so he couldn't see how Thursday's application window could possibly be met. Not when it was *his* passion project, and his signature on the paperwork. Best case, the EUNOCs might just have pulled off a blinder, especially because it was a lot cleaner to leave Grainger on the run, than in a hole somewhere, just waiting to be found. But life wasn't usually that kind to Jacobs.

As Cynthia drove around the corner and out of sight of Manson's three-bed semi, she hit the brakes and came to a complete stop at the side of the road.

'What's wrong?' asked Jacobs.

'You're what's wrong,' she replied. 'You could have just got yourselves killed.'

Jacobs appreciated that she'd waited until Manson was gone before giving him a dressing down.

'I don't get you, Bill,' she asked. 'Why would you risk everything for bloody politics. Is it *really* worth it?'

'You know the answer,' he said, avoiding eye contact.

'But do *you*?' she replied.

This surprised him. She could read him like a book – it had been that way since the beginning – but he hadn't realised she could sense the small nugget of doubt that whispered into his ears from time to time. The voice he'd done his level best to silence.

'I've come this far,' said Jacobs, 'can't turn back now.'

'Can't or *won't?*' Cynthia replied.

'Does it matter?'

'Nobody understands why this is so important to you more than me,' she said, 'but if it ends up killing you too, then they win – *again*!'

This didn't fall on deaf ears. Jacobs had met Cynthia at an anti-EEC March six years prior, back in '61 when the Harold 'Supermac' MacMillan government tried to take the UK into Europe the first time.

Cynthia was ten years younger than Jacobs and a natural stunner. He'd sworn off women after a failed marriage and a succession of one-night stands that never led anywhere of substance, but somehow Cynthia had wheedled her way into the tiny cracks in his armour and gained the unenviable role of Jacobs on/off lover and confidante.

He knew full well that she wanted more, but that was never going to happen. He'd nearly lost everything when he'd separated from his wife, Val, and to say their separation was acrimonious was an understatement. Never again would he allow a woman to have that kind of power over him – even one as delightful as Cynthia. She'd joined the movement because her father – an R.A.F gunner – had been downed on May 7 1945, one day before VE-day. Her hatred for Europe wasn't just because the War had taken her father – though that alone was more than enough to instil such vitriol – but the *context* of his death.

If he'd been killed years, or even months earlier, she'd have just about been able to come to terms with it. She wasn't stupid, she knew that an airman at war was hardly the safest profession. When people had given their lives for the Battle of Britain, D-Day, or Big Week, it had been a painful but noble fate, bestowing a sense of achievement that could never compensate for the loss, but Cynthia imagined it must have helped grieving families to at least make sense of it.

Cynthia's father, Ted, had been killed a week after Hitler had taken his own life in the Berlin bunkers while the world awaited German capitulation under the leadership of Admiral Dönitz. By then, everyone knew the War was all but over, and like households up and down the country, the family had spent the whole day celebrating the inevitable end of hostilities, and the return of their patriarch. But because the right paperwork had yet to be signed, Ted died hours before the cessation of hostilities, falling victim – as Cynthia saw it – to red tape. That began a seething resentment towards European bureaucracy, which seemed to sit at the very heart of the European Project.

It wasn't the people she despised, not even the Germans – at least most of them – because she realised they were as innocent as her father was. It was the insidious nature, as she saw it, of the nascent union, which seemed obsessed with tying member states up in needless rules, all to build its own power and influence. In this, she'd sensed Jacobs was a kindred spirit. A driven, passionate man who was articulate and headstrong, but with a sensible head on his shoulders, and a good heart.

They'd stayed in touch off and on since then, hooking up when it suited both of them, and spending time apart when their lives diverged. The news that Britain was trying to join the Common Market again had brought them back into each other's lives, but it also highlighted a change in mindsets. Where the intervening years had softened Cynthia's resolve and helped her to gain some perspective, Jacobs' views had only hardened. Guns had long-since replaced words as his weapon of choice and where once he was annoyed by the world, now he was enraged by it.

At first, she'd gone along with it – like she always had, because Jacobs was persuasive, a natural leader. People – including and especially her – wanted to follow him, even when he didn't treat them particularly well, even when they knew better. Being with him was fun – intoxicating even. There was an anarchist still buried deep within her, and when she was with Jacobs its voice grew louder, and she found herself doing things for him, things she regretted, not because of the mission, but because she wanted to impress him, to earn his love. He was her obsession. Europe was his. This meant she was following a path that no longer satisfied her head or her heart, and the dissonance had to end.

'We're so close,' said Jacobs, pleading for a little more time, a stay of execution.

'There's no we,' she replied, 'not anymore. It's not just your life you're ruining. It's all of us. If you get caught, they'll come for everyone.'

'We won't...'

'But you will, Bill,' she said, 'you will. Powerful people,

they don't let anyone take their power away. They'll hunt you down like dogs. And I can't watch that.'

He knew she was probably right, and if he'd have been a more honourable man, he'd have told her to leave a long time ago – but the truth was, he didn't want her to. She centred him, calmed him. She reminded him of the man he used to be. But he knew as soon as she said it that this wasn't the story of eleventh-hour redemption. He'd made his choice a long time ago, he was moving forwards, with or without her.

'And what if I succeed? Does that make a difference?'

'What does success even mean, Bill?' she asked. 'Think it through – you're a bright boy – they're not going to let one man, however pigheaded, stop them driving this through. Say you stall them, they'll try again – and again, until they get their way. That's what governments do. How are you ever going to *really* stop them?'

She was right. There was a good chance he'd be playing this game for years, maybe even decades, but if that kept Britain out of the Common Market in the intervening period, that *was* success, at least to his mind. After an uncomfortable pause, he shrugged his shoulders and opened his palms as if to say, "I don't know what you want me to say?"

'And there's nothing I can say to change your mind?'

'I wish there was,' said Jacobs.

She nodded. 'Then it is what it is,' she smiled. But it was a sad smile. 'Make my dad proud?'

He nodded. 'I will. I promise.'

There was an awkward pause. 'Drop me back?' he asked.

She laughed at the cheek of it. A stronger man would have gallantly walked away there and then, but this was no time for valour. He needed to get back to London to see where things were at, and she was the fastest way of achieving that goal. Even if it was a humiliating ask.

It was a painful journey back to Jacobs' factory and the silence was deafening. Not because they weren't talking – you could never hear a word either of you were saying on a motorbike with your helmet on and the roar of wind and traffic – but because they knew it was their last ride. When he let her go to dismount, he knew it was the last time he'd touch her, and he planted a kiss on the cheek. There was a lot he could have said to her – and he probably should – but that wasn't his style. Not anymore. And as he watched her drive away from the gates and fade away into the night, she became just another thing that Europe had taken from him.

40

STEED DIDN'T KNOW what to make of the Austrian-come-Swiss-come-Italian hypnotist, but he was relieved the man was still alive. Not least because he hadn't any kind of backup plan for the "Wilson problem". Mrs Peel seemed to believe Grainger's story that he was a political extremist, not a cold-blooded killer, but Steed wasn't so sure. In fairness, Mrs Peel's judgement was typically excellent and she was hardly easy to pull the wool over. Indeed, she was one of the most emotionally intelligent and brilliantly cynical people he knew. It was one of *many* reasons he enjoyed working with her so much and sharing her company. But Horatio Grainger was inherently shifty. Every word he uttered seemed measured. Carefully curated to persuade. It was never clear where his small talk ended and his hypnotic repertoire began. It reminded Steed of the Ministry's shrinks, which agents were mandated to visit from time to time. They used words as weapons, and you always had the very real sense you were being constantly analysed and evaluated.

It wasn't easy smuggling Grainger – or even Mrs Peel for that matter – into Chequers. Steed had to pull in some big favours to make it happen, such was the ring of security that surrounded the Prime Minister after recent events. And because it now seemed like Grainger himself was a target.

Steed *had* managed to pull it off – by the skin of his teeth – but the stakes were high. Steed was, in part, so popular inside the Ministry precisely because he was unorthodox. A man who favoured doing over talking. And that meant he got results others could only dream of. It was a given that, *at times*, things would go wrong, and a certain amount of collateral damage could be swept under the carpet and amortised against the enormous value Steed, and others like him, brought to the country. After all, governments would come and go, but the civil service remained as a constant safety net for Britain, defending the nation against those who would bid her harm. Nevertheless, this situation was a little different. If Grainger somehow worsened the Prime Minister's condition (though Steed wondered how much worse it could get) or it proved that he was using the whole setup as a ruse to assassinate Wilson, even Steed would have a hard time getting out of that one.

Any way you looked at it, if anything happened to the Prime Minister, nobody would forgive Steed for giving the very man responsible for this mess another chance to finish the job. The reason he'd reluctantly made the decision to bring Grainger back into the inner sanctuary was simple pragmatism and calculated risk. He knew that if he went through the official channels, it was highly unlikely that his request would be granted. Mountains of paperwork would have stretched from Chequers back to Downing Street long before clearance was afforded. Well after the window to join the EEC had expired, and perhaps more importantly for Wilson, long after the press and the public had twigged what was really going on. Steed didn't care one way or the other about European integration, but he *did* care about duty and getting the job done.

Steed, Mrs Peel and Horatio Grainger had been waiting

in the White Drawing Room at Chequers for over thirty minutes. Nobody said a word, though Steed and Mrs Peel seemed to have an entire conversation, conducted through body language alone, which Grainger found quite impressive. Frustration and flirtation notwithstanding, it broadly seemed to amount to Mrs Peel intimating that they both needed to keep their wits about them, and watch Grainger like hawks.

Thirty-seven minutes after they'd arrived, the Prime Minister's Political Secretary, Marcia Williams took them into the sitting room. Williams was a formidable woman with an impressively large blonde perm who some joked was the real power behind the Wilson Government.

'I can give you thirty minutes,' she said, 'forty at a push – after that, Dr Summers is coming to see him, and he *cannot* see any of this.'

'Understood,' said Steed tipping his bowler in appreciation. 'I owe you one.'

'Just for God's sake fix him, Steed,' she said. 'That's thanks enough.' She left the room and closed the door behind her.

Grainger wasted no time in examining Harold who looked even more afraid and bewildered than when Steed had seen him last.

'Good morning,' said Steed, removing his hat and putting it on the mantelpiece.

'Do you remember me?' asked Grainger.

'No, sir. Should I?' Harold replied, like a child meeting a police officer for the first time. 'I remember him,' he said pointing to Steed, 'he was kind to me. He told me he'd make things better.'

'That's right,' said Steed, 'I've brought this man along to help you–' he added the word, 'hopefully,' under his breath '–his name is Horatio,' Steed continued.

'Like Nelson,' said Harold.

'That's right,' Grainger replied, trying to court Harold's trust. He put his arm behind his back. 'It's on account of only having one arm, you see.'

Harold laughed at the childish ruse.

'And this is Mrs Peel,' said Steed, inviting her to come over. 'You met her before – up in Huddersfield – do you remember?'

Harold nodded.

'Nice to see you again,' she said, shaking his hand like he was an adult but pitching her voice and body language as though addressing a child.

Grainger turned to Mrs Peel. 'May I have my bag?'

Mrs Peel thought about this for a moment, before reluctantly passing over the appropriately named Gladstone bag that she'd picked up from Grainger's flat first thing that morning.

Grainger opened it and began rummaging through the brown leather satchel. Removing several books, notepads and – from a hidden compartment at the base – a vial and syringe. Steed cottoned on immediately and snatched it out of his hands.

'Are you mad?' he barked.

'It's a mild sedative,' he replied, not letting go of the needle as they each vied for control.

'Not a chance,' Mrs Peel replied, lambasting herself for missing the concealed implement, and grabbing the needle from both of them.

'Listen,' he insisted, 'the man's scared out of his mind. If I try to work on him like this, we'll almost certainly fail. Hypnotism is basically just a concentrated state of induced sleep. And like sleep, one needs to be prepared for it, eased into it. So, either you tell me how we get Wilson to peacefully nod off when he's scared for his life, locked in a place he doesn't know, and surrounded by people he doesn't much trust, or you let me get on with my job, and do what you brought me here to do.'

Steed and Mrs Peel walked across to the window – out of earshot, but close enough to keep an eye on Grainger.

'What do you think?' asked Steed.

Mrs Peel inspected the syringe, which contained a clear liquid, and held it up to the sunlight. She grabbed Steed's navy-blue pocket square from his jacket and squirted a small amount of the liquid onto the cloth and smelled it. It was completely odourless. She shook her head at Steed to indicate she couldn't be sure what drug was contained within.

'I don't see we have much choice,' she replied, 'unless…'

'Unless…?' Steed asked.

'It's a little unorthodox.'

'The Orthodoxy excommunicated me years ago Mrs Peel,' he replied.

Mrs Peel addressed Grainger. 'What drug is this?'

'Just morphine,' he answered.

'What would you say the half-life is?' she asked. 'Fifteen minutes?'

'Something like that,' he replied. 'Why?'

'Duly noted,' she said, plunging it into Grainger's leg and releasing a small amount into his blood stream.

'What do you think you're doing?' he said. But as his protestations escalated, his body gave way to the drug, collapsing into the nearest chair, on the verge of consciousness, a big smile on his face.

It felt like Grainger had been out for hours, maybe even days, by the time he properly came to, but in truth it was less than ten minutes. Poor old Harold had curled up in a tiny ball by the fireplace while it was all happening, terrified he was next in line for what could only have looked, to him, like unprovoked euthanasia. Grainger's eyes were blurry at first, before Steed and Mrs Peel's imposing silhouettes came into sharp focus, their eyes piercing into his soul. He knew he'd probably been conscious throughout, but his concoction included a few other "goodies". An old trick anaesthetists used to make sure you not only feel no pain during an operation, but you also don't remember any trauma.

'Welcome back,' said Mrs Peel. She grabbed a second syringe from Grainger's bag and passed it to Steed. 'The good news is… it *isn't* lethal.'

Grainger rubbed his eyes. 'Was that really necessary'?

'Necessary? No,' said Steed. 'Prudent? Absolutely.'

'Steed, we're running out of time,' said Mrs Peel glancing at the clock on the mantelpiece.

'Harold,' Steed said, turning to the Prime Minister who was fixated on a huge spider he could see spinning its web on the other side of the glass from his window seat, 'I have some medicine I need you to take. To make you feel better.'

Harold nodded furiously as if to say, "okay, but make it fast". Steed clumsily tapped the needle to release any air bubbles, but he realised he really wasn't best placed to deliver the injection. Mrs Peel rolled her eyes and took back the syringe, lifting Harold's sleeve, and tapping his inner arm lightly until she found a vein. Barely ten seconds later, Harold was in a state of complete calm. Deeper than sleep, but still conscious.

Steed and Mrs Peel could barely believe their ears as they witnessed Grainger's technique first hand.

'How old are you?' Grainger asked.

'Eight,' Harold answered. Half asleep, his eyes open, but his soul was dead to the world.

'No, you're not,' he replied. 'Surely, you've heard about the Wall Street Crash? It's 1929, so you've just turned thirteen, remember?'

'Okay,' said Harold. Seemingly accepting the "fact" that he was now a teenager.

'Oh, but hang on a minute,' added Grainger, 'you've left school, haven't you, Harold? You've just gone to university. Remind me where you're studying again?'

'Jesus,' he said after a moment's thought. His face turning to Steed as though he'd noticed him for the first time.

'Without the miracles or the disciples,' said Mrs Peel. Harold paid no notice and returned his stare to Grainger.

'Jesus College, Oxford,' he said, his voice soft and at peace.

'So, what year is it, Harold?'

'1934, sir,' the Prime Minister replied.

'But that means… you *can't* be thirteen, can you? How old are you, boy?' Grainger's timbre deliberately took on the tone of a schoolmaster.

'Eighteen, sir.'

'Okay, that's helpful,' Grainger paused as if walking away before turning theatrically like he was giving a performance in an am-dram production. 'Hang on though, you're a parliamentarian, aren't you? So, you mustn't be at university after all?'

Harold looked confused, his demeanour slowly becoming more animated and less anaesthetised. 'No, I suppose you're right.'

'That must make it…' Grainger deliberately hung the sentence.

'1945.'

'That's right. Of course – the War's just ended, hasn't it,' Grainger replied. 'Silly old me. So you're… what, nearly thirty now, I'd wager?'

'Yes. I must be.'

'Good good,' said Grainger, pleased with his progress. 'Oh and I meant to say…'

'Yes?' enquired Harold, suddenly communicating with the conviction of a grown man, not the boy child he was moments before.

'Congratulations on becoming leader of the Party. You must be absolutely thrilled. And at only forty-seven years of age. Quite the achievement.'

Harold picked up his pipe, opened a pouch of tobacco from his jacket and – as if through muscle memory alone – lit it with the strike of a match.

'Good of you to say,' said Harold.

'Remind me…' Grainger asked. 'Who's in power right now? In Westminster that is?'

'Well the Labour Party of course.' Harold replied confidently.

'So I suppose that would make you…'

Wilson's face came to life as he definitively answered Grainger's question, 'The Prime Minister.'

And with that, the trance was broken and James Harold Wilson – the boy from Yorkshire who had risen to the highest office in the land – was revived. The adrenaline pumped through his veins, metabolising the effects of the medications still flowing through his system, and began to revive him.

Wilson quickly clocked where he was. 'What the devil am I doing in Chequers?' he asked, looking at his watch, which displayed the time and the date. Presuming it must be wrong, he tapped the glass furiously. 'Damn thing's gone haywire.'

Steed stepped in. 'Welcome back, sir. You might want a stiff drink before I tell you this… We've got a *lot* to catch up on.'

41

IT DIDN'T TAKE long for word to reach Jacobs that the Prime Minister had left Chequers and was returning to Downing Street. His contact didn't know much, other than that Cabinet was being assembled to greet him. That could only mean one thing: Wilson had overcome his affliction. No doubt with help from Grainger, Steed and Peel.

'And there's one other thing,' said Manson. 'Our informant says there's a vote being scheduled in the House tomorrow.'

Jacobs didn't scream and shout, much to the surprise of anyone that knew him. On some level, he suspected it was inevitable. He could still turn things around; scupper the UK's chances of joining Europe, at least for now, but not unscathed. Even if he managed to evade the authorities, which he thoroughly hoped to do, there was no chance of keeping his old life. They'd hunt him for the rest of his days, and even long after he'd gone; he'd be Guy Fawkes' successor on bonfires up and down the land. It didn't matter. Not really. His life – his old life, full of love and satisfaction – back when his business was soaring, and the country was turning around its fortunes post-war had been taken from him years ago.

Ever since Mrs Peel had come sniffing, he knew his time was numbered and that even if they couldn't find the evidence – thanks to the car crusher – sooner or later they'd be back to demand their pound of flesh. No, as much as he'd have loved things to have played out the easy way, events had seemingly always been leading to this.

Steeling himself, Jacobs opened the door to his office and walked out onto to the gantry to address his men beneath.

'Time to move to Plan B,' he said, looking each and every one of them in the eye. A glance that was both threatening and pleading in equal measure.

'Which is?' asked Timpson.

Jacobs climbed down the steps to get on his men's level. He walked over to a large wooden crate hidden beneath some work benches and covered with cloths that looked like they hadn't been touched for years.

'This,' Jacobs said, grabbing a crowbar and prising the top off the pallet. Inside were dozens of blocks of gelignite.

'Are you mad?' screamed Geiger. 'How long's that lot been here?'

'It's a munitions factory, Geiger,' said Jacobs, 'use your imagination.'

'You could have blown the lot of us to buggery,' he replied.

Jacobs ignored the comment. Gelignite was perfectly safe if stored in the correct way at the proper temperature. Which Geiger would have bloody well known if he'd have paid half an interest in the business' stock in trade.

'They'll track every last one of us down,' argued Timpson, 'man and boy.'

'I'll do *anything* for my country,' said Jacobs, hoping to instil a timely dose of patriotism amongst his men, especially the veterans.

'I won't,' said Geiger, 'not anymore. It's taken enough from me already.' He pointed to the prosthesis that sat haphazardly below the shin – his real ankle shattered to bits by a German grenade.

'This is insane, Jacobs,' said Timpson. 'First, you said this was about stopping a political treaty. Then you expected us to start shooting at the Prime Minster. And now you're demanding we plunge the country into the crapper and commit high treason?'

'I'm not *demanding* anything,' Jacobs retorted. 'I'm asking for volunteers. If any of you don't have the stomach for it, then there's the door. Anyone who wants to stay loyal will – of course – be handsomely rewarded.'

'With what?' asked Geiger. 'You pay your wages late. Your fleet's rusting to bits. And this place is a fleapit. You expect us to believe you can keep us out of prison and in the lap of luxury with platitudes?'

'Let's just say we have powerful people that share our objectives,' said Jacobs, somewhat cryptically. He didn't like to talk about his financiers to the men because the risk of exposing some of the most powerful men in the country was far too high. For all concerned. These weren't principled freedom fighters who shared Jacobs' view of the world. They were simply capitalists who stood to lose a fortune if Britain entered an economic treaty with Europe. Losses which made his modest stipend look insignificant in the grand scheme of things.

The men looked at each other, each trying to read the room and find out which way their colleagues were going to sway.

'I suggest a simple show of hands,' said Jacobs. 'Who's with me?' Of the twelve men, five raised their hands, including Jacobs' loyal foreman, Manson.

Jacobs nodded. Disappointed, but not surprised by the loss of over half of his support base.

Silence filled the air and after an agonising thirty seconds, the first group of defectors started to leave, and the others soon followed.

Jacobs turned to address his remaining crew. He wasn't the kind of man that would ever say he was grateful aloud, but he was. Instead, he delivered a simple instruction, 'Let's get it done.'

42

THE PRIME MINISTER was furious. He'd barely spoken a word in the car back to Downing Street. Could everything Steed had told him possibly be true? If so, it was deeply embarrassing. He'd heard of hypnosis, of course, everyone had, and seen the odd cabaret act – people dancing on stage thinking they were chickens or being made to speak in silly accents, that sort of thing – but he'd never for a moment thought it was real.

He vaguely remembered being briefed by President Johnson about the Americans' foray into hypnosis with a top-secret project called MKUltra, but from memory, it hadn't borne much fruit. Like most people, Wilson liked to think he wouldn't be susceptible to that kind of thing, that only simpletons could be duped into becoming somebody else's puppet. To think he himself had fallen victim was painful to even contemplate – a man whose entire life had been defined by his strength of mind and character.

The last thing Wilson remembered before "waking up" in Chequers was breakfast that morning. He'd bickered with his wife, about something and nothing. And he was keen to get back to Downing Street to speak to her – though what she'd make of this tall tale was anyone's guess. He had absolutely no memory of the car journey, or the shoot-out, or his impromptu adventures back in Huddersfield. And that was probably for the best. Naturally, there would have to be a cover-up put out, but he was confident his press liaison would be drafting an alternative reality that would rival the fanciful imaginings of the very best popular fiction.

It was a good ninety-minute drive from Chequers to Number 10. Usually, Wilson would have been grateful for the time to just *be* – a moment's respite from the pandemonium of life at the helm of a declining empire, trying its best to stay relevant in the new world. But today, the drive felt painfully slow, such was his desire to get back to the capital and reassert control of the situation.

'How are you doing, sir?' asked Steed, who was sitting in the back of the car with Wilson.

'I'll be okay,' he replied, so lost in his thoughts that he'd forgotten anyone was with him.

Steed glanced out the back window to check Mrs Peel was still following them in her Lotus. And she was.

'Is it really necessary for you both to be babysitting me?' Wilson asked.

'Let's just say we've become a little nervous of Government drivers,' said Steed.

Their chauffeur didn't seem best pleased by the comment, adopting a look, out of sight of his passengers, that seemed to say "bloody cheek".

Dark grey rain clouds were descending over London as the lights of the Post Office Tower finally came into view. Wilson glanced over to his bowler-hatted bodyguard, who cut an imposing figure, and he realised he knew next to nothing about his saviour.

'I suppose I should say thank you,' said Wilson. 'By all accounts, it sounds like you've gone above and beyond to serve the Government–' he paused, '–and me.'

'You're very welcome, sir.'

'Remind me of your name.' Wilson asked.

'Steed, sir. John Steed.'

'And the woman?'

'Mrs Emma Peel.'

'Steed and Peel. Why do those names sound familiar?'

'We helped you once before, sir,' he answered. 'A little while back – a spot of bother on a train.'

'Yes, that's right,' said Wilson. 'Well, the nation owes you a great debt of gratitude.'

'Not at all,' said Steed. 'All in a day's work.'

Suddenly a memory popped into Wilson's head. 'Hang on… I called on you both that day to invite you to a shindig. Cocktails, plaudits, that sort of thing – I'd even prepared a speech.'

'You did, sir?' said Steed feigning ignorance.

'And not a dicky bird. You'd disappeared off the face of the planet.'

Steed was hoping he hadn't remembered that part.

'Duty called most likely,' Steed replied, omitting the fact that they'd spent some days in the north of France to avoid the spotlight. After all, fawning politicians were – in Steed and Mrs Peel's professional opinion – the most dangerous adversaries of all.

Steed spotted Big Ben's clock tower coming into view now as they drove over Westminster Bridge. 'Nearly home,' he said.

Wilson nodded. 'Tell me, Steed,' he said, 'I've been bloody-minded since I was knee-high to a grasshopper.'

'I remember,' Steed replied.

'Well, quite. So you'll understand when I tell you I *never* like to be told what to do.'

'Not many people do.'

'I mean it, Steed. If someone tries to cajole me, proselytize, beat me into submission, I push back. Do the exact opposite. Keep 'em guessing.'

'I'm a little like that myself,' Steed admitted, unsure where this was going.

'So, what would you do if you knew one madman had been hypnotising you into doing something, and another psychopath was ready to kill you if you did?'

Steed thought for a moment. 'I suppose I'd do what *I* wanted to do.'

'That's just the problem though, isn't it, Steed?' said Wilson. 'Before all this, I'd have been confident I knew what that was. But now... I'm not so sure. What if, *even now*, I'm still under his spell? If I vote yes, they'll say I've been tricked into it. If I say no, I'll be accused of running scared to save my own backside...'

Steed empathised. Wilson's doctors and psychologists were fairly sure he *was* free from Grainger's influence. But how could they be entirely sure? 'Well, how long have you been supporting the idea of European Unification?' asked Steed.

'On and off for years.'

'On and off?'

'Well. It's... complicated,' said Wilson. 'I shan't pretend I don't have my concerns, but providing we enter in the right way – on the right terms – I think it's in this country's best interests. It was in our manifesto last year.'

'Well, there you go then,' said Steed. 'Grainger wasn't even in the country until the beginning of this year. And knowing the EUNOCs *might* pose a security risk didn't seem to put you off back then. I'd say that's your answer.'

'So you think his hold over me is broken?' said Wilson.

'For what it's worth, I do,' Steed confirmed.

Wilson nodded appreciatively as the car pulled up outside his electoral home and he could see his wife and two adult sons waiting for him along with a dozen ministers. 'Then I know what I have to do,' he said climbing out of the car.

As Wilson was embraced warmly by the crowd, Steed joined Mrs Peel who had parked behind the Prime Minister's saloon.

'You think that's the end of it?' Mrs Peel asked.

'Do you?' he replied.

'Not a chance. If Jacobs is still at large, he'll try again.'

'I'm inclined to agree,' said Steed. 'It's time to bring him in.'

'Agreed,' said Mrs Peel. 'There's no doubt he arranged the Prime Minister's ambush *and* tried to kill Grainger.'

'Not to mention the hospitality he showed towards *you*,' added Steed.

'The application's due Thursday,' said Mrs Peel, 'and the vote's tomorrow. So, we've got to keep him alive, and compos mentis for at least another–' she gently grabbed Steed's wrist to take a look at his watch, '–forty-eight hours give or take.'

'I'll stick to the Prime Minister like a limpet,' said Steed, 'he trusts me.'

'Okay,' agreed Mrs Peel. 'I'll go back to the police. This time they'll *have to* listen.'

Steed shook his head, 'I've got a better idea.'

43

SUSAN PICKERING HAD never seen anything like it in her eighty-three years on this earth. She'd taken successive dogs for their evening walk along this route for nearly fifty years precisely because there was barely any traffic, save for the odd delivery. But tonight, she'd already seen half a dozen vehicles racing away from the old Travis munitions factory, almost clipping her prized pug, Rosie, in the process. And now, not twenty minutes later, a convoy of army vehicles piled into the very same complex. A menagerie of khaki trucks whose camouflage wouldn't have been effective against the industrial backdrop even if it hadn't have been pitch black.

At first, Susan wondered if the factory was supplying arms to the military. Just like it had during the War if memory served, but peering through the gates, she could see the trucks weren't for carrying guns, they were for transporting people. She watched in horror as dozens of uniformed troops piled out of the vehicles and into the factory, each one armed to the teeth.

After a few minutes, the last of the soldiers arrived and joined their comrades inside. Only one person remained outside. A woman in an orange jumpsuit.

The factory grounds looked far more sinister in the dark. Mrs Peel could barely walk without stumbling as she attempted to navigate the clapped-out obstacles that cluttered the grounds. Her ankles attached themselves almost magnetically to every divot. She'd been ordered to remain outside until Jacobs was in custody, and the factory was secured. It rankled to be commanded by anyone – especially a toff in uniform – but convincing the generals to allow her to ride along in the first place had been an uphill battle, so she bit her lip. Within seconds of arriving, she knew their trip had been futile. They were too late. All of the vans that littered the grounds last time she'd been here were gone and the convoy's headlights were shining through the factory windows, revealing there wasn't a soul in sight. Naturally, that hadn't stopped the army bulldozing their way in, but Mrs Peel knew they'd come back empty-handed. Despite Steed's best efforts, copious ribbons of red tape had prevented them drafting in the squaddies any sooner. And while she wasn't expecting Jacob's nine-to-fivers to be around at this hour, she'd hoped the militant arm of the operation might have been caught unawares.

But where had Jacobs gone? Not – she suspected – clocking off early for a pint down the local. He and his men were mobilising.

As she pondered her next move, Mrs Peel heard a voice whispering to her. She squinted her eyes to try to make out the silhouette of a man, hiding in the overgrown shrubbery.

'You're with the Government, yes?' the mystery man asked.

'Perhaps,' said Mrs Peel. 'Who wants to know?'

'My name's not important,' said Boskins – one of the last to join Jacobs' bandits, and one of the first to leave. 'There's something you need to know.' He paused, seemingly conflicted about whether or not to rat out his former boss.

'Spit it out then!' said Mrs Peel.

'If you want to save a lot of lives,' he continued, 'get to the Houses of Parliament pronto.'

'And why's that?' she asked.

'He's going to blow it up.'

This surprised Mrs Peel. She knew Jacobs was a violent extremist, but she hadn't imagined he would go *that* far. 'And why are you telling me this information?'

'Because I'm not a murderer, lady,' said the Welshman. 'Just here for the money, I was.'

'Blow it up, how, exactly?' she asked.

'I don't know the specifics, all I can tell you is that fifty pounds of explosives were here this morning. Now they're not. And he's heading for the Palace of Westminster.'

'He'll never get past security,' said Mrs Peel, knowing full well that everyone was on high alert following the events of recent days. And as she spoke, she edged forward, closing the ten yards or so between them without him realising, in case he made a run for it.

'Oh yes he will,' Boskins asserted. 'How do you think he's always one step ahead of you?'

'Enlighten me,' said Mrs Peel, conceding it was a fair question.

'It's the *cars*,' said Boskins, 'they're bugged. He's got a man on the inside, so he has. A mechanic or something. I don't know the details, but he has a pass to come and go as he pleases. He'll be able to drive right through those gates, no questions asked.'

Mrs Peel realised the significance of what she was hearing.

'Is there a phone here?' she asked.

'Yes, it's up in the–' A shot rang out and Boskins slumped face first into the dirt. Mrs Peel dropped to the floor to avoid the crossfire as soldiers piled out of the factory, firing their weapons in the direction of the assassin, apparently in one of the old outbuildings. She couldn't tell whether Jacobs had stationed a few sentries to keep watch, or whether he'd somehow rigged the whole place up to discharge a lifetime of ammunition. Either way, it was having the desired effect, with bullets raining down all around her, puncturing flesh, tyres, glass and steel indiscriminately. She gauged her options.

Running into the factory wasn't an option. She'd be cut down long before she made it to the doors, and the army trucks were now well and truly shot to pieces. Her only hope was a Triumph motorcycle she could see propped against a wall through the gaps in the trucks, on the other side of the convoy. Keeping low to the ground, she shimmied her way across to the vehicles and rolled under the trucks and across to the other side. The vehicles – what was left of them – *should* offer her enough cover to reach the bike, she reckoned.

After catching her breath, she took her chance and sprinted over to the motorcycle undetected. Luck was on her side as the keys were still in the ignition, not that the simple task of hotwiring it would have posed her any difficulties. She didn't doubt the army would eventually overcome their attackers, but not anytime soon. So, Mrs Peel accelerated towards the gates as fast as her two wheels would carry her and headed to Westminster alone.

44

STEED WAITED PATIENTLY with Grainger outside the Cabinet Room at Number 10. The two men had barely said a word since he'd been brought in by the authorities. Steed had argued they needed to keep him close for the next few hours, in case the Prime Minister had a relapse. That was the only reason he wasn't behind bars at this very moment. The debate had become heated, but Steed had assured Callaghan and the others that as soon as the application was safely made, and the announcement given, he, Mrs Peel – and especially Grainger and Jacobs would be out of their hair for good. The Cabinet had been sequestered for hours now, and Steed had a good mind to go barging in and remind them that Wilson was hardly in a fit state to be working past ten so soon after his recovery. But if he knew the Prime Minister – and he was beginning to feel like he did – he knew he'd be making up for lost time.

'What's he going to do in there?' asked Grainger, breaking the silence. 'Did he tell you?'

'Perhaps,' said Steed, remaining aloof.

'If I know Wilson, he'll go ahead.'

'You seem very sure,' said Steed.

'He'll convince himself it was his idea of course. That I was only convincing him of something he wanted to do all along.'

'Are you saying that's *not* the case?' Steed asked.

'Perhaps,' said Grainger, deliberately echoing Steed's dismissive language.

'Well, it's above my head now,' said Steed. 'I don't get involved with the politics.'

'Nobody ever does, Mr Steed,' Grainger said. 'That's why Europe's destined to carry on tearing chunks out of itself for evermore while polite society turns the other way.'

Steed chose not to respond.

'Where will I be taken?' Grainger asked. 'The Tower of London?'

'You're about five hundred years too late for that,' said Steed, 'unless your punishment is overpriced tea, death by tourists, or being eaten one morsel at a time by ravens.'

'Where have they bid you take me then?'

'What makes you think they'll tell me?' Steed asked.

'Obvious isn't it?' Grainger replied. 'I finished my work with the Prime Minister two hours and forty-seven minutes ago. Yet here we still are. Inexplicably bound together. You could have had me taken off in chains by your bobbies on the beat by now, or frog-marched by the fifty-first battalion of something or other. But no, I'm still stuck to you like a nursemaid. You're keeping me around for something. I wonder what it is.'

'Just a little insurance,' said Steed.

'So, you want to keep me alive long enough to check I'm definitely… dispensable,' Grainger summarised.

'Something like that,' Steed replied.

'Sensible,' Grainger conceded. 'So, what have they told you to do with me? When it's all over?'

Steed wasn't prone to lying if he didn't have to, and there was something about Grainger that made you warm to him, despite the fact he was quite clearly a crackpot.

'It depends,' said Steed.

'On?'

'On what cover story they run with...'

'Are you telling me the establishment would hide the truth from its own citizens?' asked Grainger sarcastically.

'I couldn't possibly comment,' said Steed.

'Best case...' guessed Grainger, 'I think you'll ship me off back to Italy. Or Switzerland. Or France, Belgium, Austria – wherever you think I "belong". Worst case? Well, I can imagine some very dark things indeed, Mr Steed. Something tells me they won't put me on trial...'

'For hypnotising the Prime Minister?' said Steed. 'I'd say it's unlikely.'

'Doesn't play well for the democratic process, does it?' said Grainger. 'My guess? I'll mysteriously disappear...'

Steed neither confirmed nor denied.

'Not my decision to make, I'm afraid.'

Grainger nodded, his manner communicating that he understood Steed's position and that he hoped the feeling would be reciprocated. That's when he grabbed the hypodermic he'd concealed in his sock back at Chequers and plunged it into Steed's thigh.

It took a moment or two for Steed to register what had just happened. Ordinarily, he'd have never allowed someone to smuggle a weapon into Downing Street, but Steed himself had bypassed all the usual checks in the interests of time. He'd known the risks but underestimated the odds.

'You told Mrs Peel you were a pacifist,' Steed said, blindsided.

'Desperate times I'm afraid, Steed.' Grainger dashed for the exit and practically bounced onto Downing Street's first-floor landing.

Steed just about made it to his feet to follow him, but his knees buckled, and his gait shook like a marionette being puppeteered for the very first time.

He should have dropped to the floor immediately, but

years of training and a bloody-minded refusal to be a victim kept him standing longer than most. As Grainger's foot navigated the first step of the staircase, Steed threw all of his might atop the man, sending them both tumbling down the historic stairwell, knocking monochrome portraits of former prime ministers crashing to the ground.

Grainger got to his feet and kicked Steed back down as he tried to do the same. 'You haven't the strength,' Grainger said, encouraging Steed not to mount a second attempt.

But Steed tried anyway. By now though, his strength was abandoning him, and he barely got himself upright before Grainger easily pushed him down the next flight of stairs. In a final noble effort to put mind over matter, Steed grabbed one of the portraits from the wall and threw it towards Grainger, like a frisbee. It hit his head, and the broken glass gashed his cheek. Steed attempted to stand one final time, but Grainger's concoction was well and truly doing its job. As Steed saw Grainger disappearing, he lost consciousness, sliding down the wall and causing a final photograph to tumble to the floor, shattering down upon his skull as it fell.

It didn't take long for Downing Street security to arrive on the scene, alerted by the commotion, but by the time they had, somehow Grainger had evaded them.

'What the hell happened here?' said Sergeant Withers, a military man who was on rota. In the lobby, he found a guard called Gibbins who was supposed to be on duty, asleep on the job.

'I… I…' said Gibbins, clearly disorientated.

'Well spit it out, man,' said Withers, a man whose bushy moustache eclipsed his tiny lips.

'I don't remember, sir. There was a man, he…'

'Get out the way,' said Withers, shoving Gibbins to one side to survey the carnage on the staircase. Spotting Steed, he rushed over to help him and found him unconscious. Withers retrieved Steed's bowler from the stairs and gently tapped his cheek to rouse him. Steed opened his eyes and greeted Withers with a huge, maniacal smile.

'Are you okay, old chap?' Withers asked.

'Perfectly,' said Steed.

Withers recognised the man's face. Their paths had crossed from time to time, and he knew the gentleman lying battered and bruised at the bottom of the stairwell had the very highest security clearance – higher even than his own – but he'd *never* seen him like this before.

'Pardon my asking, sir,' said Withers, 'but what in the name of all that is holy happened here?'

Steed looked at the battlefield around him, as if seeing it for the very first time.

'Oh dear,' he said, 'that's quite a mess, isn't it?'

Withers didn't know what to make of it. 'You'll think me terribly rude,' he said, 'but I've forgotten your name.'

Steed thought about this and realised he didn't have a clue. But that didn't trouble him, in fact he let out a small laugh. 'Your guess is as good as mine,' he said.

Getting to his feet, Steed's shoes stepped on splintered glass beneath them. He looked down to see what he was treading on and everything was suddenly clear. He bent down to scoop up the black and white portrait of Sir Winston Churchill, taken by Walter Stoneman in 1948, which showed the former prime minster dressed in a suit and waistcoat, with a signature white pocket hanky and a spotted black bow tie. Steed looked at the photo of the legendary wartime leader who saved Britain from the Nazi menace as if staring into a mirror. He turned the portrait around to proudly display it to Withers. 'What's wrong with you, Sergeant?' said Steed at last. 'Don't you recognise your prime minister?'

45

MRS PEEL BURST into the Palace of Westminster like Oliver Cromwell leading a charge, but without an army of Roundheads behind her.

In St Stephen's Porch was a man who looked well beyond retirement age, eating an egg sandwich and reading a copy of *The Economist*. Such were his praetorian abilities that he'd barely even noticed Mrs Peel's arrival, let alone a stealthy attack from a bad actor.

'Have any vehicles entered the Estate?' she demanded. Still out of breath from the sprint, she slammed her triple-starred security pass on the counter.

'How should I know?' said the nightwatchman. 'That's Fred's domain downstairs.'

'Phone him,' said Mrs Peel, 'tell him *no* vehicles are allowed to enter the underground car park. No exceptions. Even if they have the right clearances.'

The watchman continued eating his sandwich, but he did at least have the courtesy to put down his newspaper, furling the edge of the page for quick reference later.

'And phone the police,' she added, 'tell them to find John Steed at the Ministry and tell him Jacobs is planning to blow this place to kingdom come.'

The sandwich fell out of the old man's mouth.

'And that would be very, *very* bad,' she said glibly, pleased she'd finally got the man's undivided attention.

She ran down St Stephen's Hall and into the Central Lobby – a beautifully crafted octagonal space designed by Charles Barry as a meeting point between the two Houses of Government. It was decorated – as was most of the Palace – in a Gothic Revival style with incredible arched windows, mosaic tiled floor and exquisite masonry. Mrs Peel span 360 degrees, pondering where to start. The place was as quiet as the grave as it was approaching midnight now, and Parliament wasn't due to sit for another ten hours.

Mrs Peel looked all around her for *any* signs of activity. To one side, she found a large chamber with rows upon rows of empty red leather benches. This, she recognised as the House of Lords. Next, she opened a handful of doors leading to rooms running off the Peers' corridor. Again, she found nothing. Realising the House of Commons must be on the opposite side of the building – the west wing of the Palace – she ran back through the Central Lobby and onto the Commons' Corridor. That took her to the famous entranceway to the lower house of Government. She pulled open the battle-scarred wooden doors, bruised and dented from hundreds of years of abuse from "Black Rod".

Inside was a room much like the chamber in the Lords but with benches of green, not red. The benches were laid out adversarially so that the Government of the day could duke it out face to face with Her Majesty's Opposition. In the centre of the benches was the Speaker's Chair and the Clerks' table, which held a number of legal books and a ceremonial golden mace that had been carried into the Chamber ready for the House to sit in a matter of hours.

As Emma looked across the room and up to the galleries, all seemed quiet, but something felt wrong. Suddenly, a man appeared behind her, scaring her half to death, dressed in a blue boiler suit.

'Can't be in here, miss,' he said urgently. 'Security sweep ahead of tomorrow's parliamentary session. We've had a tip off trouble's brewing.'

'Is that so?' said Mrs Peel, doubting the man's legitimacy. For a start his clothes looked suspiciously like the outfits she'd seen Jacobs' henchmen wear during her impromptu detainment days ago. Plus, the nightwatchman would have surely told her if security services had got there just moments before.

As she debated whether to confront him, she spotted, out of the corner of her eye, a flash of blue, peeking out from behind the green benches, like a butterfly resting on a field of grass. Then she spotted another, and another. It was the same indigo colour the man in front of her was wearing.

'Fair enough,' said Mrs Peel, turning as if to leave, but as she did so she deployed a step through martial arts move, followed by a roundhouse kick she had learned in her very first week of training back when she was a teenager. The man guarding the door fell like a deck of cards, but as he did so, five other men emerged from behind the Government benches.

Jacobs had just finished placing the last of his explosives beneath the Prime Minister's seat and was almost pleased to greet his visitor.

'You're too late, Mrs Peel,' he said.

Mrs Peel turned to leave, but Ruskin, the burly man she'd immobilised, had dragged himself back up to his feet and closed the doors behind them.

So, that left her with little choice but to run across to the Opposition benches and hold the pursuing marauders at bay by hurling Erskine May, Standing Orders and Hansard books at them like shrapnel.

They'd held off firing at her until now, because they knew the sound of gunfire would almost certainly alert the authorities, but Manson figured they might get away with a warning shot to show Mrs Peel it was useless to resist. The single shot flew no more than a foot away from her shoulder and pierced the green leather bench behind, sending its innards into the air like a stream of candyfloss.

Mrs Peel instinctively dropped to the floor, using the benches for shelter just as her attackers had done when she'd arrived. But this gave them time to cross the floor, and before long she had two men flanking her, so she jumped back up to her feet and offered each a wrist, feigning surrender. As they moved in to detain her, she grabbed each of them and yanked them towards each other, causing them to collide like marbles. They crumpled to the floor, where she gave them a swift kick to render them unconscious. But by the time she'd overpowered one set of crazies, another two were on her tail, led by the sole female in the group, Lord Hagley's assassin, Caroline Kirk, who Jacobs had paid a small fortune to assist. The two women locked horns, fighting with a ferociousness that made even Manson keep his distance.

As they each paused to recover their breath, Mrs Peel quipped, 'Ever think you're hanging around with the wrong kind of men?'

'I could say the same about you,' said Kirk, wiping away the blood from her split lip.

Emma shrugged her shoulders as if to say, "touché".

Then Manson piled in and Emma knew she couldn't keep up the fight indefinitely. She calculated the probability of jumping from her current position on the third row of benches back down to the centre where she might find something to fight back with. She was far from convinced she'd make it without breaking her back on one of the benches, but she took a chance and leapt into the air, just about making it to the chamber floor. But by the time her feet touched the carpet, Jacobs was waiting and had a gun trained point-blank against her head.

'A valiant effort,' Jacobs conceded, 'but it's over, Mrs Peel. Stand down.'

'Even if you kill me,' said Mrs Peel, 'you can't win now. Even if you blow us all sky high, you won't get a single politician. I've already alerted the authorities. And – a little tip for you – if the Chamber's full of bullet holes, people ask questions.'

'Then we'll have to take our victories where we can get them, Mrs Peel,' he said, cocking the gun that was still pointing at her head. 'Something tells me Brussels might get a little nervous of getting into bed with us when they see this historic place has been razed to the ground.'

Given she'd seen nothing from Jacobs to indicate he wasn't prepared to kill her in cold blood, she had a split-second decision to make: freeze, flee or fight. Freezing wasn't really Mrs Peel's style. And fleeing wasn't really viable. Which left one option. As she glanced down she saw the golden ceremonial mace sitting on the table in front of her and reckoned she could probably just about reach it. She only needed Jacobs to take his eyes off her, just for a moment.

And that's when the mother of all distractions came along. Dozens of armed officers piled onto the elevated galleries that ran along the sides of the Commons Chamber, a gun trained on each and every one of the people in the room. As Jacobs calculated what to do next, Mrs Peel wasted no time in grabbing the mace, and clocking Jacobs round the head with it, knocking the gun out of his hands as she did so. This discharged a bullet, which blew a hole in the Speaker's chair as the gun clattered to the floor. Realising the game was up,

Jacobs raised his hands in abject submission, as did the rest of his crew – at least those still conscious.

Exhausted, Mrs Peel collapsed into the battle-damaged Speaker's chair, grabbing a white peruke and placing the wig on her head.

That was when Steed walked into the room, wearing a Homburg hat, smoking a cigar and holding his hand aloft with two fingers placed in the "V for Victory" position. He walked straight up to Mrs Peel and shook her hand warmly. She hadn't a clue why he was aping Winston Churchill, but the purple bump on his forehead told her he'd clearly been hurt.

'I'm the Prime Minister,' he said cheerfully, 'and who might you be…?'

46

AT NUMBER 55 Rue du Faubourg Saint-Honoré in Paris, a Citroën DS pulled up to some black gates decorated with gold leaf. Above the ornate gates were two intertwined letters: an F and an R, which stood for République Française.

The driver paused at the gates and waited for the gendarmes to approach the car. Winding his window down, he passed his identification across to the policemen who checked everything was above board.

'*Je suis le chauffeur du président*,' the driver said.

The gendarme nodded and opened the gates.

The driver smiled as he took back his ID that named him as Monsieur Jean Claude Phillipe, rather than his real name – Horatio Grainger. As he stowed the paperwork back inside his jacket pocket, he headed down the gravelled driveway and all the way up to the Élysée Palace.

47

STEED WAS RECOVERING from a bad case of concussion in his apartment at 3 Stable Mews in central London. As he sipped a glass of Laurent-Perrier from a *very* good vintage – the '59 – there were three loud knocks at his front door. Steed put down his drink to attend to his guest, but before he'd made it to the door, another three knocks came, this time louder than the first. And as Steed pressed his hands to the catch, a final set of knuckle raps reverberated around the flat, only this time, on the third and final knock, the glass from the side window next to his front door shattered and a golden mace poked through like a child emerging from the womb. Through the broken glass, Steed could see Mrs Peel dressed as Black Rod – wearing a black trouser suit, an elaborate white neckerchief, a gold chain and black leather gloves.

'Oops,' she said, as Steed swung the door open to let her in properly.

'That's quite an entrance, Mrs Peel,' he said.

'Open up,' she said, her tongue firmly in cheek, 'in the name of the Queen.'

'And what, exactly, does my queen want?' he asked.

'What are you offering?' she asked.

'You know me, Mrs Peel,' said Steed, 'simply ask and I

shall oblige…' he pointed to his bruised forehead, '*if* I'm up to it.'

'Well,' said Mrs Peel, still standing on the doorstep, 'are you going to let me in?'

Steed declined, choosing to honour the long-held tradition of slamming the door shut in Black Rod's face.

'That's fair,' said Mrs Peel, who used the golden mace to break the remaining shards of the side window free from the frame, and stepped through the gap into Steed's apartment, 'in that case, I'll settle for a large brandy.'

Steed collected two cubes of ice en route to his chair, one for Mrs Peel's drink and another to wrap inside a cloth and place on his aching head.

'Have you seen the papers?' she asked, inspecting his head wound to check she was happy with how it was healing.

Steed nodded and showed her the headline from the newspaper beside him. It showed a picture of Harold Wilson evading photographers and looking decidedly deflated. The headline read: "WILSON WINS LANDSLIDE VOTE…" but beneath, in smaller letting it added, "BUT DE GAULLE LIKELY TO VETO BRITAIN JOINING THE COMMON MARKET… AGAIN. WILSON HOLDS HIS BREATH."

Mrs Peel skimmed the article, which seemed to suggest that, although they wouldn't have a definitive answer until November, the mood music was that the French president was still inclined to block the United Kingdom's accession. The article quoted him as saying: *"this great people, so magnificently gifted with ability and courage, should be on their own behalf and for themselves achieve a profound economic and political transformation, which would allow them to join the Six Continentals."*

'You know what they say, Mrs Peel,' said Steed, 'If at first you don't succeed…'

'Skydiving's not for you?' she joked.

'Quite!' Steed replied.

'Now you're feeling better, will you join me in the *other place*?' Mrs Peel asked.

Steed looked honoured. 'The House of Peers?' he asked expectantly.

'The public house.'

'On one condition,' Steed said.

'Which is?' asked Mrs Peel.

Steed offered his arm to his old friend. 'Let's not talk politics.'

THE END

ACKNOWLEDGEMENTS

With special thanks to: Susan de Christofaro at Warner Bros. Entertainment Group and Massimo Moretti at Studio Canal for making this novel possible. Richard Jackson and Daquan Cadogan at Titan for commissioning and editing the book. My loving dad, Ian Crichton for introducing me to *The Avengers* as a boy and fact checking all things historical and football-related. And Chris Trengove for helping me polish the very first chapters back when it started life as a Covid lockdown project.

The book is dedicated to the late, great Raymond Thompson MNZM who encouraged my creative career from the very beginning and was unwaveringly supportive of my writing.

ABOUT THE AUTHOR

David is a professional writer who spends most of his time crafting marketing copy for clients in his role as Creative Director at an award-winning brand and digital agency. He's a published non-fiction author who's turning his hand to novels with the release of *Death in Downing Street.* Dave wasn't even born when *The Avengers* finished its television run in the 1960s, but like many others, he fell in love with the programme during repeats in the '90s. He lives in the Midlands with his wife and daughters, who indulge his addiction to vintage TV.